ACCLAIM FOR KATHLEEN FULLER

"Fuller's inspirational tale portrays complex characters facing real-world problems and finding love where they least expected or wanted it to be."

—BOOKLIST, STARRED REVIEW, ON A RELUCTANT BRIDE

"Fuller has an amazing capacity for creating damaged characters and giving insights into their brokenness. One of the better voices in the Amish fiction genre."

—CBA RETAILERS + RESOURCES ON A RELUCTANT BRIDE

"This promising series debut from Fuller is edgier than most Amish novels, dealing with difficult and dark issues and featuring well-drawn characters who are tougher than the usual gentle souls found in this genre. Recommended for Amish fiction fans who might like a different flavor."

—LIBRARY JOURNAL ON A RELUCTANT BRIDE

"Sadie and Aden's love is both sweet and hard-won, and Aden's patience is touching as he wrestles not only with Sadie's dilemma, but his own abusive past. Birch Creek is weighed down by the Troyer family's dark secrets, and readers will be interested to see how secondary characters' lives unfold as the series continues."

—RT BOOK REVIEWS, 4 STARS, ON A RELUCTANT BRIDE

"Kathleen Fuller's A Reluctant Bride tells the story of two Amish families whose lives have collided through tragedy. Sadie Schrock's stoic resolve will touch and inspire Fuller's fans, as will the story's concluding triumph of redemption."

—SUZANNE WOODS FISHER, BESTSELLING
AUTHOR OF ANNA'S CROSSING

"Kathleen Fuller's *A Reluctant Bride* is a beautiful story of faith, hope, and second chances. Her characters and descriptions are captivating, bringing the story to life with the turn of every page."

—AMY CLIPSTON, BESTSELLING AUTHOR OF *A SIMPLE PRAYER* AND THE KAUFFMAN AMISH BAKERY SERIES

"The latest offering in the Middlefield Family series is a sweet love story, with perfectly crafted characters. Fuller's Amish novels are written with the utmost respect for their way of living. Readers are given a glimpse of what it is like to live the simple life."

—*RT BOOK REVIEWS*, 4 STARS, ON *LETTERS TO KATIE*

"Fuller's second Amish series entry is a sweet romance with a strong sense of place that will attract readers of Wanda Brunstetter and Cindy Woodsmall."

—*LIBRARY JOURNAL* ON *FAITHFUL TO LAURA*

"Well-drawn characters and a homespun feel will make this Amish romance a sure bet for fans of Beverly Lewis and Jerry S. Eicher."

—*LIBRARY JOURNAL* ON *TREASURING EMMA*

"*Treasuring Emma* is a heartwarming story filled with real-life situations and well-developed characters. I rooted for Emma and Adam until the very last page. Fans of Amish fiction and those seeking an endearing romance will enjoy this love story. Highly recommended."

—BETH WISEMAN, BESTSELLING AUTHOR OF *HER BROTHER'S KEEPER* AND THE DAUGHTERS OF THE PROMISE SERIES

"*Treasuring Emma* is a charming, emotionally layered story of the value of friendship in love and discovering the truth of the heart. A true treasure of a read!"

—KELLY LONG, AUTHOR OF THE PATCH OF HEAVEN SERIES

AN
UNBROKEN
HEART

Also by Kathleen Fuller

The Amish of Birch Creek

A Reluctant Bride
An Unbroken Heart
A Love Made New (available September 2016)

The Middlefield Amish Novels

A Faith of Her Own

The Middlefield Family Novels

Treasuring Emma
Faithful to Laura
Letters to Katie

The Hearts of Middlefield Novels

A Man of His Word
An Honest Love
A Hand to Hold

Novellas included in

An Amish Christmas—A Miracle for Miriam
An Amish Gathering—A Place of His Own
An Amish Love—What the Heart Sees
An Amish Wedding—A Perfect Match
An Amish Garden—Flowers for Rachael
An Amish Second Christmas—A Gift for Anne Marie
An Amish Cradle—A Heart Full of Love
An Amish Market—A Bid for Love
An Amish Harvest—A Quiet Love (available August 2016)

The Mysteries of Middlefield
Series for Young Readers

A Summer Secret
The Secrets Beneath
Hide and Secret

AN UNBROKEN HEART

KATHLEEN FULLER

THOMAS NELSON
Since 1798

To my husband, James, and my children,
Mathew, Sydney, and Zoie. I love you
more than you'll ever know.

Published in Nashville, Tennessee, by Thomas Nelson. Thomas Nelson is a registered trademark of HarperCollins Christian Publishing, Inc.

Thomas Nelson titles may be purchased in bulk for educational, business, fund-raising, or sales promotional use. For information, please e-mail SpecialMarkets@ ThomasNelson.com.

Unless otherwise noted, Scripture quotations are taken from THE HOLY BIBLE, NEW INTERNATIONAL VERSION®, NIV®. Copyright © 1973, 1978, 1984, 2011 by Biblica, Inc.® Used by permission. All rights reserved worldwide.

Publisher's Note: This novel is a work of fiction. Names, characters, places, and incidents are either products of the author's imagination or used fictitiously. All characters are fictional, and any similarity to people living or dead is purely coincidental.

Library of Congress Cataloging-in-Publication Data

Names: Fuller, Kathleen.
Title: An unbroken heart / Kathleen Fuller.
Description: Nashville, Tennessee : Thomas Nelson, 2016. | 2015 | Series: An Amish of Birch Creek novel
Identifiers: LCCN 2015035927 | ISBN 9780718033187 (softcover)
Subjects: LCSH: Man-woman relationships--Fiction. | Accident victims--Fiction. | Bereavement--Fiction. | Forgiveness--Fiction. | Amish--Fiction. | Grief--Fiction. | GSAFD: Christian fiction. | Love stories.
Classification: LCC PS3606.U553 U53 2016 | DDC 813/.6--dc23 LC record available at http://lccn.loc.gov/2015035927

Printed in the United States of America

16 17 18 19 20 RRD 6 5 4 3 2 1

GLOSSARY

ab im kopp: crazy, crazy in the head

ach: oh

aenti: aunt

appeditlich: delicious

boppli: baby

bruder: brother

bu/buwe: young man/young men

daag/daags: day/days

daed: father

danki: thank you

Dietsch: Amish language

dochder: daughter

dummkopf: idiot

Englisch: non-Amish

familye: family

frau: woman, Mrs.

geh: go

gute nacht: good night

haus: house

herr: man, mister

kaffee: coffee

kapp: white hat worn by Amish women

kinn/kinner: child/children

kumme: come

lieb: love

maedel: girl/young woman

mamm: mom

mann: Amish man

mei: my

mudder/mutter: mother

nee: no

nix: nothing

schee: pretty/handsome

schwesters: sisters

seltsam: weird

sohn: son

vatter: father

ya: yes

yer: your

yerself: yourself

yung: young

Be strong and courageous. Do not be afraid;
do not be discouraged, for the LORD your
God will be with you wherever you go.

JOSHUA 1:9

CHAPTER 1

T*his has to be a trick.*

Joanna Schrock had been fooled once before—and again and again and again. As Thomas Yutzy stretched his closed hands out in front of him, a familiar knot of dread formed in her stomach.

She'd decided to spend her lunch recess alone on this warm spring day, reading under the cool shade of a huge oak tree in the school yard. Then less than a minute after she'd become engrossed in the book she started last night, Thomas approached her and asked if she wanted to play a game.

She should ignore him, but that would be rude. She also couldn't resist the thought that this might be the one time he was telling her the truth. She set down her book and stood.

"C'mon, Joanna." His small gray eyes were round with fake innocence. What a lousy liar. "Which hand has the candy?" He moved closer to her as the noonday sun brightened the cloudless sky.

Joanna glanced around the school yard. She could see her

classmates Andrew Beiler, Christopher Beachy, and Asa Bontrager standing near a maple tree a few feet away, waiting to see what she would do. The rest of the students were playing baseball in the field behind the schoolhouse while *Frau* Miller supervised the game.

Christopher whispered something to Asa, and both boys laughed. Joanna's cheeks burned. Then she saw Andrew. His face remained impassive, with his light blond hair poking out from beneath his straw hat.

Thomas continued to grin, clearly not caring if she knew his true intentions. Then again, everyone knew she was easy to fool. Although she was twelve years old now, that didn't mean she was less gullible. In third grade she'd believed the moon was made of cheese. Swiss, to be exact. In fourth grade she'd been told a real live monster lived in the gentle flowing waters of Birch Creek. She'd been afraid to swim in the creek until her father reassured her that the monster didn't exist. Then he had taken her fishing to prove it.

Her classmates, mostly the boys, had also pulled several pranks on her. A few had been harmless, like the time Asa had taken her math book and hidden it under the teacher's desk. She hadn't minded that . . . too much. "We're only funning you," some of them would say after she'd been duped again. "Only kidding," others would tell her. She accepted their excuses. Hid her hurt feelings. And never admitted there was nothing funny about being the butt of the joke.

Sometime during the last year, the pranks had become cruel. The tack in her chair. The dozen pieces of chewing gum on the bottom of her desk, which she had to scrape off after school because she was responsible for keeping her desk clean and tidy.

She refused to cry as she took the dull butter knife and removed the nasty, hardened globs.

"You're too nice and sweet," her sister Sadie had told her when they walked home later that day.

"That's why the *buwe* pick on you," her other sister, Abigail, said.

Sadie added, "You should stand up for yourself, Joanna. Don't let them walk all over you."

So it's mei *fault.* Which wasn't fair. She didn't want to confront the boys. She wanted them to leave her alone.

But as she stared at Thomas's grimy knuckles, she realized this might be the time to make a stand. "I don't want to play." She backed away from him.

"Aw, Joanna. Don't be like that." Thomas's grin revealed overlapping front teeth. He would have been a bit nice looking if he wasn't so annoying. "Be a *gut* sport. Pick a hand."

Perspiration formed on the back of her neck. She should pick so he would have his laugh and leave her alone. She started to point to his left hand, squeezing her eyes shut and steeling herself for what would happen if she chose wrong.

"Let her be, Thomas."

She opened her eyes. Andrew strode toward them with confident steps. He was shorter than the rest of the boys in their grade, and he was stocky. Solid, like the trunk of a thick, unyielding oak tree. He stopped in front of Joanna and calmly slipped his hands into his pockets, his gaze never leaving Thomas.

Thomas scoffed. "We're just playing a little game. You stay out of it."

"Doesn't seem like she wants to play."

Joanna's words left her. She didn't need Andrew to fight her battles, but she had to admit a small part of her liked that he was willing to. Andrew was not only very *schee*, he was also very nice. She lifted her chin, his presence bolstering her confidence.

Ignoring Andrew, Thomas faced Joanna again, pushing his fists toward her. "Pick," he ordered.

Andrew shook his head, confirming what she already knew—she wouldn't like either choice. Knowing he was beaten, Thomas opened both hands and tossed two small toads at Joanna. Like tiny rubber balls, both animals bounced off her face and shoulder and landed on the ground. She gasped and jumped back.

Thomas's laughter rang in her ears. Asa and Christopher were also giggling.

Her face flamed, her eyes stinging with tears she dared not shed. The last time she'd cried at school, even a few girls had called her a crybaby. Only when Sadie and Abigail had told them to shut up did they stop. *I will not cry . . . I will not cry . . .*

Joanna focused on the toads as they hopped away in the grass. Thankfully they weren't harmed by Thomas's cruelty. She couldn't face her tormentors—or Andrew. He was probably laughing at her too.

"Fight!" Asa yelled.

Joanna whirled around. Andrew was gripping Thomas by the front of his pale yellow shirt. "I told you to leave her alone," Andrew growled, his voice much deeper than she'd ever heard it.

Thomas replied with a punch to Andrew's face.

Joanna gasped again and brought her hands to her mouth. Andrew stumbled from the blow yet managed to remain on his feet, his hands fisted at his sides. But he didn't retaliate. Before things could escalate, two eighth-grade boys stepped between them.

"Enough!" Joel Zook, the tallest kid in school, pierced both boys with a warning look. "*Ach,* you want the teacher to know about this? She'll tell *yer* parents and you'll both be in big trouble."

Andrew took a step back, the red mark on his cheek glowing against his fair skin. "*Nee.* We had a misunderstanding, that's all."

"It won't happen again," Thomas added.

"Better not, or I'll take you to *Frau* Miller myself." Joel gave each of them a hard look before he and the other boy walked away.

As Thomas went to stand by Asa and Christopher, Joanna wiped the part of her cheek the toad had landed on, fighting off the tears. If she had gone along with Thomas to begin with, none of this would have happened. Everything was worse now. She picked up her book and proceeded to the schoolhouse, eager to get away from all of them.

Andrew appeared beside her. He walked with her a few steps, then moved to stand in front of her. "Are you okay, Joanna?"

Surprised, a funny feeling appeared in her tummy when she met his gaze. Oh, he was definitely nice looking. "I should be asking you that question." She rubbed her nose. "I'm sorry I caused so much trouble."

"It's not *yer* fault Thomas is a *dummkopf,*" he said with a nonchalant lift of his shoulders. "If those guys or anyone else bothers you, let me know. I'll take care of it."

She looked at his swollen cheek. "I don't want you to get hurt again."

He chuckled. "This?" He pointed at the dark red mark. "He only landed that punch because he caught me off guard." The smile slid from his handsome face. "There are better ways to handle an argument than using fists. Thomas needs to learn that."

He sounded wiser and far older than his twelve years. Andrew, his sister, Irene, and their mother were new to the district, having moved to Birch Creek almost a year ago. There were rumors that his father had left the family for an *Englisch* woman. Joanna had never asked Andrew about it. His family had the right to their privacy and didn't deserve to be gossiped about.

Andrew suddenly reached toward her. When she flinched, he said softly, "This is a *gut* trick. I promise." He brushed his fist against her ear, then drew back his hand and opened it.

Her eyebrows lifted at the acorn in his palm. "How did you do that?"

His lips tipped up in a half-smile. "I can't tell you all my secrets."

Frau Miller rang the bell, and the students scrambled back to the schoolhouse. Andrew walked with Joanna. "What are you going to tell *Frau* Miller about *yer* cheek?" she asked, rubbing her nose again.

He shrugged. "I'll think of something."

Their teacher had given both Thomas and Andrew a questioning look when they entered the school building, but she didn't say anything. Joanna suspected *Frau* Miller had an idea about what had happened between the boys but for some reason chose not to do anything about it. As the children sat in their seats and school resumed, Joanna leaned back, relieved nothing else awful had happened.

The rest of the day went by without incident. Joanna tried to focus on her schoolwork, but she was unable to resist sneaking a few glances at Andrew, who sat three seats away. Unfortunately, he didn't seem to notice. She bit her lip, disappointed. What he'd done for her at recess was special. He'd stood up for her when no one, other than her sisters, had ever done so. He'd been her hero.

At the end of the school day, Joanna gathered her books and her lunch pail and met Sadie and Abigail outside, forgetting about Andrew and focusing on what she would do when she got home. After she finished her homework, she would start on supper. She'd taken over the cooking chores this year so her mother and sisters could work more hours in their family-owned grocery store. She didn't mind. She liked to cook and loved to bake. *What's Andrew's favorite dessert?* She shook her head at the sudden thought. *So much for getting him out of* mei *mind.*

She was deciding whether to make hamburger casserole or chicken pot pie when Andrew appeared by her side. Butterflies danced in her stomach. He remained quiet as they continued down the dirt-packed shoulder of the road. Slowing her pace, she lagged behind her sisters. When his stride lingered with hers, the butterflies ramped up. There was something comforting and protective about his presence. They passed by sun-warmed fields and gardens, the freshly turned earth ready and waiting to be seeded with corn, tomatoes, beans, and other varieties of vegetables and grains.

When they reached her house, the ease she'd felt with him disappeared. Should she thank him for walking her home? Would she sound stupid if she did? Her stomach tightened as she wondered if he would say anything to her. If he did, how would she respond? She wasn't sure she could even talk, not when her mouth was drier than a parched garden.

While all these thoughts ran through her mind, he gave her a nod, turned, and walked in the opposite direction toward his home. She sighed. As she watched him leave, a part of her fell in love with him.

CHAPTER 2

Joanna's heart thrummed as she searched for Andrew among the crowd of young people gathered in the Troyers' basement. This had been their ritual for the past two months. They would arrive at a singing separately, seek each other out, then send a silent signal so they could meet in private. Her anticipation always grew as she tried not to reveal she was looking for him. She couldn't help frowning when she didn't see him right away.

Finally she spied him standing on the opposite side of the room. The warm smile he aimed at her created the usual tiny butterflies that tickled her stomach, easing the tension from listening to her sisters argue on the way here. Sadie was upset. She never went to singings but had reluctantly agreed to go this time, and her mood was foul by the time they had arrived. Abigail had given up trying to reason with her and had disappeared as soon as she exited the buggy. Now Sadie stood alone in the corner, a

8

sour look on her face, which wouldn't do much to attract the few eligible young men attending tonight.

Abigail had no problem mingling, though, especially with Joel Zook. Joanna saw her flirting with him, and from the full grin on his face, he was enjoying the attention.

Joanna put her sisters out of her mind and met Andrew's gaze again. His blond eyebrow lifted above his left eye. Their signal. He tilted his head in a small gesture for her to come to him. She gave him a tiny nod, the butterflies now swirling in a frenzy.

"Hello," he said as she drew near.

She stood close to him but not too close. He had to lean over to say his next words.

"Will you meet me behind the barn?"

He was always so polite with her. Never demanding and thoroughly respectful. She pulled back, her cheeks hot, savoring the thought that once again Andrew wanted her alone.

But part of her was growing impatient. Andrew's respect also translated into keeping her at arm's length, even when they were by themselves. After waiting eight years for him to finally show his romantic interest, she wanted more than conversation.

He left the room first. Several moments later she followed, dashing up the basement stairs and through the door that led to the backyard. In the dusky light she saw him disappear behind the Troyers' white barn. She hurried, a little breathless by the time she caught up to him. She found him leaning casually against the barn wall.

"You look nervous," he said.

"Not . . . nervous." She rubbed her nose.

"Definitely nervous." He removed her hand from her nose. "You don't have to be skittish, Joanna. It's just me."

He would never be just Andrew to her. He was her protector, her savior . . . her love. She looked at his face, barely seeing the muted tangerine and lavender clouds streaking the sky behind him. He'd taken off his hat and left it inside the Troyers' house. His thick, wavy blond hair was streaked with pale highlights from the sun. He always took her breath away.

Without a word he reached behind her ear, the soft brush of his finger on her earlobe making her breath hitch. He'd done his one and only magic trick several times before—pulling out quarters, acorns, even a stick of gum. But this time he withdrew a flower on a short stem, a lovely light blue blossom the size of a new dandelion. He handed it to her.

"How sweet." She smiled at the romantic gesture. Maybe they were making progress after all. "I like this better than acorns."

"I thought you would."

She gently cupped the flower in her hand. She'd take it home and press it into a small book, then place it in her treasure box where she'd kept everything he'd given to her over the years.

A long moment passed, and then the awkwardness between them began, as it always did when they were alone. As friends they could talk about anything. Now that they were dating, they struggled to hold a normal conversation. She wished he would show her some affection. A kiss on the cheek. Or on the lips. Instead he glanced at the ground, kicking a tuft of grass with the toe of his shoe.

In every other aspect of his life, Andrew was confident. Everything about him was strong, from his large, barrel-like chest and hard biceps to his loyal character and devotion to his family and faith. But when they were together like this, she felt on shaky ground, even though he was the one who had started their courtship two months ago.

She drew in a deep breath. It was now or never. It had taken more than two weeks to gather her courage, ever since the idea had popped into her mind while she was asking God what to do about her relationship with Andrew. Tentatively she stepped forward and touched one of the black suspenders that ran over his thick chest. He wasn't very tall, but neither was she. She liked that they could meet eye to eye.

"Joanna." He whispered her name, sending a shiver down her spine. His blue eyes darkened a bit, and his voice, which had deepened to a rich bass over the years, grew even huskier. "What are you doing?"

She froze, her courage suddenly faltering despite seeing that her simple touch had an effect on him. All her life she'd been told to take a stand, to stop being such a mouse. To go after what she wanted. What she wanted was Andrew. She was rubbing her nose again, and she forced herself to stop. She wanted to be confident, to show Andrew how she truly felt about him. She moved closer, close enough that she could kiss him if she wanted to. *I really want to.*

"What if someone sees us?" he asked, sounding a little breathless.

"I don't care." Her own breathing quickened. She drew her fingertip down the length of his suspender.

His smoky gaze cleared, his mouth forming a frown. "Is something wrong, Joanna? This isn't like you."

"That's the point." Being herself wasn't getting her anywhere with Andrew. She had to show him she wasn't the insecure girl he'd always known. "Andrew," she said, her voice sounding thicker than a wool sock, "will you marry me?"

His eyes widened as if he'd seen a cow doing a backflip in the pasture. He stepped back, forcing her to drop her hand from his chest. "What?"

Oh no. She opened her mouth to speak but no sound came out. Her courageous moment had passed, and now she was back to timid Joanna, afraid of her own shadow. Her face the temperature of a bonfire, she turned from him, prepared to flee.

He put his hand on her arm. "Wait. Let's talk about this."

She halted but didn't face him. She had messed up everything. But hadn't God led her to this point? Hadn't he given her the courage she needed to propose to Andrew? Now she could see she'd been very, very wrong. "We should *geh* back to the singing," she mumbled, desperate to stew alone in her embarrassment.

"Please." His voice was soft and husky, a bone-melting tone she'd never heard him use before. "Don't leave."

Turning, she forced herself to look at him. At least he seemed less bewildered now. He ran his hand through his hair and stuffed his other hand in his pocket.

"I'm sorry," she managed to squeak out.

He paused, a half-smile on his lips. "Don't be." He went to her but still kept a respectable distance. "I'm flattered."

Flattered? That was the last thing she wanted to hear.

"But we've only been seeing each other for a few weeks," he added.

"Two months," she said under her breath. She'd kept track of every day, practically every minute.

"And they've been a great two months." His smile widened, yet he didn't move closer. "I thought you didn't mind us taking things slow. Then again, we never talked about it." He sighed. "We don't talk about much lately, do we? Guess that's *mei* fault."

"I don't understand."

Andrew met her eyes with an intense gaze. "I need to be sure about this, Joanna. About us. I don't want to rush into anything."

Eight years hardly seemed like rushing. Then again, he was still catching up.

"I care about you." He removed his hand from his pocket and touched her cheek for a brief second, then pulled back as if her skin burned him. "And I'm saying that it's possible, that maybe sometime in the future when the time is right, we could talk about, uh, being more serious."

Joanna fought the urge to roll her eyes. She wasn't embarrassed anymore. In fact, she was a little annoyed. Why wasn't he willing to take a chance with her? Didn't he know how deeply she loved him? She'd never gone home with any other boy after a singing. She'd never been out on a date. She had spent any free time she had with him over the years. She baked his favorite desserts and took them to his house to surprise him, although she made sure to make plenty for his mother, Naomi, and his sister, Irene, so they wouldn't get suspicious. She'd listened to him talk about his farrier business until she was sure she could shoe a horse herself. What other ways could she show him how she felt? Why did she have to try so hard with him?

"I need to get back inside before *mei schwesters* notice I'm gone," she said flatly. This time when she turned around, she wasn't going to let him stop her. It ended up not mattering, because he didn't even try.

Andrew watched Joanna walk away, still shocked by her proposal and still kicking himself for how he handled it. Ever since he'd made the decision to court her, he'd bungled their relationship. He'd known for years that she liked him. He had always cared for her too. She was sweet, pretty, and so devoted, not only to their friendship but to her family and faith. She was everything he wanted in a woman. Yet for years he'd put off asking her out for one reason—he was scared. He didn't know how to date. He didn't even know what a romantic relationship was supposed to be. It wasn't as if his father had been a sterling example.

So he thought he needed to be respectful. To make sure he kept his own feelings and desires in control around Joanna. They were young, barely twenty. He wasn't ready for marriage. But if he had been paying more attention, if he knew what he was doing in this relationship, he would have realized Joanna was.

He kicked at a clod of dirt. He'd go after her and offer to take her home tonight so they could talk more. Not that he had any idea what to say. But he had to fix this. He couldn't let her believe he didn't love her—because he did. He wasn't ready to say the words yet. The time had to be right. The moment special. She needed to feel cherished, loved, and secure. He needed to be the loyal man his father had failed to be.

He went back to the basement and searched for Joanna. He found her talking to Abigail, who was still standing next to Joel. Maybe he should ask him for advice. He would have gone to his best friend, Asa Bontrager, but he and his family had moved to Indiana years ago. Andrew knew he needed to talk to someone before he permanently ruined his future with Joanna.

As he reached her, Sadie came rushing to them. "We have to leave," she said, looking flustered and out of sorts.

"Now?" Abigail asked.

"Right now."

Andrew looked at Joanna. She nodded to her sister, glanced at Andrew, then left without a word.

As he watched her walk away, he prayed their relationship wasn't permanently broken.

⌒

The next morning Joanna sat in the backseat of her parents' buggy as they headed for the apple orchard. They would pick the apples, then sell them at the family store, Schrock Grocery and Tools. This was the first trip to the apple orchard, and they would go a few more times before the apple-picking season ended in October. She and her sisters took turns helping with the picking, and this year it was her turn to go.

But she wasn't thinking about apples right now. She rubbed her nose, still upset over what happened last night with Andrew. To his credit, when he'd returned to the Troyers' basement he had seemed upset too. More upset than she'd ever seen him. He also looked like he wanted to talk. Then Sadie had shown up, and Joanna was glad for the excuse to leave. She had been embarrassed enough for one night.

Abigail wasn't happy about leaving, however, and had peppered Sadie with questions on the way home.

Joanna had kept quiet, barely listening to their bickering as she replayed every moment of her botched proposal. How could she have been so stupid?

Her father's horse moved along at a brisk clip, the fall air warm and pleasant, the rich smells of full gardens and grazing livestock surrounding them as they traveled to the apple farm. The peaceful beauty was a stark contrast to her sour mood. Maybe last night had been a sign that she should finally give up on Andrew, that she would grow old and gray before he made up his mind about her. Yet she couldn't imagine herself with anyone else. She didn't want to.

"Joanna, what's wrong?"

She met her mother's over-the shoulder gaze. *"Nix."*

"You're rubbing the skin off *yer* nose. Is there something you want to talk about?" She glanced at *Daed*, who was staring straight ahead, his attention on the horse and the surrounding traffic, which was light today on the back roads.

Joanna put her hands in her lap. The buggy lurched as one of the wheels dipped into a pothole. The bright sun warmed the interior of the buggy. Or maybe it was her irritation making her face heat. "What's the point?" she muttered.

"What?"

Ugh. She hadn't meant to say the words out loud.

"Does this have something to do with Andrew?"

Stunned, Joanna gripped her fingers together. "Andrew?" She let out an awkward chuckle. "Nothing's going on with me and Andrew."

"If you say so." *Mamm* smirked.

Joanna sighed. Clearly she hadn't done a good job of hiding her feelings, at least from her mother. "How did you know?"

"A mother figures these things out." Her tone turned serious. "He hasn't hurt you, has he?"

Not on purpose. "Nee, Mamm. He hasn't. He's just . . . slow."

"Slow? I always thought he was pretty smart."

"I mean cautious. Overly cautious."

"Like I said, smart."

"What do you mean by that?"

Mamm turned more fully around in her seat. "Joanna, I know you've been carrying a torch for that *bu* for years. Which is okay. But you're both *yung*. There's *nee* reason to get serious right now."

Even her mother thought she was wrong to think about marrying Andrew? "What if I want to get serious?"

Her mother's face paled. "He didn't propose to you, did he?"

"Nee." She crossed her arms, feeling more defiant than she had in her whole life. "I proposed to him."

"Joanna!"

"I didn't rob a bank, *Mamm*. I just asked him to marry me."

"What did he say?"

She averted her gaze. "He said he wanted to talk about it."

Her mother breathed out a long sigh. "I'm glad one of you has some sense. I'm surprised at you. You're barely twenty years old. You have *nee* business getting married. How long have you and Andrew been dating, anyway?"

"A little over two months." Saying the words out loud made her feel sheepish. Still, she lifted her chin.

"Two months? How could you be so foolish? Marriage is not something to take lightly. You will be with *yer* husband the rest of *yer* life."

"I already know that," she replied, unable to keep the bite out of her tone.

"You don't want to rush into anything."

"How can eight years be rushing?" she blurted.

"Eight years?" *Mamm's* eyes grew wide. "I didn't realize you'd had a crush on him for that long."

"It wasn't—it's not—a crush. I love him, *Mamm*. I always have."

Mamm looked at *Daed*, who still remained focused on driving. But Joanna could see the muscle in his right cheek twitching hard. He was just as upset as *Mamm*. Disgusted, Joanna flopped back against the seat. "You and *Daed* have been trying to get Sadie married off for years."

"That's totally different."

"Why? Because Sadie's smarter? She's got more sense than I do?"

"In some ways . . . *ya*."

Joanna slumped farther in her seat. Her parents didn't trust her, despite her never giving them a single reason not to.

"Sadie's older," *Daed* added.

"You and *Mamm* were eighteen when you got married."

"We knew what we were doing." *Mamm* pressed her lips together.

"Why is it that you two knew what you were doing but I don't? Or that Sadie and Abigail are ready to get married but I'm not?"

"We worry about you, *lieb*. You've always been too trusting. So sweet and—"

"Gullible." She scowled.

"*Ya*. That too. Those aren't bad qualities. They simply show how pure *yer* heart is."

Joanna huffed. "That's supposed to make me feel better?"

"If you and Andrew are meant to get married, it will happen. But not now."

"Then when? When I'm forty?"

"Don't be ridiculous. *Yer* childish behavior right now is starting to prove our point."

Joanna knew that was true, but she was so angry she couldn't help it. "How old will I have to be before you trust me to make *gut* decisions?"

"We don't want you to get hurt, that's all."

"Andrew would never hurt me." But hadn't he last night? Then again, she had opened herself up for getting hurt by proposing. He hadn't even kissed her yet, and she was already pushing him for marriage. She put her fingertips to her temples. All she wanted was to be strong for once. To make something happen with Andrew instead of waiting eight more years before he would finally commit to her. She was ready to live her life. To be treated as a grown-up, not as a child.

But it didn't matter what she did. Her parents would always see her as a naive little girl. "Maybe Andrew and I will elope," she mumbled. The words sounded stupid to her own ears, and now she was really acting like a child. But she was furious, not only with them but with herself. She couldn't stop herself from digging a deeper hole. "If Andrew and I want to get married, we will get married, whether you like it or not."

Daed turned and looked at her, his eyes flashing with anger. "You will not speak to *yer mudder* that way—"

Suddenly everything became a blur. The buggy tilted violently. Joanna was in the air, then slammed to the ground. Her cheek stung and burned. *"Mamm? Daed?"* They didn't respond. She tried to get up but couldn't move. Pain shot through her hips and black spots danced in front of her eyes. She heard a weird noise. Tires squealing?

She collapsed and her world went black.

CHAPTER 3

Four weeks later

Andrew handed the taxi driver a twenty-dollar bill. "I'm not sure how long I'll be inside," he said as he opened the car door.

Marjorie, the driver, took the bill and nodded. "Take your time. You can call me when you're finished. I'm not doing anything else today." She glanced at her wristwatch. "I think I might have lunch at Mary Yoder's restaurant while I'm waiting."

Andrew nodded, barely hearing the woman. His stomach rebelled at the thought of food.

She patted her short, silver-colored hair. "Would you like me to bring you anything back?"

"Nee." As nice as Marjorie was—she lived in nearby Langdon and was a familiar driver among the Amish in Birch Creek—Andrew was eager for her to leave. "I'll be fine."

"All right. Give me a call when you're ready to be picked up."

As Marjorie drove off, he stood in front of the rehabilitation center and took a deep breath. Since the accident nearly a month ago, Joanna had rebuffed his attempts to contact her. He was tired of leaving messages, so he came here as a last resort. If she didn't want to see him, she would have to tell him to his face.

Gathering up his courage, he walked into the building, asked the woman behind the information desk for Joanna's room number, then headed for the elevator. Two other people got on at the same time. They were *Englisch*, of course. He steeled himself for their curious glances, but they stared straight ahead at the elevator doors. Then he remembered that *Englisch* folks in Middlefield were used to the Amish. They mixed and mingled like a tossed fruit salad in this atypical Ohio town.

The doors opened. Andrew excused himself and walked onto the floor. He gulped and went in the direction of Joanna's room. He knew she'd be surprised to see him, but would she be happy? The last time they were together, he'd refused her marriage proposal. He intended to right that wrong, but not today. This morning he only wanted to see her. To make sure she was okay. They could talk about the future when she returned home.

Unless she never wanted to see him again.

He ditched that thought and knocked on the door to her room. He heard a loud grunt and had to force himself not to barge in. Was she in pain? Did she need help? At the second grunt, he couldn't stop himself. He opened the door a crack. "Joanna?"

Silence met his voice. Now he was genuinely concerned. He opened the door wider. "Joanna? It's Andrew." How stupid. Of course she knew who he was. "Can I come in?"

Another long pause. Had he gotten the wrong room number?

He should have written it down. But he had a good memory for numbers, so he hadn't felt the need. Still, he could have made a mistake—

"*Ya.*"

He stilled. Her voice was weaker than it used to be. And uncertain. But she was still Joanna. He leaned against the door for a moment before walking inside. He passed by an empty bed, then peeked around a curtain that divided the room in half. "Hi," he said, then stopped, shocked by what he saw.

She was in a wheelchair. He didn't know why that surprised him, considering he knew she had broken her pelvis and had to have surgery. He also noticed she was thin. Very thin. Joanna had always been slender, but now her cheeks were gaunt and he could clearly see her collarbone under the neckline of her dress. Beads of perspiration dotted her face, and the pink kerchief fastened to her rich brown hair was damp at the edges. Her light blue dress was also sweat soaked.

"Are you okay?" was all he could think to say. Then he wanted to kick himself all the way back to Birch Creek. Of course she wasn't okay. She'd been in a terrible accident. Broken her pelvis. Lost her parents. He couldn't comprehend what she was going through, even though he understood what it was like to have your entire life upended without warning.

He had lost his father—not because he died, but because the man chose another woman over his family. Andrew knew about loss, what it was like to lose someone you loved, but not to the extent Joanna did. More than anything he wanted to take that pain from her. But he didn't know how. All he knew was that she shouldn't have to go through the heartache alone.

She turned her head to the side, not looking at him. "*Ya.* I'm fine." Her cheek, rosy from whatever exertion she'd been doing, was begging to be kissed. He didn't care that she was sweating or in a wheelchair or not even looking at him. He was grateful she was alive. He hadn't lost her. *Thank you, God.*

Despite wanting to go to her, he held back. He'd always tried to be respectful toward her, and now he knew he had to be careful, too, until she healed. He didn't want to do anything to set back her recovery. "Hi," he said again.

"Hi." Her voice was barely above a whisper, and she still wasn't looking at him.

"Did I interrupt something?"

She paused, then nodded. "I was doing some of *mei* exercises." She sighed. "I can't do them all yet. Once I can, they'll let me *geh* home."

He nodded, relieved that she was getting closer to being released. He missed her and he wanted her home. "I called you. Several times," he couldn't help but add.

"I know. I'm sorry." She turned slightly toward him, her chestnut eyes meeting his. He still couldn't see the other side of her face. It was as if she was hiding it from him.

"It's okay. I know you've been . . . busy." He swallowed an unexpected lump in his throat. If she'd allowed it, he would have been by her side every day. But at least she hadn't been alone. Her sister had been with her. "Where's Abigail?"

"Getting lunch. She's been cooped up with me all morning." Joanna glanced at him again. "You didn't have to *kumme* here, Andrew."

He took a step toward her. "I wanted to." He glanced around the sparse room. Had she received his flowers? He didn't see them anywhere. Maybe they'd died already. He should have gotten her

23

a plant instead. They lasted longer. He scratched his eyebrow, feeling more ill at ease with her than ever before.

She turned her chair toward the window, keeping her back to him, her gaze fixed on the closed blinds.

"Do you want me to open those for you?" He moved toward the window.

"*Nee.*"

He stopped, took off his straw hat, laid it on the crisp white sheets of her neatly made hospital bed, and threaded his fingers through his hair. He knew this would be hard, but he hadn't expected to feel this much distance between them, even though they were only separated by a few feet. Maybe he should leave. But hadn't he spent enough time apart from her? Hadn't he hurt her enough? "Joanna," he said, sitting on the edge of the bed, "are you mad at me?"

She paused for the briefest of moments and shook her head. "I'm just tired."

His shoulders sloped with relief. At least she wasn't upset with him, even though she had a good reason. "I'm sorry about what happened. *Yer* parents . . . the night at the Troyers' . . ."

Her lips pressed together until they were white. "It's . . . okay."

"*Nee*, it's not. I didn't mean to hurt *yer* feelings."

"You didn't."

But he knew she was lying. Why else wouldn't she look at him? He gripped the edge of the bed, his fingers digging into the sheets. "Joanna, I want—" He swallowed again. "I need to ask you something."

She wiped the sweat off her forehead with the back of her hand, then nodded.

"I want us to get married." He froze. Where had that come

from? That wasn't what he'd intended to say. He wanted a chance to apologize and tell her he loved her, the words he should have said the night before the accident. He wanted to find out if she still loved him. *Why did I propose instead?*

But hadn't he been thinking about her proposal—and his stupid rejection of it—since that night at the Troyers'? Hadn't he replayed the scenario over and over in his mind, telling her yes instead of breaking her heart with his refusal? Wasn't asking her to marry him now the right thing to do?

When she didn't say anything, he held his breath. He'd made another mistake. Why couldn't he do anything right when it came to her? All he wanted was for Joanna to know how much he loved her. Instead, he proposed to her in a rehab center while she was still healing from surgery and grieving her parents' deaths. Talk about rotten timing.

She continued to stare at the white vertical blinds as if they held the answer to his question. He was about to stand up and tell her not to worry about answering him now when she whispered, "All right."

He leaned forward until he almost fell off the bed. Had he heard her correctly? "What?"

Slowly she turned the chair to face him. But she still wasn't looking at him directly, and he still couldn't see her entire face. Then he realized why. Her scar. He remembered Abigail informing him at her parents' funeral that Joanna's face was injured when she was flung from the buggy. He was about to tell her she didn't have to hide anything from him. That she was perfect the way she was—

"I'll marry you." Her voice was a little louder and stronger this time.

He rose from the bed and walked to her, then knelt in front of the wheelchair, putting both hands on the arms of the chair. His uneasiness disappeared as he looked into her beautiful eyes. He wanted to take her into his arms and kiss her until they both couldn't breathe. But he wouldn't do that, not now. He had to show her how much he respected her. Honored her. Loved her. So as he'd always done with her, he held his feelings close inside, not wanting to scare or overwhelm her. She was fragile, and never more so than right now. "*Danki*, Joanna."

She brushed back a stray lock of brown hair that had escaped from beneath the kerchief. She had shadows under her eyes, and there was a lost look about her that didn't sit well with him even though she had said yes to his impulsive proposal. She had agreed to marry him, but she looked anything but happy about it. *Cut her some slack. You can see she's not feeling well.* He couldn't stop himself from leaning forward and kissing her uninjured cheek. "I love you," he said before pulling away.

"I . . . I love you too."

"When do you think you'll be home?"

"Maybe a week." She glanced up at him. "I hope."

"We can talk about the wedding then." He didn't want to push her any more than he had. "Do you need anything from home? Or I can come and spell Abigail for a while—"

"I wouldn't want to put you out. I'll be busy with therapy."

"But I want to help—"

"I'll be home in a week." She finally smiled. "Like you said, we can talk then."

He had the distinct feeling he was being dismissed. "Are you . . . sure?" He wasn't only referring to their future discussion of the wedding.

After a pause she said, "*Ya.* I'm sure." She lifted her hand toward her face as if she was going to rub her nose, then gripped the wheelchair wheel. "I need to rest, Andrew."

He got the hint. "Okay." He stood and backed away. He didn't want to tire her or keep her from healing as quickly as she could.

"I'll see you when I'm home."

He would cling to that promise until then. He retrieved his hat from the bed and put it on his head. "Call me when they release you, *ya*? I can *kumme* with Sadie when she picks up you and Abigail."

"I will."

Andrew looked at her one last time before leaving her room. When he got downstairs, he pulled out his cell phone, which he only used in emergencies, and dialed Marjorie's number.

"That was quick," the older woman said over a bite of food. Andrew heard her swallow before she asked, "Is everything all right?"

"*Ya.*" He and Joanna were getting married. That fact hit him like a hay bale in the chest, shaking him to the core. He'd always wanted to be sure about everything, especially marriage. It was the reason he hadn't said yes to her at the Troyers'. But despite his nerves, he believed he was doing the right thing. He loved Joanna. And God had not only answered his prayer to keep her alive, but also that she still loved him enough to marry him. That's what mattered, not his apprehension. He finally smiled, his first time since arriving in Middlefield. "*Ya*," he repeated to Marjorie. "Everything is *gut*."

27

ONE WEEK LATER

Teeth clenched, Joanna wiped the back of her hand over her sweat-slicked forehead as she did her morning exercises for her hips and legs. Her physical therapist had warned her not to do too much, but Joanna ignored the advice. The quicker she regained her strength, the faster she would get rid of the stupid crutches she was so dependent on. Her hips ached as she lay on the pink-and-gray woven rag rug Abigail had made for her last year. She did three extra leg lift sets until her lower body trembled with fatigue.

Her breathing still labored, she pushed herself to a sitting position. Homer, the stray dog Sadie and her new husband, Aden Troyer, had adopted while Joanna was at the rehabilitation center, sauntered into the room. He sniffed her right calf, gave it a quick lick, then jumped onto her bed.

"Homer, off."

He put his chin on his paws and closed his eyes.

Joanna half-smiled at the stubborn mutt, but she didn't reprimand him. Sadie didn't want the dog on the furniture, but this was Joanna's room—a makeshift one since she couldn't go up the stairs to her own bedroom. Homer could do what he pleased here. She had been unable to resist him since she'd returned home two days ago. When she was growing up, her family couldn't have a dog because of *Mamm's* allergies. Homer, with his brown spots on half of his white coat, and his tongue always hanging out of this mouth, seemed to like Joanna. She enjoyed the dog's company too.

Her legs still too weak to support her body, she stayed on the floor and surveyed her room. Anything so she didn't have to think about Andrew . . . or his proposal. Had she been *ab im kopp* when she agreed to marry him? That had to be it, or else she wouldn't have answered him so quickly, and so foolishly. But at the time she would have said anything to get him to leave. He'd seen her at her worst—sweating, weak, and in pain. She'd never wanted him to see her that way. And his response to her helplessness had been to propose. It didn't make any sense. What had made him switch from wanting to wait to talk about marriage to suddenly proposing?

Guilt. The accident. Pity. All of the above.

She pushed Andrew from her thoughts and focused on her temporary bedroom. Because of her injuries, Aden and his older brother, Sol, had added the small room to her family's house while she'd been in therapy in Middlefield for the past month. The room was simple and had the basic necessities—a twin-size bed shoved against a white wall, her nightstand from her room upstairs, a small bureau, and a pegboard Sol had constructed from spare lumber. She used it to hang her dresses. It was strange to think that Sol and Aden were now part of her family. They had helped her sisters make sure Joanna had a safe and comfortable room until she was well enough to walk upstairs. Not only did her sisters care about her, but the family Sadie had married into did too. Their thoughtfulness didn't ease the sorrow she experienced every time she thought of her parents, but it did help . . . a little.

Feeling a bit stronger, she placed her hand on the mattress to steady herself and rose to her feet. She pushed the white strings of her prayer *kapp* off her shoulders so they lay against the back of her light green dress. Homer's huge brown eyes tracked her movements. As if in sympathy, he licked the tops of her fingers.

She patted his soft head before turning off the battery-operated lamp on her nightstand. Morning darkness engulfed the room, but she knew exactly where her crutches were. She put them under her arms and started for the door. Everyone would be up soon, and she wanted to have breakfast ready. The activity would also help keep her thoughts away from Andrew. *I hope.*

She hobbled to the kitchen and turned on the gas lamp suspended from the ceiling, then gathered what she needed to make breakfast. She could still cook and bake, but now it was more of a chore than a joy. Breakfast this morning would be simple— reheated cinnamon rolls from the batch she'd made the day before, ham steaks, sliced pears, and coffee. Gathering the food required overcoming a series of obstacles that turned a fifteen-minute task into almost an hour ordeal.

By the time the rolls were warming in the oven and the steaks were sizzling in a cast iron skillet on the stove, she was already tired and achy. But she also felt a small sense of satisfaction. She could prepare a meal. She wasn't useless.

Aden walked into the room a few minutes later. She glanced at her brother-in-law, still getting used to the idea that he was Sadie's husband. Sadie had explained to her sisters that their parents' deaths were the catalyst for the quick marriage. The decision made sense, of course. Aden now did a lot of the physical work her father had done around the house and the store. In some ways he and Sadie had taken the place of their parents, at least when it came to the family business.

But Joanna struggled with Sadie's surprise marriage, mostly because she'd been in rehab and hadn't been a part of the ceremony. Abigail hadn't either. That was Joanna's fault too. Jealousy also lurked. Sadie had her happy ending, romantically speaking.

Joanna wondered if she'd ever have hers. If she could ever trust that Andrew's marriage proposal was sincere. He hadn't wanted to marry her when she was normal and whole. Why would he want to be with her now that she was scarred and broken?

More important, what right did she have to be happy when her parents were dead?

"Morning," Aden said, drawing Joanna out of her thoughts. He took a mug from the cabinet, then paused. "Everything all right?"

She nodded and shuffled to him, offering to take the mug. "I'll bring you *yer kaffee* and breakfast."

"I don't mind getting *mei* own *kaffee*."

But she wanted to get it for him. She could do little else right now. Then she remembered today was different. "Sadie told me yesterday that today's *yer* birthday. You deserve special treatment."

A slight rosy hue appeared on his cheeks. Joanna didn't know Aden well. Not only was he almost three years older and Sadie's age, but he had also kept to himself over the years. From what Joanna could tell so far, though, he was a kind man who loved her sister, and he was nothing if not humble.

Aden sat down, and she poured his coffee. She'd bake him a birthday cake for dessert tonight. They were expecting his brother, Sol, and their mother, Rhoda, for supper, and Joanna would find a way to make the meal extra special.

She leaned one of her crutches against the counter and made her way to the table, balancing the coffee mug and putting her weight on the single crutch. She'd learned the hard way yesterday not to fill the mug to the top. Pleased she didn't spill a drop, she handed the mug to Aden. "Happy birthday."

"Birthday *kaffee*." Aden grinned at her. "That's a first for me."

Sadie walked into the kitchen. "Good morning." She touched Aden's shoulder as she passed by him.

Joanna saw the loving looks Sadie and Aden exchanged and felt a jolt of envy. She and Andrew had never been as comfortable and loving around each other as Sadie and Aden were. If that day he showed up at the rehabilitation center was any indication, things between them were even more strained than before. That was why she hadn't kept her promise to call him when she was released, and why she hadn't seen him since she'd been home.

She couldn't face him right now. She knew she should be celebrating their impending wedding. She'd finally gotten what she wanted—a commitment from Andrew. Yet she felt anything but satisfied. Or happy. She couldn't even tell her sisters she was engaged. That's not normal. Then again, she wasn't normal anymore.

With another hard shake of her head, she shoved Andrew and her engagement out of her mind. She'd focus on getting well, and then she'd make things up to Abigail, who had spent weeks at her bedside while Joanna was in the hospital and in rehabilitation. When she was able she would join her sisters and work in the store, along with making sure Abigail, Sadie, and Aden had delicious food to eat every day. From now on she would put her family first, not her own selfish desires.

Yet she couldn't help but wonder that if things were different, if the accident that was partly her fault hadn't happened, that Andrew wouldn't have asked her to marry him out of obligation. That eventually, someday, he would have proposed out of love.

Ugh. She rubbed her nose. Somehow she had to figure out a way not to obsess about him. She went back to check on the steaks. She had flipped two of them over when Abigail entered the kitchen, her expression unusually somber.

"Joanna, someone's here to see you."

Joanna lifted an eyebrow. Sadie and Aden seemed surprised too. "Who would be visiting this early in the morning?"

"Andrew."

Joanna froze, the sizzle and popping of the steaks the only sound in the kitchen. "Why is he here?" she whispered.

"For you. He's here to see you."

⁓

Andrew's palms were slick as he shifted the bouquet to his free hand. He wiped his damp hand against the leg of his work pants. It was early, ridiculously early, but he couldn't stay away from Joanna any longer. He'd bought the flowers yesterday after work, resisting the urge to stop by her house last night and give them to her. He wanted to see her face light up the way it always did when she received something from him. This time she was getting a nice arrangement, not a silly acorn or a pitiful flower.

He'd promised himself he would wait, mostly because he had to come to terms with her broken promise. He kept telling himself that he couldn't blame her for not calling him when she was ready to come home. It wasn't her fault she hadn't contacted him, even though she'd been back in Birch Creek for two days. She was busy, she was getting settled, she was tired . . . He continued providing her with a litany of excuses. He was trying to be understanding. He had to be understanding.

But this morning he'd had enough of sleepless nights and waiting on her. He'd planned to see her later today after he finished work, but when he got up this morning he didn't even bother with breakfast. He hooked his horse Fred to his buggy and drove over here before there was a hint of daylight in the sky.

The longer he waited in the living room, the faster his hope fell. He suspected something was wrong when Abigail had frowned at the flowers, although the look had been so fleeting Andrew almost missed it. Had Joanna told her about their engagement? He would be surprised if she had. Before the accident they had kept their romantic relationship a secret from everyone. At the time that had felt right, especially since Andrew had wanted to take things slow with Joanna. But since then everything had changed. Now he knew what real fear was. He'd almost lost her. *I'm not wasting any more time.* He would shout out his feelings from the top of the Schrock barn if she asked him to.

Abigail came out of the kitchen. He straightened, smiling. The flowers seemed to wilt in his hand when he realized Abigail was alone.

"I'm sorry, Andrew. Joanna doesn't want to see you right now."

His fingers clenched around the delicate green paper surrounding the bouquet. He'd made sure to pick out her favorites: three pink carnations and three pink roses. He didn't know squat about flowers, but he knew she liked pink, and these were the pinkest ones he could find.

"She's been through a lot," Abigail continued.

Andrew shifted on his feet. He guessed Abigail didn't know anything about the engagement. Andrew wouldn't be the one to tell her. "I just want to see her for a few minutes." *I need to see her.*

"But she's not ready to see you."

His jaw twitched as he tried to accept Abigail's words. Had

Joanna changed her mind? A slight jolt of relief ran through him. Then he shook his head. Relief? He wanted to marry Joanna. He was sure of it . . . wasn't he?

"Andrew?"

He looked at Abigail, still dazed. *"Ya?"*

"Why don't you come by tomorrow? I'm sure she'll be up to a visit then."

But he could see she was lying. The sting of rejection burned. He handed the flowers to Abigail. "Give her these." He walked out the front door, letting it slam behind him, and started down the planked steps, only to jerk to a stop on the bottom step. He took in several deep breaths. Turning around, he went back to the house and knocked on the door again. Abigail opened it, the bouquet held loosely in her hand, as if she'd expected him to return right away.

"I'm sorry," he said. "I didn't mean to be rude."

"It's all right."

"Nee, it's not. I'm worried about her, that's all. I thought if I could see her for a few minutes . . ." He shook his head. "Never mind."

Kindness entered her brown eyes. "You need to be patient with her." She frowned a little. "We all do. It's hard because we care so much about her. We want our sweet Joanna back."

Andrew wasn't naive or thoughtless enough to believe that Joanna hadn't been changed by the accident and the deaths of her parents. But what did her sister mean about getting Joanna back? Had she changed that much? If only Joanna would give him a chance to find out.

Abigail was right. He did need patience, which he normally had in abundance. *Joanna's not the only one who's changed.* Even if she wouldn't see him, he needed to remind her of what was on his heart. "Would you please give Joanna a message?"

"Of course," Abigail said with a small, compassionate smile.

He was glad to have one sister on his side. He gulped, shocked by the emotion suddenly constricting his throat. "Tell her I love her. Tell her I'm not going anywhere. She can count on that." Then he took off, not waiting for a response.

⟶

LANGDON, OHIO

Seated on his beat-up sofa, Cameron Crawford looked around the tiny one-bedroom apartment. His gaze landed on the morning's local paper, which lay on the warped coffee table. The headline screamed at him: REWARD FOR HIT AND RUN INFORMATION. He didn't have to read the article to learn the story. He *was* the story.

He pushed the paper off the table and pulled on his steel-toed boots. He shoved the accident out of his mind, only to have the memory replaced with a bittersweet one: the day six months ago when he and Mackenzie had first moved in. She'd protested when he'd carried her over the threshold, saying that at seven months pregnant she was too heavy for him to lift. Of course she wasn't, and the delight in her eyes when he held her close and they walked into their first apartment together had made him believe in miracles and happy endings.

He didn't believe in them anymore.

He rubbed his palms over his worn jeans, picked up the plain brown picture frame on the coffee table, and ran his finger over the glass. His beautiful Mackenzie. He'd snapped the picture with his camera phone right after she delivered Lacy. That was the second happiest day of his life. The first was when he and Mackenzie married. He'd never felt such joy, the kind that exploded in his chest and kept a permanent smile on his face. Mackenzie and Lacy. His precious girls. The loves of his life.

Cameron touched his lips, remembering how he'd kissed Mackenzie's pale, damp forehead when the nurse took Lacy from her. "She's perfect," he'd said to Mackenzie. "You're perfect."

Then the machines started to beep. The nurses rushed around, panicked. Cameron could still hear their words . . . Blood pressure is dropping . . . She's lost too much blood . . . Prep for surgery . . .

His throat pinched and he set down the photo. He didn't only need to leave Langdon because of what had happened six weeks ago. He also needed to escape the memories that haunted him like a relentless ghost, taunting him about what he had lost . . . and how much he still had to lose.

Mrs. Rodriguez walked into the living room from Lacy's bedroom, holding the baby in her arms. "Say good morning to *Papi*, sunshine."

Despite his melancholy, Cameron smiled. He couldn't help it when he saw his daughter's sweet face. "Are you sure you don't mind watching her today? I can still drop her off at day care."

"Mind? Of course not. I jump at the chance anytime I can watch this little cutie pie." She kissed Lacy's cheek. His landlord and part-time babysitter, Mrs. Rodriguez, was the classic grandmother type—loving, cheerful, and wonderful with Lacy. Since his daughter didn't have any grandparents in her life, spending time with Mrs. Rodriguez had been good for her, even if that time had been short. He was glad Mrs. Rodriguez benefited from the relationship too.

She handed Lacy to Cameron. "I'll fix her bottle."

Cameron cradled Lacy in his arm while Mrs. Rodriguez prepared Lacy's breakfast. He would be leaving soon for his job at Barton Plastics, where he'd worked since he and Mackenzie had moved into the apartment. Eight hours a day, six days a week. He was relieved Mrs. Rodriguez was willing to watch Lacy on a Saturday. He'd found a day care that was open on Saturdays, but they charged double the rate. This would save him money, something he desperately needed.

He kissed the top of Lacy's head, fierce love filling him. More often than not he felt helpless and unworthy of taking care of this tiny baby who had become his reason for living. Light blonde fuzz covered her tiny scalp. Mackenzie's hair. His was dark, nearly black, and he kept it long and in a ponytail because Mackenzie had liked it that way. He stared at Lacy's blue eyes—a trait she'd inherited from both him and her mother.

"I can't thank you enough for everything you've done for me and Lacy," Cameron said to Mrs. Rodriguez.

"It's my pleasure," she called out from the kitchen, which was only a few feet from the living room. The apartment, and the furniture he and Mackenzie had purchased from a thrift store, was about two decades out of date. But it had seemed like paradise when he and Mackenzie settled in.

Mrs. Rodriguez went to Cameron and took Lacy from him, holding the baby's bottle in one hand. "She's such a sweet baby. No trouble at all."

"I don't want to impose." Cameron pulled at the sleeves of his shirt, making sure the cuffs didn't roll past his forearms. He hadn't worn a short-sleeved shirt in years, except when he was with Mackenzie. He didn't want to face the questions the cigarette burns and penknife scars covering his upper arms and torso always instigated. *Thanks, Mom and Dad.*

Settling her plump frame into an orange-and-brown-plaid chair, she shook her head at him. "For the thousandth time, you're not imposing. Besides, this is good practice for when my own children have their babies. Of course, they'll have to get married first." She sighed. "Unfortunately all three of them are too *busy* to find a spouse."

Cameron had only met Mrs. Rodriguez's three sons a couple of times before Lacy was born. They were older than he was, in their late twenties and early thirties. Here he was, barely twenty, a widower with an infant to take care of, plus a new thundercloud hanging over his head, threatening to drown both him and Lacy. But his days were numbered at Barton Plastics, and in Langdon. He would have to skip town soon. He'd put it off for too long. His throat pinched. He'd thought he finally found a stable home here. A place where he could escape his past and build a new future. This town, even this tiny apartment that most people would have thumbed their noses at, had held so much promise for him and Mackenzie. Now every moment he stayed here reminded him of what he lost.

But he wouldn't reveal all this to Mrs. Rodriguez. He wasn't going to draw her into his nightmare. Somehow he'd have to live with what he'd done. Not just to the Amish family—he refused to think of them by name—but also with the choices he'd made since then. He stood and grabbed his keys off the coffee table. "I'll be back by five. Call me if something happens." His gaze remained on Lacy as she contentedly sucked on her bottle.

"Cameron." Mrs. Rodriguez's voice and expression were somber. "Don't worry. Nothing will happen to your daughter."

Nothing was supposed to happen to Mackenzie either. He would never stop worrying about Lacy, because he knew life was fragile and could be snuffed out at any moment, whether in a hospital maternity ward or on a back road in Birch Creek.

CHAPTER 4

Joanna clung to the edge of her bed as she heard a soft knock on her bedroom door.

"Joanna?" Abigail said from the other side, her voice tentative.

Sighing, Joanna stroked Homer's back. He'd followed her into her bedroom after she told Abigail she didn't want to see Andrew. She didn't care that she'd left the ham steak on the stove and the cinnamon rolls in the oven. All she'd wanted was escape.

But she couldn't escape Abigail. Her sister was tenacious, and she would stand outside her door until next week if Joanna didn't let her in. "Come in."

Abigail entered carrying a lovely pink bouquet. "Andrew brought you these." She eased next to Joanna on the bed and handed the bundle of flowers to her. "You're not going to throw them away this time, are you?"

Joanna looked down at the delicate pink blooms. Her chest

felt heavy, like a huge rock was resting on it. Andrew had also sent her flowers shortly after she arrived at the rehabilitation center. In a fit of anger and confusion, she'd tossed them in the trash and regretted it right afterward. But at the time the bouquet didn't cheer her up. It had served as a reminder of her rejected proposal and the argument she'd had with her parents.

The flowers he'd brought this morning were stunning, just like the previous bouquet. It was so like him to make sure the blooms were her favorite color. She didn't have the urge to throw them away this time, but they did spur her guilt again. Yet deep inside her heart she was touched. Her throat constricted with confusion and, to her surprise and frustration, longing. *Lord, why am I so flustered about everything?*

"Why wouldn't you see him?" Abigail asked gently.

What was she supposed to say? *I don't want to see him because I embarrassed myself by asking him to marry me. Oh, and then I fought with* Mamm *and* Daed *about it right before they died. And then he asked me to marry him and I said yes, even though I'm pretty sure I made a huge mistake . . .*

Instead she looked away and said nothing.

"He said to tell you he loves you."

Joanna froze. He had told her he loved her in the rehabilitation center, but she wouldn't allow the words to nestle in her heart. She'd been certain that after he had time to think about marrying her, he would not only take back his proposal but also his declaration of love.

Yet he had repeated it, this time to her sister. That blew their privacy—and the status of their relationship—out into the open. What happened to taking things slow?

This wasn't like Andrew. He didn't do things on impulse. And that worried her more than anything.

Abigail put her hand on Joanna's arm. "He also said he isn't going anywhere."

She gaped. "He told you that?"

"*Ya.* I didn't realize you two were so serious." Abigail stuck out her bottom lip in an exaggerated pout. "First Sadie kept Aden a secret, and now I find out you and Andrew were courting." She sighed. "At least I've been upfront with you and Sadie about how much I like Joel Zook."

Joanna met Abigail's gaze. "We're not serious." She rubbed her nose.

"And pigs fly upside down." She pointed to Joanna's nose. Joanna immediately stopped the rubbing motion. "He was really upset that you wouldn't see him. He went to all the trouble to bring you those pretty flowers before the sun was even up."

She looked at the mix of carnations and roses in her hand again. "You know Andrew. He's nice. Polite. He was just being thoughtful."

"What's going on, Joanna?"

Joanna could feel something inside her almost break in two. A part of her wanted to tell Abigail everything. Maybe her sister would have some insight. But she held back. Abigail and Sadie had enough to worry about without dealing with Joanna's doubts and fears about her relationship with Andrew. She glanced down at the flowers again and shook her head.

"All right. I won't pry. I'm showing a huge amount of restraint, by the way." Abigail chuckled, but Joanna couldn't even bring herself to smile.

"I told him to stop by tomorrow," Abigail added.

Joanna grimaced. "Why?"

Abigail held up her hands. "I thought it was a *gut* idea at the time. You do want to see him eventually, right?"

She paused, then nodded. Because despite her confusion and misgivings, she missed him. She missed his steady presence in her life. The sweet little tokens he used to give her when he was doing his corny magic trick. The easy talks they used to have before everything between them changed.

Her sister took the bouquet from Joanna. "You know, if Joel showed up here and brought me flowers and proclaimed his undying love, I'd be doing cartwheels in the backyard—" She brought her hand to her mouth. "Joanna, I'm so sorry. I didn't think. That was wrong of me to say."

"It's all right." Abigail's words had barely made it past Joanna's haze. "Honestly, don't give it another thought."

But Abigail looked stricken. "I'll just take my foot out of *mei* mouth. Make that both feet."

Joanna lifted her lips in a half-smile. "I promise, Abigail. You didn't say anything wrong. I'll be doing cartwheels soon enough."

"That's the spirit." Abigail stood. "Still, I'm going to stay out of *yer* business from now on." She glanced at the flowers. "I'll put these in water. Do you want to keep them in *yer* room? They would look so pretty on *yer* dresser."

The last place she wanted them was in her room. "They would be nice on the kitchen table. That way everyone can enjoy them."

"You're sure?"

"Positive."

"Have it *yer* way, then." Abigail smiled. "I'll walk back with you to the kitchen. Those cinnamon rolls smell *gut*."

"You *geh* ahead. I'll be right behind you."

Once her sister was out of sight, Joanna bit the inside of her bottom lip. Andrew loved her. Wanted to marry her. She'd spent months—years, actually—waiting for him to feel the same about her as she felt about him. Yet all she could do was sit on her bed and feel doubt, dread, and a good dose of apprehension. Now what was she supposed to do? Andrew would be back tomorrow. She couldn't avoid him again.

But what could she tell him? What *should* she tell him? Her mind spun in bewilderment. Was love supposed to be this complicated? This difficult?

Straightening, she took her crutches and focused her mind on the day's work. She still had time to figure things out, if that was even possible.

A few moments later Joanna limped to the kitchen. Aden had already eaten breakfast and gone to work outside. Sadie was finishing up her coffee while Abigail used the side of her fork to cut through one of the three cinnamon rolls on her plate. Joanna's gaze went to the bouquet at the center of the table. The sunlight streaming through the windows dappled spots of light on the soft petals of the roses. She stumbled through a quick turn and headed for the stove. She might be able to choke down a cup of coffee, but little else. She hadn't had much of an appetite since the accident.

"Are you still planning to work in *Daed's* office today, Sadie?" Abigail asked. "Oh, wait, Joanna. Let me get that for you."

Remembering she couldn't manage both crutches and the coffee, she let Abigail take the mug from her. Ugh, once again she needed help. She hid her frustration as she hobbled to the table and lowered her achy body into one of the chairs. Abigail set the coffee down in front of Joanna, then sat next to Sadie as they resumed their conversation.

"*Ya,* I plan to work on organizing the file cabinets," Sadie said. "That will take all *daag.* There's still so much that needs to be done."

Abigail fiddled with her fork. "I never knew *Daed* was such a pack rat."

"Me either. But I don't mind. Going through *Daed's* things . . ." Sadie touched the top edge of her coffee mug, her voice cracking. "It's almost like he's still here."

Joanna nodded and Abigail pushed her plate away. They sat in silence for a moment. Joanna couldn't bring herself to talk about her parents, even with Sadie and Abigail. The hurt was still too fresh.

Sadie finally spoke. "Abigail, are you sure you don't mind working the front of the store by yourself? Aden will be around if things get busy."

Abigail shook her head. "I can handle a few customers. It will be *gut* to work for a change."

Joanna pushed away the guilt that was becoming a familiar part of her life. Of course Abigail would be eager to return to the store. Anything was better than being stuck at Joanna's side day in and day out. *Stop feeling sorry for yourself.* But it was hard to halt the negative train of thought once it got rolling.

She wished she could join her sisters at the store. The whole family had always run the grocery together. She hadn't been as involved as Sadie and Abigail, mostly because she liked to be in the kitchen preparing meals, canning vegetables, and baking treats for neighbors, friends, and church services. Her favorite task when she did work in the grocery was creating displays that would grab customer interest, such as pairing marshmallows, graham crackers, and chocolate bars for s'mores. If she tried to do that now, she would only be in the way. She'd probably knock something over with her crutches too. But as soon as she was physically able, she would pull her fair share of shifts in the store.

The kitchen grew quiet again. "I miss them." Abigail's voice was barely above a whisper.

"Me too," Sadie added. She took Joanna's hand but didn't say anything else.

Then Abigail cleared her throat, took a hefty forkful of cinnamon roll, and held it in front of her mouth. "These hit the spot." She practically inhaled the huge bite.

"You should think about selling them in the store, Joanna." Sadie released her hand. "When Aden gets his honey business going again, we're going to sell his products. We're getting a steady stream of *Englisch* customers, and I've had a lot of them asking if we carry baked goods or Amish-made items."

"I was thinking about selling a couple of my rugs." Abigail stood and picked up her plate and napkin. "They're so easy to make. Do you think they'd sell?"

"Absolutely." Sadie glanced at Joanna, then at Abigail again. "And while you two create *yer* masterpieces, I'll do the accounting."

"Sounds exciting," Abigail said dryly.

"I like it." Sadie folded her napkin and set it on her empty plate. "Aden says I have a knack for it."

Abigail smirked. "I'm glad one of us does." She put her dish in the sink. "I'll *geh* open the store."

Joanna expected Sadie to follow Abigail, since she was usually eager to start work first thing after breakfast. But her sister stayed in her seat, leisurely sipping her coffee. Only when Abigail had left the kitchen did Sadie speak.

"Joanna, can we talk?"

"Have I done something wrong?" Maybe sending Andrew away had upset Sadie.

Sadie shook her head, giving Joanna an encouraging smile. "Of course not. Although I'm worried you're doing too much work in the kitchen. You've only been home two *daags* and you seem tired. Abigail and I can help with the cooking."

"I can handle it." She sounded shorter than she meant to, and she could tell from Sadie's expression that her sister was taken aback. To soften her words, Joanna added, "I'm tired because I was up early this morning." She leaned forward, giving Sadie her full attention. "What do we need to discuss?"

"While you were at the rehab center, I discovered something. A secret *Mamm* and *Daed* kept from us."

Joanna gripped her coffee mug, which was still nearly full.

"There are natural gas rights attached to our property. I don't know why *Mamm* and *Daed* didn't tell us about them, but I'm sure they had their reasons. I recently got the paperwork, and Aden's been in talks with one of the gas companies that want to purchase the rights from us."

Joanna relaxed a little bit, glad the secret wasn't something devastating. She couldn't take any more bad news. "Does Abigail know?"

"I told her about it yesterday. Once we get a fair price for the rights, the money belongs to all of us. We'll use it to pay off our debts first."

Joanna blanched. Those debts were because of her. "I'm sorry," she said, staring at the lukewarm coffee.

"The bills aren't just from the accident. That's not *yer* fault, anyway."

But Sadie didn't understand. The accident was her fault, at least partly. She had distracted both of her parents with her bratty behavior. She'd have to live with that the rest of her life.

"We'd pay any amount of money for you to be alive and healed, Joanna. Don't doubt that for a minute."

Her sister's words were little comfort. The hospital and rehabilitation bills had to be a fortune.

"The store is in debt," Sadie continued. "That was something else we didn't know about. There's *nix* we can do about that, other than accept that they didn't want us to know about their money troubles. The point is, after the debts are paid, we need to discuss how to divide the money equally between the three of us. You don't have to worry about that now, of course. I wanted you to know, that's all."

"*Danki* for telling me."

"I—all of us—want you to focus on healing. Don't worry about bills or about doing so much work around here. God has taken care of us so far."

But he still allowed the accident to happen. Joanna tasted bitter bile climbing her throat.

"I'll help you with the dishes before I *geh* to the office." Sadie rose from the chair.

Joanna shook her head. "I'll do them."

"Did you hear what I just said?" There was an impatient bite in Sadie's voice. "You focus on getting better."

She nodded and kept the rest of her thoughts to herself. She didn't want to upset Sadie or anyone else.

"*Gut.*"

Sadie gave her an encouraging smile before leaving the kitchen. Once she was alone, Joanna rubbed her temple. First Andrew's abrupt change of heart, and now she learned her parents had kept secrets from the family. Was nothing as it seemed? Her entire life was turned around and upside down.

Rejoice in suffering.

The words intruded into her thoughts. A fragment of a scripture verse. Absently she touched the scar on her face. *How am I supposed to rejoice about this? Or my parents' deaths? Or my doubts about Andrew?*

She got to her feet, knowing that she had to keep busy or her thoughts would drive her crazy. She reached for the crutches and started to clear the table. She paused as her gaze landed on Andrew's bouquet.

Despite herself, she couldn't resist touching one of the delicate pink rose petals.

For the rest of the morning Andrew threw himself into his work. Anything to keep his thoughts away from Joanna. But it was proving impossible. He'd already banged his hand with his hammer and nearly pinched his finger with the nippers. He hadn't made those kinds of mistakes since he'd been an apprentice.

After lunch he arrived at Freemont Yoder's. Freemont was the new bishop of Birch Creek. His roan mare needed a full set of new shoes. Andrew tried to keep his attention on the work, only to wonder yet again if Joanna had changed her mind about the wedding. "Ow!" He missed tapping the final nail into a horseshoe and banged the top of his thigh with the hammer.

He groaned. He could shoe horses in his sleep. Apparently he couldn't shoe them while Joanna was on his mind.

"Everything okay?" Freemont asked, leaning against the stable wall.

Andrew gently released the horse's foot. She was a sweet old mare. He patted her flank. "Lost *mei* concentration a bit."

"Unusual for you." Freemont straightened and put his hands in his pockets. "Um, anything you want to talk about?"

Andrew's brow lifted.

"Seeing I'm now the bishop and all . . ." He cleared his throat. It was no secret that Freemont was uncomfortable in his new role. "Anyway, if you need to talk to someone, let me know."

"Danki." Andrew wiped his hands on his leather apron, then put his hammer into his tool belt. Surely Freemont didn't know anything about the proposal. And right now Andrew didn't want him to, not while Joanna kept pushing him away. "I'll keep that in mind."

"I hope you didn't think I was, uh, prying. I wasn't meaning to, anyway."

"I didn't think you were."

That seemed to put Freemont more at ease. "How much do I owe you for the shoeing?"

"Nix." Andrew led the horse back to the stall. He wasn't going to charge Freemont, and not only because he was the bishop. He knew the man had experienced some financial difficulties of late. Their former bishop, Emmanuel Troyer, had kept a tight rein on the community fund despite being aware of Freemont's crop failures and the large family he had to support. Since Emmanuel had left Birch Creek, everyone in the district now knew the fund was flush with money. Freemont was also

getting back on his feet. Still, Andrew didn't feel right charging him.

"I gotta pay you something," Freemont said.

Andrew sized up the man, who was in his early forties and had a huge amount of responsibility resting on his slim shoulders. He could have easily accepted Andrew's refusal to charge him. But Andrew understood, probably better than most in their district, that a man didn't want something for nothing. It was one thing to get help from the community fund since everyone contributed to it. It was another to receive a service without giving some kind of compensation. "We could use another chicken," Andrew said, having noticed at least a dozen free-range birds pecking around in the front yard.

Freemont grinned. "Chickens are something I've got plenty of. Rooster or hen?"

"Hen. We've already got one rooster."

"One rooster is all anyone needs, unless you're going to sell the ornery things." He chuckled. "I'll have one of *mei buwe* bring you a *gut* laying hen later on today."

"*Mei mamm* would like that."

"How is she doing?" Freemont asked.

"*Mamm*'s fine. Irene is too." He could see Freemont wasn't going to let up on his bishop duties. Emmanuel had always been fairly hands-off when it came to Andrew and his family, and Andrew had liked it that way. He'd been taking care of his family since he was eleven years old. But it was good to know that if he or his mother and sister did need help, Freemont would be there for them.

"Do you all need anything?" Freemont asked.

"Not right now. I'll let you know if we do."

"*Gut.* Things need to be a little different around here than they have been in the past. I want to make sure everyone in the community is taken care of."

Andrew nodded. "We all appreciate that." Freemont might doubt himself, but Andrew could tell the man was going to be a fine bishop.

After leaving Freemont's, Andrew headed for his next job, but to get there he had to pass by Macon Road, Joanna's street. He gripped the reins, the leather digging into his skin. Her behavior continued to baffle him. What if she really had changed her mind? What if she didn't love him anymore? *How am I supposed to wait until tomorrow to find out?*

He was a few yards past her street when he pulled on the reins and slowed down. He couldn't stand this anymore. He had to find out the truth—even if it was something he didn't want to hear. Anything was better than dealing with the constant ping-ponging thoughts. It was starting to affect his work, and he couldn't risk an injury.

Moments later he pulled into her driveway and guided his buggy past Schrock Grocery and Tools. A few cars plus a couple of horses and buggies were in the parking area. If they were that busy, Joanna might be inside helping her sisters. He clambered out of the buggy and tied his horse to the hitching rail, trying to decide if he should go to the store first or knock on the back door of the house. Then he saw a flash of movement through their kitchen window. His throat turned dry as he recognized Joanna's profile.

With quick steps he went to the door and knocked on it, tapping his fingers against the doorjamb as he waited for her to answer. He heard the unsteady thump of footsteps, and his fingers moved faster. When she finally opened the door, he stilled.

She stood motionless, leaning on her wooden crutches, her chestnut-colored eyes wide with surprise and . . . wariness?

"Andrew," she whispered, turning her head slightly away from him.

He craned his neck, trying to meet her gaze. It was as if she were talking to the door instead of him. She was still trying to hide her scar from his view. She must have forgotten he had already seen it at the rehabilitation center. It was another reminder that he'd have to tread gently with her. If she was self-conscious about her face, he wouldn't draw attention to it. "I need to talk to you." He struggled to steady his voice.

She stiffened, but she also turned toward him, enough that he could clearly see the raised ridge on her cheek.

But the marred skin scarcely registered in his mind. All he saw was the woman he wanted to be with for the rest of his life. "Can I come in?" This time he couldn't keep the tremor out of his voice.

For a long moment she didn't say anything. She didn't move. After what seemed like a lifetime, she finally said, "Yes."

CHAPTER 5

J oanna forced her pulse to slow as Andrew walked into the
kitchen. Why had she let him in? She regretted it as soon as he
shut the door. Could he hear her heart pounding? She was sure
he could, because it was roaring in her ears.

She went to the kitchen table. Cake ingredients were spread
out on top. She stared at them, every sense heightened as she
heard Andrew move to stand behind her. She had missed him so
much, and seeing him, feeling his warmth as he stood close . . .
She almost turned around and leaned against him. Yet her feet
refused to move, refused to seek comfort from the one man who
could give it to her.

"Joanna?" When she didn't move or answer him, he said,
"Please look at me."

Just as she couldn't turn him away again, she couldn't refuse
his request. She swallowed and faced him, steeling herself for
his negative reaction when he saw the ugly, raised ridge on her
cheek.

But he didn't seem to notice. In fact, his gaze didn't leave her eyes. The blue depths drew her in, eliciting the tingling warmth of attraction she used to feel when she was around him. It was faint and hidden in a fog of conflicting emotions, but the spark was there. She couldn't ignore it even if she wanted to.

Still, she tried. She snatched the wooden spoon from the bowl and turned her back on him. A rude gesture, but she couldn't sort her feelings with him looking at her with so much . . . love.

Love motivated by pity. She had to remember that.

"Joanna, I . . ."

His warm breath brushed against her bare neck, and she froze. Did he have any idea how he affected her? How for years she had wished he would be this physically close to her? She tossed a cup of flour into the cake batter and started stirring, needing to lean against the table for support. Her legs, already wobbly from the morning's work, were now like jelly. But she refused to collapse in front of him.

Then his hand covered hers with a light, firm touch that made her skin tingle. She glanced at his tan skin against her pale flesh, the roughness of his calloused fingers and palm a familiar sight but not a familiar feeling. With every movement he was confusing her further, weakening her resolve. "I need to finish this cake."

"You have the whole afternoon to bake that cake."

"Unlike you," she said, her sudden resentment not allowing her to soften her words, "it takes a long time for me to get things done."

"Then let me help. All you have to do is ask."

She stopped stirring the batter and closed her eyes. His kindness, which he had always possessed in abundance, started to unravel her tormented thoughts.

His strong hands touched her shoulders and turned her to face him, the heat of his palms passing through the light green cloth of her dress, warming her skin. "I want to understand what you're thinking," he said. "What you're feeling. It's hard, I'll admit. I don't have any idea what you're going through. I won't pretend I do." He leaned forward, his voice low. "But I do know this. I love you, Joanna, even though you're pushing me away. Have you"—his Adam's apple bobbed in his throat—"stopped loving me?"

She fought the tears that threatened to fall. Again, he was seeing her at one of her weakest moments. She couldn't lie to him, though. "*Nee*, Andrew. I still love you."

He blew out a long breath, then smiled. "You had me worried for a minute." His smile faded. "Can I hold you, Joanna?"

All she could do was nod. He kept his gaze locked with hers as he slipped the crutch from underneath her arm and leaned it against the table. Then he enfolded her against him.

She could feel the rise and fall of his chest, smell the leather and hay on his clothes.

"I should have done this a long time ago," he said in a low voice.

Ya, you should have. The bitter words came unbidden, but they were the truth. She also should have felt safe in his embrace. Loved, because he had finally given her what she wanted—commitment and a moment of physical touch. And she did feel some security, but she couldn't completely shake her misgivings. *He wouldn't be holding me if he didn't feel sorry for me.*

He pulled back a bit, his hands still resting on her waist, his smile sweet and gentle. His gaze landed on her scar. He leaned forward, hesitated, then planted a quick kiss on her opposite cheek.

A fresh lump appeared in her throat. He couldn't even acknowledge that her face was forever ruined.

"I almost lost you," he said. "That made me realize I can't live without you." He took in a deep breath. "Joanna, my proposal stands. I still want to get married. I need to know if you do too."

Why was he acting like everything was normal? That she hadn't changed? That he wasn't different too? *I need to tell him no . . . that I'm not ready . . . that we're not ready. Can't he see how wrong this is?*

But if she said no she would lose him forever.

Naturally he'd be hurt at first. But it wouldn't be long before he realized the real reason for his hasty proposal and that it didn't have to do with love. He might even thank her for knocking some reality into him.

Would any of that matter if she was alone? If she lost him forever? Could she stand by and watch him get married to someone else? Because if anyone deserved a happy marriage, a *whole* wife, it was Andrew.

In the end her selfishness won the mental battle. *"Ya,"* she said, barely hearing herself say the word. She had to force herself not to rub her nose. Andrew was familiar with her annoying tic that never failed to reveal her true feelings. "I . . . I still want to get married."

He gave her the biggest grin she'd ever seen. Then before she could take another breath, he picked her up and whirled her around. And for that one brief moment she felt sheer freedom at being spun around in his strong arms. She squeezed his biceps as he set her down gently, his eyes growing wide.

"I'm sorry," he said, his brow creasing with concern. "I

wasn't thinking." He peered at her intently. "I didn't hurt you, did I?"

She shook her head. He hadn't hurt her, only surprised her with another whimsical move, one that before the accident would have thrilled her.

"*Gut.*" Then he looked down at his feet. Within seconds the awkwardness that had dogged them from the moment they started dating returned. Finally he lifted his head and gave her a shy smile. "*Danki*, Joanna. You've made me a happy *mann.*"

Had she? Or had she assuaged his guilt?

"How does two weeks from Tuesday sound for the wedding?"

Her legs started to shake. "That soon?"

"I don't think we should wait." He paused, a flash of fierce intensity appearing in his eyes, only to disappear just as quickly. "Bishop Yoder can announce it next Sunday at church."

She nodded, although it felt like her lungs were collapsing in her chest. But what else could she do? She was committed now, and she wouldn't go back on her word. *I can't disappoint him.*

"I'll build an addition on *mei haus.*" He said the words as if he'd just thought of them. "It will be small, but we can add to it later. Irene and *Mamm* won't mind. I'm sure they'll both be happy about the wedding." He stepped away from her. "Do you want to tell them together?"

She made herself focus on him instead of the anxiety building in her chest. Everything was moving so fast. "All right."

"I can pick you up tomorrow morning." He took in a deep breath. "I better get back to work. I'll see you tomorrow?"

She could feel beads of sweat forming on her forehead. *Please don't let him notice.* "Tomorrow, right."

He went to the door, opened it, then turned to her. "I love you."

"I . . . love you too."

As soon as the door closed she collapsed against the table, her legs trembling. She needed to sit down, but she couldn't move. A few moments later Abigail burst through the back door. Joanna jumped and nearly fell, managing to hang on to the table as she fought to steady herself.

"I see Andrew was here." Abigail walked over to her, a wide grin on her face. "I guess you two talked."

"*Ya.*" She was still looking down at the table, fighting for strength.

"He looked happy." Abigail chuckled. "Very happy. Any particular reason why?"

"We're getting married," Joanna mumbled, finally looking at her sister.

"Married?" Abigail's eyes widened.

"*Ya.*"

"When?"

"Two weeks."

Abigail's mouth dropped open. "What?"

"He said he wanted to get married right away." The words were coming easier now, and her heartbeat started to slow.

"Joanna, are you sure?"

She hung on to the edge of the table. Maybe getting married wasn't a bad thing after all. Perhaps after they were married everything would be right again. She and Andrew would be together forever. For better or for worse. Her chest started hurting again.

Abigail pulled out one of the kitchen chairs. "Sit down."

Joanna sank onto the seat. With the back of her hand she wiped her damp forehead.

Her sister moved a chair closer to Joanna and sat. "Let's think about this for a minute. This morning you didn't want to see him. Now all of a sudden you're getting married in two weeks?"

Joanna nodded.

Abigail leaned back, shaking her head. "I don't get it."

"Andrew doesn't want to wait."

"Obviously. But what about you? Are you ready for this?" She peered into Joanna's eyes. "What do you want?"

Andrew. She had always wanted Andrew. But now she realized something else. *I don't want to be alone.* Joanna touched the smattering of flour that had spilled on the table. When she saw her finger shaking, she pulled back. "I want what he wants," she said, unable to admit her fear.

"You're dodging the question."

She tightened her fingers into fists under the table. "We're getting married. I'm sorry if you're upset about that."

"I'm not upset." Abigail's voice was calm and steady, the way she had been throughout Joanna's stay at the rehabilitation center. "I'm happy for you *if* this is what you truly want and *if* you're not feeling pressured."

Pressure pressed down on her from all sides, but she couldn't acknowledge that out loud. She could only try to manage the strain. She relaxed her tense shoulders, attempting to create a confidence she didn't feel. "Marrying Andrew is what I want."

"Then congratulations!" She gave Joanna a quick hug, then pulled away. A rueful grin formed on her lips. "Seems that when it comes to marriage, both *mei schwesters* don't waste any time. Joel better hurry and catch up." Her smile disappeared. "I haven't seen him since we got back. I know he's been busy working at Barton Plastics, and then he's been helping his older *bruder* finish building his new *haus*. I thought maybe he would stop by the store today, but so far he hasn't."

"I'm sure he'll visit soon." Joanna patted Abigail's hand, glad for the change of subject. "He cares about you, Abigail." Before the accident she had seen the two of them together, mostly after church services and during singings. They made a striking couple. He was tall, blond, and fair, while Abigail was petite and had dark hair and an olive complexion.

"I think he does." Uncertainty crept into her expression, then she shook her head, her brown eyes regaining their prior sparkle. "Never mind about me and Joel. We were talking about you. We have a wedding to plan, a dress to make, people to invite, food to prepare . . ."

As Abigail continued to tick off what seemed to be a never-ending list of things to do for the nuptials, Joanna silently prayed. *I've finally gotten* mei *heart's desire, God. But I never expected it to happen like this.*

"You're going to have a beautiful wedding," Abigail said. "These next two weeks are going to fly by. Before you know it, you'll be Mrs. Andrew Beiler."

Joanna turned and embraced her sister, trying not to cling to her as if she were a life raft. *Lord, what have I done?*

⌒

Irene Beiler hung up the last pair of Andrew's pants on the line. Her brother went through clothes at twice the rate she and *Mamm* did, but that was to be expected because of his job. Once his pants were hung, she stepped back and let the fall breeze fan her face. The clothes fluttered like colorful flags on the line. Her dresses, her mother's dresses, and her brother's shirts and pants would be dry in a short time if the cool dry air continued throughout the day.

She turned away from the clothesline, but instead of picking up the plastic basket, she turned it over and sat down, using the basket as a stool. It was too nice to go inside and start lunch. She wanted to spend a few moments in the fresh air, alone with her thoughts and the twittering sounds of the birds that were taking turns at the three feeders she'd filled up yesterday. She loved to watch the different species—chickadees, swallows, finches, and her favorite, brown creepers. Those little birds were adorable.

After a few moments she stood, picked up the laundry basket, and began to head inside. As she turned she saw a man walking up the driveway. She frowned. She wasn't expecting anyone. As he neared her jaw dropped. "Asa?"

Her brother's childhood friend waved as he strode toward her. He smiled, stopping in front of her and shoving his hands into the pockets of his pants.

Irene kept gaping. She hadn't seen Asa for five years, since he left Birch Creek for a job opportunity in Indiana. His family had followed him soon after. Asa had been sixteen, and even then he had been the most gorgeous boy she'd ever seen. She wasn't the only one who thought so—every one of her friends had a crush on him at one time or another. But he wasn't a boy anymore. He was a man. A stunningly beautiful one, with black wavy hair, thick eyebrows, and pale gray eyes surrounded by so many dark, long eyelashes it wasn't fair. Still, she'd never felt an attraction to him and had always considered him part of their family, at least until he had moved away. At twenty, he was two years younger than she was, and she'd always seen him as her little brother. There was nothing little about him now.

"Hey, Irene," Asa said, his voice deeper than she remembered, his gaze flickering off to the side. That part of him hadn't changed. He'd always tended to be quiet and a little shy. Now he also seemed unsure around her. Odd, considering how close they'd been growing up.

She had to break this strange ice between them. Grinning, she went to him. "Is that any way to greet me?" she asked, throwing her arms around him and squeezing tight. He hugged her back, harder than she'd expected. His embrace was almost desperate. When she pulled away, the curve of his smile was a little bigger, reminding her of the kid she used to know.

"*Gut* to see you too," he said.

Irene watched as his gaze surveyed the house and yard. A couple of chickens were near the front flower bed, pecking at the ground. "Not much has changed around here I see."

She nodded but didn't say anything. While outwardly their community seemed to remain the same, everything had changed. Asa would learn soon enough what had happened to Bishop Troyer and Solomon. She bit her bottom lip at the thought of Sol Troyer. She had been interested in him for a while. It was hard not to be, with his gorgeous green eyes and mischievous smile. But Sol was trouble—and she had vowed to stay away from him.

She pushed the Troyers from her mind. "What are you doing here? Are you back for a visit?"

"*Nee*. I'm back for *gut*."

Irene pushed one of the strings from her *kapp* over her

shoulder. "Andrew will be glad to hear that. What about the rest of *yer familye*? Have they returned too?"

"They're staying in Indiana."

She waited for him to give more of an explanation. When he didn't she decided not to pry, despite her curiosity. Andrew would talk to him soon, and she'd rather badger her brother for information than quiz Asa. He was more at ease than he'd been a few minutes ago, but he still wasn't the confident, easygoing teenager she remembered.

"Is Andrew here?" Asa asked.

"*Nee*. He's out working."

"Still a farrier?"

"*Ya*, and he probably will be for the rest of his life."

Asa nodded. "I remember how much he liked the job when he was apprenticing. Can you let him know I'm in town? I'm staying at *mei* parents' old *haus*."

She looked at him askance. "I thought they sold the place."

"They did." He didn't add more details.

Irene had never thought of Asa as mysterious, but he was doing a good job of being intriguing. Again, she kept her questions to herself. "You're welcome to stay for lunch. I was just getting ready to make some roast beef sandwiches."

"That sounds *gut*, but I can't stay. I've got a lot of work to do at home." He removed his hands from his pockets and took a few steps back. "Tell Andrew if he's got time he's welcome to stop by. I'll be around."

"I will. Asa?"

He paused and looked at her.

"Welcome back."

Flashing her a grin that would easily have all the single

women in Birch Creek swooning, he nodded before walking away.

Irene watched him leave. Why couldn't she be attracted to someone like Asa? She was starting to feel the pressure to find someone, especially since most of her friends were either married, engaged, or in a relationship. The pickings in Birch Creek were slim since the young women outnumbered the young men. Very few males were unattached in their small district.

Again, Sol unceremoniously popped into her mind. Before he'd admitted to the entire congregation that he'd been a thief and a drunkard, she thought there might be a chance for something between them. Even now she could feel a slight pull of attraction whenever she thought of him. Eventually that would go away. At least she hoped it would. She wouldn't get involved with a man of questionable integrity. Her father had already abandoned her. She wouldn't allow herself to be hurt that deeply again.

She picked up the laundry basket and headed back to the house, determined to put Sol out of her mind.

Easier said than done.

CHAPTER 6

LANGDON

Cameron paced back and forth in his tiny apartment as he waited for Mrs. Rodriguez to arrive. He'd put Lacy down for the night, although she would probably wake up in a few hours around midnight. Once she was asleep, he'd called Mrs. R., leaving a message on her voice mail. He'd decided earlier that evening to tell her he was leaving. He didn't want to spring the news on her at the last minute.

A few moments later he heard a knock on the door. He opened it and she burst inside.

"I got your message," she said, panting slightly after climbing the flight of stairs from her apartment to his. "Is everything all right? Nothing's wrong with Lacy, is it?"

"No," he said, surprised at her panic.

"Thank God." She collapsed into his only living room chair as Cameron shut the door. She fanned herself, her bright green shirt and navy-blue pants clashing with the orange-and-brown-plaid chair. "When you said you needed to see me and it was important, I thought something had happened to the baby."

"She's fine. I'm sorry I worried you." He sat down on the sofa near the chair. It would be so hard to leave this woman, who had been more of a mother to him than his own mom ever was. He tugged at a loose upholstery thread, unsure how to tell her he was leaving.

"Cameron?" She leaned forward. "You look upset. Just tell me what's going on."

He met her concerned gaze. "I'm sorry, Mrs. Rodriguez. I need to break my lease."

Her fingers touched her red lips. Then she put her hands on each arm of the chair. "You're moving?"

"Yes."

She touched her mouth again, as if in thought. "Cameron, if you're having trouble with the rent, I can lower it. I own the building. I can do whatever I want."

Her generosity touched him. "The rent is fine. More than reasonable, actually. You should probably raise it after I leave."

"I don't care about money. I care about my tenants." She leaned back in the chair. "Where are you going?"

"South." He refused to be more specific. He didn't want to drag her into his mess if the police came around asking about him.

"South Langdon?" she said, her tone hopeful.

He almost smiled. There wasn't a South Langdon, but he understood what she meant. "Farther south than that." He wished he could tell her he had family somewhere in Texas or Florida. Or friends. Or a job. But he didn't want to completely lie to her.

And he had decided to go to West Virginia, which was technically south from here. "I need a fresh start." It was the closest he could come to the truth.

She angled her plump body toward him. "It's the memories, isn't it?" She sighed. "When my Diego passed away ten years ago, I wanted a fresh start too. But no matter how hard you try, you can't outrun the past. Or the pain. They'll always be there, although the ache will fade with time." She pressed her hand over her heart. "And you'll always carry the beautiful memories you have here, in your heart. I know it seems impossible right now, but someday you'll be able to think about your Mackenzie with joy instead of sorrow."

He looked away, stupid tears stinging his eyes again. How many times had he cried since Mackenzie's funeral? He'd been alone with her before the cremation while the funeral director's wife took care of Lacy. There had been no service. No visitation. No phone calls, even though Cameron had reached out to Mackenzie's mother and told her what happened. He'd gotten her voice mail. He hadn't wanted to leave that devastating message. Although he'd never met the woman and knew Mackenzie had hated her for caring more about scoring drugs than about her, he felt a duty to let her mother know she'd lost her daughter. He shouldn't have been surprised not to get a call back.

There was no one to mourn Mackenzie but Cameron. His sweet wife had deserved more than that, more than the short, mostly unhappy life she'd had. No, he didn't believe the ache would ever go away.

Neither would the guilt for what he'd done. He would never think about his wife without anger, or about the buggy accident without guilt.

Mrs. Rodriguez looked up at the ceiling, said something in Spanish he didn't understand, then peered at him. "I realize it's not my place to pry into your business, but I have to say my piece. I know you aren't religious . . ."

Cameron drew back. Mrs. Rodriguez was a faithful attendee of her local Catholic church. Both Cameron and Mackenzie had never attended church, although when they were in the group home a pastor came by every once in a while to talk to the kids. Cameron usually ignored him. If God was real he wouldn't have let Cameron or Mackenzie get stuck in foster care. They would have had loving parents and families, not broken ones. *God would have never let my wife die.*

". . . but I promise you, God is telling me to tell you that you need to stay."

Okay, that was a surprise. Cameron had never heard of God directly speaking to someone. He'd always thought of him—which was rarely—as some intangible spirit thing hovering above, waiting to punish people. Like a ghost on steroids or something. "He's talking to you right now?"

"Not in words so much. But I feel it in my heart. And when I feel something in my heart, I know God has put it there."

Cameron nodded, but more out of politeness than agreement. He respected Mrs. Rodriguez too much to dismiss her beliefs, even though he didn't accept them. "I appreciate the thought—"

"It's not a thought, Cameron. It's real. If you leave Langdon, you'll bring trouble on yourself."

This wasn't how he'd expected the conversation to go. He'd assumed she might try to convince him to stay, but not with some kind of religious mumbo jumbo. Besides, how much more trouble could happen? He'd already lost his wife. *And taken the lives of two innocent people.*

If he stayed, the risk was too great that the cops would figure out he was the one who had plowed into the Amish buggy almost six weeks ago. He'd been thinking about Mackenzie as he'd left for work that morning. Then he realized he'd forgotten his wallet at home and had to turn back. Even now he could remember his anger—how his foot pressed on the pedal, how his car raced down the winding road as if the speed would pull the agony and fury out of his body. By the time the buggy came into view, he hit the brakes too late. His head had slammed against the steering wheel of his beat-up Chevy truck. Panicked, he'd backed up and driven off, blood dripping down his face.

He called in sick to work and spent the day freaking out in his apartment, trying to figure out what to do. All he could think about was Lacy and how his arrest would put her into the system that had nearly broken him if he hadn't met Mackenzie. His daughter would be alone, and he couldn't allow that to happen. Not because of his careless stupidity.

He squirmed in the chair and forced the memories from his mind. He had to focus on the present. "I can pay you whatever the penalty is for breaking the lease."

"Forget that." She looked at him for a long moment, then shook her head as if she was disappointed in him. She couldn't possibly be more disappointed in him than he was in himself. "I can see you're determined to go. When are you leaving?"

"Thursday morning. My last day of work is Wednesday, and I plan to pack up everything that night."

"At least let me make you a pot roast tonight. As a going away present."

He smiled, glad she wasn't upset with him. "You know I'd never turn down your pot roast."

"And you don't worry about taking Lacy to day care. I'll watch her until you go. I won't have much time left with the little one." She rose from her chair. To Cameron's surprise she touched his shoulder. "I'll also be praying for you. Not just this week, but after you leave." She wiped the tears that had spilled from her eyes. "I know it sounds strange because we haven't known each other for very long. But you're like a son to me. I truly believe God brought you and Mackenzie and Lacy into my life at the perfect time for all of us, even if you don't see it that way." She pulled away from him. "I hope if you ever need anything in the future, you won't hesitate to call. I'll always be there for you and Lacy."

His chest expanded with gratitude for her kindness. He hadn't done anything to earn it, yet she was giving it to him without strings attached. He wasn't used to such selflessness. "I won't," he said, fighting another burning round of unshed tears. He had no intention to follow through with his promise, though. She didn't rate getting mixed up in his disaster of a life.

Her eyes were shiny. "I'll bring you that pot roast tomorrow night." She drew in a stuttering breath, then turned and rushed out of the apartment.

With a forceful jerk Cameron yanked the thread out of the upholstery. If only things were different, he could stay. He wanted to stay. He wanted Mackenzie sitting next to him on this old sofa, her head against his shoulder, her slim fingers entwined with his. If she were here, there would never have been an accident. He wouldn't be a coward about to go on the run.

He wouldn't be a murderer.

He slammed his fist on the coffee table, almost breaking the old wood in two.

⁓

Joanna was past exhausted by the time Aden's brother, Sol, and his mother, Rhoda, arrived for Aden's birthday supper. Aden, in his typical humble way, had said he didn't want anyone to fuss over him. But a nice supper with his family—with the exception of his father—wasn't going overboard. Every birthday, *nee*, every day, was precious. Aden deserved a little bit of extra attention tonight.

"Can I help?" Rhoda Troyer asked as she walked into the kitchen. Sol wasn't with her, and Joanna assumed he was outside somewhere with Aden. Joanna knew that since Bishop Troyer had left Birch Creek, Sol kept close vigil on his mother, as if he were afraid of leaving her alone. Aden had also gone to see his mother and brother three times in the two days Joanna had been back home. She hadn't realized the Troyer family was so tight-knit. She'd always detected an underlying strain between the brothers. Then again, perhaps that was due to their father leaving them and the community he had promised to serve. Tragedy had a way of bringing people together.

Or tearing them apart.

The words slammed into her brain, unbidden. Busy all afternoon, she hadn't had much time to think about Andrew and the wedding, which meant she didn't have to continue chasing away her doubts. She had put all her focus and energy into preparing tonight's meal and baking Aden's cake.

"Joanna?" Rhoda stood next to her, puzzlement in her eyes. "Are you okay?"

She wasn't, but she nodded anyway. She was leaning heavily on both of her crutches, her legs weak and her hips aching. Tonight she would rest her body, but for now she would hide her pain.

Rhoda looked at her intently, and Joanna thought Aden's mother didn't believe her. Then she realized Rhoda's gaze was focused on the scar.

She fought the urge to turn away and hide her face. *I have to get used to the stares.* Not just because of the scar, but her crutches, too, at least until she got rid of them. She rallied and gave Rhoda a sweet smile. "I promise, I'm fine. You can pour the iced tea if you like."

Rhoda nodded eagerly, as if grateful to have something to do. She took the tea pitcher, and then Joanna limped to the oven and opened the door. A wave of heat hit her as she pulled out the pan of yeast rolls, golden brown on top. She set the tray on the stove, then slathered melted butter over the rolls.

"Smells *appeditlich*," Rhoda said as she filled one of the tea glasses.

"*Danki.* I hope Aden will like them."

"I'm sure he will. He's always been easy to please. When he was a little boy . . ."

Joanna detected the sadness in her voice. Was that because of her husband's absence? Or was she recalling more difficult memories? Although Emmanuel Troyer had been the bishop of Birch Creek Joanna's entire life, she'd always sensed a distance between the Troyers and the rest of the community. They had kept to themselves, especially Aden, which was one of several reasons why Sadie's marriage was such a shock. Joanna hadn't been aware that Sadie and Aden were friends, much less courting.

Joanna thought she and Andrew had been private about their relationship, but they had been overly conspicuous compared to her sister and new brother-in-law.

"We're almost out of tea," Rhoda said, holding up the pitcher. "Would you like me to make some more?"

"*Ya*. Fresh tea would be great." Joanna arranged the rolls in a basket lined with a kitchen towel to catch the dripping butter.

Rhoda filled the kettle and placed it on the stove. "Let me take the rolls to the table for you."

Joanna was tempted to do it herself, but she was so tired she didn't resist. Rhoda had just set the basket down when Sadie, Abigail, Aden, and Sol entered the kitchen.

"Everything looks and smells amazing, Joanna," Abigail said, coming up to her. She leaned closer and whispered, "Promise me you'll eat tonight."

With a jerk of her head Joanna looked at Abigail. "I always eat."

"Picking at *yer* food is not eating." Abigail gave her a sharp look. "And I'll get the dishes after supper."

"But—"

"No arguments. I can tell you worked hard to make supper special. Don't be so stubborn."

Joanna nodded, unable to refuse her sister. She couldn't refuse anyone anymore, not after they had done so much for her. She owed them everything, and all she could give them was a good meal. It seemed so little in comparison.

She started to take her place at the table but paused, surveying the seating arrangements. Aden was sitting at the head of the table, Sadie at the other end. The same places where her mother and father used to sit. Her heart compressed as her sister and brother-in-law's faces blurred into her parents. Would the grief ever subside?

Reminding herself that this was a happy occasion, she glanced at Sol, who was sitting next to Rhoda and opposite Abigail. He'd been silent since his arrival, and there was a seriousness to him that Joanna had never noticed before. Not that she had known him very well. He was nearly ten years older than her. But she'd always thought he'd had a reckless, bold air to him. When she'd heard about his confession from Abigail, she'd been surprised but not shocked. She also didn't judge him. Everyone made mistakes, and he had not only asked for forgiveness, but he seemed to have turned his life around, at least from what she could tell. Again she was reminded of how much had changed in the past month and a half.

When she noticed she was the last person standing, Joanna hurried to take her seat beside Abigail. Her sister's brow lifted knowingly, and Joanna nodded. She would eat, if only for Abigail's sake.

On Aden's cue everyone bowed their heads for silent prayer. When the prayer was over moments later, she opened her eyes and saw Abigail holding out a platter of meat loaf. Her sister put a large slice on Joanna's plate and smiled. "Enjoy."

Picking up her fork, Joanna stared at the steaming portion. She'd used her mother's recipe from the cookbook she'd found in her parents' bedroom the day she returned from Middlefield. She took a small bite. Her stomach lurched a bit, but the food was tasty.

Abigail nodded her approval, then finished filling her own plate with mashed potatoes, cooked cabbage, and broccoli salad, plus two rolls.

"Sol and I have started building the bee frames," Aden said above the low clatter of silverware and plates being moved around.

Joanna looked at her brother-in-law and curled her fingers tightly around her fork. Her father had always initiated supper conversations, just as Aden was doing. Another moment of grief touched her soul.

"We should have them done by winter," Aden continued. He looked at his brother. "It's been nice having the help."

"I've learned a lot about bees." Sol scooped up a forkful of mashed potatoes.

"More than you wanted to, I'm sure," Sadie said.

Sol froze, the potatoes halfway to his mouth. He looked at Sadie, who was smiling. Aden was also grinning widely. Sol's shoulders eventually relaxed, as if he'd had to figure out if Sadie was serious or not. "*Ya.* You could say that."

Aden shrugged. "I can't help it. I like bees."

"You love bees." Sadie laughed.

"Admit it, you're starting to love them too."

"Barely tolerating them is more accurate."

"There's *nix* to tolerate, since I don't have any right now," he pointed out. "Besides, you can't deny that you love the honey."

She nodded. "And when that comes in, I will fall in love with the bees."

Everyone chuckled, even Joanna.

"Promise?" Aden asked, a touch of seriousness in his voice.

Sadie smiled. "Promise. *Yer* honey is going to be a big seller in the store. I'm sure of it."

"Maybe." Aden glanced down at his nearly empty plate.

"It will. Everyone knows it's the best honey around."

Joanna saw the small flush of pleasure on his face at the compliment. Sadie had always been a forthright person, so she wouldn't hesitate to compliment her husband, even though it might be considered a bit prideful. This wasn't the first time she'd said something complimentary about Aden in front of Joanna, and he seemed to soak up the words like a man dying of thirst.

Joanna had also noticed that the love Sadie and Aden shared had softened her sister. She didn't spend as much time in the store after hours, the way she used to before the accident. She seemed happier than Joanna had seen her in years. And when Aden looked at Sadie, his heart was in his eyes—the same way Andrew's had been in his when he asked Joanna to marry him. But Joanna knew Aden's love came from the heart. She couldn't shake the thought that Andrew's came from his conscience.

She looked down at her plate, unable to take another bite. Why couldn't she have peace about marrying him? *Why can't I be sure of his love?*

Joanna pushed around her food until everyone was nearly finished with their meal. Desperate to get away from the table before Abigail nagged her about not eating, she picked up her crutches, stood up, and put them under her arms. "I'll get the cake ready."

"Let me help you," Sadie said, starting to get up.

Joanna shook her head. "*Geh* ahead and finish *yer* meal."

Sadie shook her head and was now standing. "I—"

"I can do it!" Joanna bit the inside of her cheek.

"All right," Sadie said quietly, sitting back down.

Joanna's face filled with heat. Everyone was looking at her, except for Sadie, who had exchanged a worried glance with Aden. Gathering her wits, Joanna turned around. She'd show them she didn't need their help. But her legs started to wobble when she took her first step toward the counter. The short time she'd sat at the dinner table hadn't given her body enough recovery time. Yet she continued, determined to get that cake and bring it to the table.

She gripped the handles of the crutches and forced her limbs to cooperate. After a few more steps, her legs gained some strength. When she reached the counter, she leaned her left crutch against the lower cabinets and picked up Aden's dessert—a triple-layer fudge cake with cream cheese icing. She balanced it on the palm of her hand and started to turn around.

Without warning her legs buckled beneath her. Powerless, she crashed to the floor.

"Joanna!"

Abigail crouched on one side, Sadie on the other, Aden in front. Sol and Rhoda stood behind Aden, looking down at her, their eyes wide with surprise.

"Are you okay?" Sadie asked.

"You shouldn't have carried that cake yourself," Abigail admonished.

"Let me help you up," Aden offered.

But Joanna couldn't move. Triple fudge cake was everywhere—on the floor, on her dress, on her hand. Then she saw the lovely white plate her mother had used specifically for birthday cakes. Now it lay broken on the floor into four large, jagged pieces. A combination of physical pain and shame welled inside her. "I'm sorry," she whispered, looking down at her cakestained dress. "I ruined everything."

"You didn't ruin a thing." Sadie put her arm around Joanna's shoulders.

Joanna ignored her. She tried to push herself up from the floor, but her legs wouldn't cooperate. What kind of wife would she be to Andrew if she couldn't even get up off the floor on her own?

"Here," Aden said, moving in front of Abigail and reaching around Joanna's shoulders. "I've got you."

Tired of fighting everything, she let Aden help her to her feet. As soon as she could reach her crutches she grabbed them and went to her bedroom as fast as she could. She shut the door behind her, plunked down on her bed, and started to sob.

Minutes later a knock sounded at the door. "Joanna." It was Sadie. "It's me and Abigail. Please, let us in."

She closed her swollen eyes. They wouldn't leave until she agreed. She quickly dried her tears. "*Kumme* in."

The door opened and Sadie poked her head inside. "Are you all right?"

"Of course she isn't." Abigail blew past Sadie and walked into the bedroom. She knelt on the floor in front of Joanna. "That was quite a tumble you took. Are you hurting anywhere?"

Every muscle in her body throbbed, but she shook her head. What she really hurt was her pride, which again was foolish since she wasn't supposed to be prideful. Knowing that didn't dispel her embarrassment at falling down in front of her sisters, Aden, and his family. As she had done several times that day, she collected her faculties and tried to smile. "I'm just a little sticky."

Abigail frowned but didn't say anything as Sadie sat next to Joanna on the bed.

"I'm sorry for ruining Aden's birthday," Joanna said to Sadie.

"You didn't ruin anything. We had a delicious supper, and Aden mentioned this was one of the best birthdays he's ever had."

Joanna wasn't fooled. "He said that because he's nice."

Sadie looked at her with all seriousness. "Trust me. He didn't say that to make anyone feel better. Aden is nice, but when it comes to family, he wouldn't fib about something like that. And as far as the cake," she added, a smile twitching on her lips as she turned to Abigail," "it's not like you're the first person to drop a dessert in the kitchen."

"Excuse me." Abigail lifted her chin as she stood. "*Nee* one told me *Mamm* had just waxed the floor."

"Four hours earlier." Sadie snickered. "That floor wasn't slippery. You were clumsy."

"Humph." Abigail crossed her arms over her ample chest. "I'm sticking with my waxy build-up theory."

Joanna remembered the incident. Two years ago the family was eating supper when Abigail remembered that she'd left a blueberry pie in the buggy, a gift from Joel Zook's mother. Abigail had dashed out to retrieve the dessert, then run back inside and tripped over her feet, falling headfirst into the pie. At the time it was funny, but right now Joanna couldn't muster a chuckle.

"You were the only one who got to taste it," Sadie continued, her cheeks flushed with mirth. She looked at Joanna. "See? Compared to blueberry pie, a little fudge cake on the floor is nothing."

"I'll make Aden another one. I promise." Joanna started to get up despite her body rebelling against the movement. "And I'll clean up the mess—"

Sadie put her hand on Joanna's shoulder. "Aden and Sol are taking care of it. Rhoda's doing the dishes. Everything in the kitchen is under control."

"You can surrender *yer* domain," Abigail said with a slight smirk. "At least for now."

"Besides," Sadie added, "you need to rest."

Abigail's smile widened, her eyes filled with silent knowing. "It's been a big *daag* for you. *Ya?*"

Joanna clutched the skirt of her cake-covered dress and gave Abigail a warning look. Obviously she hadn't said anything to Sadie about Andrew's proposal. Joanna should tell Sadie herself, but not right now. The thought of talking about her impending marriage made her want to hide under the covers. *I'll tell Sadie tomorrow.* "All right. I'll take it easy for the rest of the night."

"Thank you for finally listening to reason." Abigail went to the dresser. "Do you want me to bring you *yer* nightgown?"

"*Nee.* I can do it."

Sadie stood and joined Abigail at the door. "If you're too tired in the morning, don't worry about making breakfast."

Joanna clenched her teeth. She knew her sisters meant well, but their hovering was getting on her nerves. "I'm sure I'll be fine in the morning."

Abigail and Sadie exchanged a glance. "All right, then. *Gute nacht,*" Abigail replied, and both she and Sadie left.

Joanna's sore shoulders slumped with relief. She looked at the cake on her dress and sighed. She'd have to take a shower, but she wasn't ready to get up yet. The muscles in her legs were still shaking. She took off her *kapp* and put in on the bed. Cake crumbs clung to the strings. She was too tired to do anything but lie down and close her eyes. Only for a few minutes, then she'd get up and take her shower.

Her eyes flew open as Andrew entered her thoughts. She still couldn't shake the feeling she was traveling the wrong path.

But how could that be when marrying Andrew was what she had always wanted? *Lord, help me get through the next two weeks and the wedding. I love Andrew. Please give me peace about marrying him.*

CHAPTER 7

As soon as Andrew arrived home from work, Irene told him about Asa's return. He'd changed his dirty work clothes, wolfed down his supper, then headed to Asa's house. As he walked there, his mind turned to Joanna. Not to his proposal, but to how good she had felt in his arms when she reassured him she still wanted to get married. Picking her up and swinging her around hadn't been too smart of him, but he'd been so caught up with relief that he'd lost his senses for a bit. And that wasn't the only time in the kitchen that he hadn't been thinking straight.

He was finding it harder to keep himself respectful around her. From the moment she'd let him near her, he'd wanted to do more than touch her hand, hug her, or kiss her cheek. He'd wanted to show her how much he loved her. Every part of her, including the scar, including her unsteady legs, including the pain she carried inside from the accident and losing her parents. But once again he held back, reminding himself he had to be careful. Joanna was like a fragile flower—she needed to be handled delicately and fully appreciated for her beauty and sweetness. He didn't want to make another huge mistake with her. Yet that hadn't stopped him from pushing for a quick wedding—again, something else he hadn't planned on.

Now that he'd had time to think about it, he had to battle a creeping fear that despite his intentions, he'd made another big error. Was this the right time to rush into a wedding? Then again, was there really any reason to wait? They loved each other. And she had agreed to his rushed timeline. If she hadn't she would have told him no.

On the way to Asa's, he tamped down his growing fear. The thought of not spending the rest of his life with Joanna scared him more than a fast wedding. No, he'd done the right thing. Whatever jitters he felt now would disappear once he and Joanna were married.

When he reached Asa's house, he expected his friend to be as glad to see him as he was to see Asa. And that was true. But what Andrew hadn't expected was for Asa's place to be a complete wreck. As a child Andrew had spent a lot of time at the Bontragers', and their house was always neat and tidy. Now there were fist-size holes in the living room wall, the wood floor was stained black in spots, and graffiti marked everything from the baseboards to the ceiling.

"What in the world happened?" Andrew asked once he'd stepped inside.

Asa sighed, running his hand through his black mop of hair. "I'm still trying to figure that out. The former owners let the *haus* go into foreclosure before they left. Christopher Beachy let me know. When I stopped by a month ago—"

"You were in Birch Creek and didn't tell me?"

"Just to check out things. It was a quick trip."

Andrew frowned. Asa wasn't meeting him in the eye, and it wasn't like his friend to come to town and not contact him or anyone else. If he had, Andrew would have heard about it. "You could have asked me to watch the *haus*. I would have made sure *nix* happened to it."

"I didn't want to impose."

"Asa, we're friends."

"First thing I saw was that the back door was busted. I don't know if there were squatters here or if the former owners did the damage. Doesn't matter. I still have to clean it all up."

So Asa was ignoring his offer of help. That wasn't like his friend, either.

Asa blew out a breath and put his hand on his hip. "I cleaned up the garbage they left behind. Let me tell you, it was a lot."

Andrew glanced around the empty living room. What used to be a cozy area where the Bontragers gathered was now bare. "Where are you staying?"

"In *mei* old bedroom upstairs."

"You got furniture up there?"

"*Nee.* There's a sleeping bag, though. It's pretty comfortable."

Andrew crossed his arms and looked at Asa squarely. "All right, out with it. And don't tell me *nix* is going on, because I know that's not true."

Glancing away again, Asa said, "It's a long story. I'd offer you a seat, but . . ." He gestured around the living room, then shoved his hands into the pockets of his pants. He was stalling, which also wasn't typical behavior from Asa.

"Is *yer familye* okay?" Andrew asked.

"*Ya.* Both *mei schwesters* are married and live in Shipshewana."

The mention of marriage brought Andrew's engagement back into focus. He'd planned to tell Asa about it after he and Joanna told his mother and Irene tomorrow. Soon enough everyone in the district would know, but Andrew wanted the most important people in his life to hear the news first. While he hadn't kept in touch with Asa over the years, he still considered the guy his closest friend. But for now, he was more concerned with getting to the bottom of Asa's peculiar behavior. "That's great to hear."

"Yep. *Mei* parents moved in with Hannah and her husband six months ago. Everyone's happy and content in Indiana."

"But you weren't?"

Asa shrugged.

Getting Asa to talk was like pulling out a stubborn nail from a rusty horseshoe. "You didn't like Indiana?"

"I liked it fine. Had a girlfriend, a serious one. Talked about getting married, even." He tilted his head and looked at Andrew. "I'm not making much sense, am I?"

"*Nee*, not a bit. If this *haus* is in foreclosure and you're planning to get married, why are you here?"

"I bought the *haus* last month."

Andrew's eyebrows raised. "So you're getting married and moving to Birch Creek?"

"*Nee*. I broke up with *mei* girlfriend three weeks ago."

"What happened?"

Asa pressed his lips into a tight line for a moment before answering. "*Nix*. She was nice. Pretty. I loved her . . . at least I thought I did." He glanced away. "I reckon she's not happy with me right now."

Rubbing his chin, Andrew said, "Asa, I really don't understand this."

"Neither do I." Asa ran his hand over his face. "You're going to think I lost *mei* mind. Everyone else does."

Andrew gave him a steady look. "I'm sure I won't."

"God spoke to me, Andrew. Like, in words. I heard them in *mei* head, plain as I can hear you talking to me now."

"Okay." Andrew nodded. So far his friend didn't sound crazy.

"There's more. God said I had to leave everything and everybody behind and come back to Birch Creek. Do you know how hard that was? *Mei* life was perfect. A great job, an amazing girlfriend, *mei familye*, lots of friends . . . and he wanted me to walk away from it all."

"Why?"

"I don't know!" Asa started to pace. "This was right after Christopher contacted me about the *haus*, and I came to check on the place. I figured I was homesick and all the stuff I was hearing was in *mei* head." He stopped and looked at Andrew. "I meant to let you know I was in town. I was looking forward to seeing some old friends, checking things out around here, and then returning to Indiana and *mei* girl. But the *daag* I arrived, God spoke to me, right in the middle of piles of rotting garbage. He told me to stay. That I *had* to stay." His voice cracked. Then he cleared his throat and gave Andrew a half-grin. "Told you. Crazy."

Andrew didn't know what to say. Sure, he'd felt God's presence in his life. Had thought he'd even "heard" his voice, although it wasn't in words. His mother had talked about God speaking to her, so he wasn't completely taken off guard. This seemed different, though, and whatever Asa had heard had upset him. Andrew put his hand on his friend's shoulder. "Couldn't you and *yer maedel* have gotten married and moved here?"

Asa shook his head, pain in his eyes. "When God told me to leave everything, he meant it. I had to come here with nothing. That sleeping bag I've got upstairs? I found it in the *haus* with the rest of the trash. I don't have a job, a horse, or a buggy. I sold everything I owned."

He was sleeping on the floor? "Asa, I can get you a bed. You can borrow *mei* buggy when you need it. Whatever is mine is *yers* until you get back on *yer* feet."

"I can't borrow anything. Or take charity."

"It's not charity."

"That's not how this works. I have to allow God to provide."

Now he really wasn't making any sense. "How do you know for sure this is what you're supposed to do?"

"Because I tried to ignore God. I went back to Indiana and got fired from *mei* job. *Mei* boss didn't tell me why, just said I wasn't needed anymore. The *haus* I was building for Susanna and I to move into after we got married? Burned down to the ground. The axle on *mei* buggy broke, and *mei* horse went lame . . . but I didn't start listening until Susanna got sick." His eyes welled up with tears, something Andrew had never seen before. "Pneumonia. She was in the hospital. For three *daags*. I prayed for her to be healed, and she wasn't getting any better. That's when I heard God again, and I knew if she was going to get well I would have to do what he said. I ended things with her. I broke her heart." He swallowed. "When I left for Birch Creek, she came home from the hospital."

Andrew couldn't believe what he was hearing. Then an uncertain thought entered his mind. Was he following God's will by marrying Joanna?

"I know what you're thinking," Asa said.

You have nee *idea.*

"You're wondering how I bought the *haus* if I don't have any money. I used all *mei* savings, including what I'd put aside for the wedding." He wiped at his eyes, and when he looked at Andrew the tears were gone. "I don't know what I'm doing here. All I know is that God wants me in Birch Creek. Don't tell anyone what brought me here. I don't want people to think I've gone off the deep end. I didn't even explain it to *mei* parents."

"I won't say a word," Andrew promised, still trying to wrap his head around what Asa was saying. If God told Andrew to leave everything and everyone he treasured, could he do it? After almost losing Joanna and now knowing they would be married soon, he didn't think he'd have the strength, even if it meant ignoring God's will. But when he joined the church, wasn't that what he'd promised? To follow God's will? Asa was doing just that, and it cost him everything. Andrew gained a newfound respect for his friend.

"Enough about all that," Asa said. He leaned against a graffiti-decorated wall. "What's been going on in *yer* life?"

Glancing away, Andrew wasn't sure what to say. How could he tell Asa about Joanna? It would be like tossing salt into a gaping wound.

"Now look who's dodging the subject. What aren't you telling me?" Asa crossed his arms with a wry grin. "Let me guess—you're getting married."

Wincing, Andrew said, "Um . . . *ya.*"

"Congratulations," Asa said, sounding genuinely pleased. "Who's the lucky *maedel*?"

Taking his cue from Asa, Andrew finally smiled. "Joanna Schrock."

"Really?"

His smile dimmed. "You sound surprised."

"I guess I shouldn't be. You were always looking out for her in school." He frowned. "I was such a jerk to her."

"You weren't as bad as Christopher and Thomas." His jaw twitched at the memory of how his friends used to pull pranks on her. Even though that was in the past and Christopher and Thomas were both really great guys, he could still remember the shame on her face and the pain in her eyes as she'd tried not to show how deeply they hurt her.

"I still feel terrible about it. She's a nice *maedel* and didn't deserve the teasing." Asa tilted his head to the side. "I heard about the accident while I was in Indiana. Is she okay?"

"She was hurt pretty bad." He grimaced at the thought of her on crutches and the scar on her face. "She's healing, though."

"And she's okay with having the wedding so soon after the accident?"

Andrew nodded, pushing away another niggle of unease. "*Ya.* We didn't want to wait." *I kept her waiting long enough.*

Asa clapped Andrew on the shoulder. "When's the big event?"

"Two weeks. I'd like you to stand up for me, Asa." He hadn't given much thought to the details of the wedding. But now that Asa had returned, his friend was the natural choice to stand by his side while he married Joanna. Still, he was unsure Asa would agree, considering his own broken engagement. "I'd understand if you don't want to."

"Of course I want to." He grinned. "Looks like I returned just in time." He glanced down at his clothes, which were covered with a coating of dust. "Don't worry. I did bring *mei* church clothes."

His words brought Asa's circumstances back in focus. "Are you sure I can't do something for you?"

"I'm sure. I've got to follow God's will. I learned the hard way what happens when I don't. I am looking for work, though."

"What did you do in Indiana?"

"Factory work. I learned some machining at *mei* old job."

"Barton Plastics opened up three years ago in Langdon. Several men in the community have jobs there." Andrew paused. "That's not giving you too much help, is it?"

"Nope. I have to get the job myself."

Andrew was glad to see Asa's typical good humor was back. A miracle, considering what had happened to him. "Can you come to supper Monday? *Mamm* would like to see you."

Asa paused, as if mulling it over. Finally he said, "*Ya*. I can do that."

"*Gut*. I'll let her know."

With a relaxed smile Asa said, "Looking forward to it."

As Andrew walked home from Asa's, he realized his friend would be okay despite his struggles. And although Asa believed he had to do everything on his own, Andrew vowed to be there when or if he needed him.

When he reached his house, Andrew stopped by the barn and took care of Jack and Fred, his two horses. The chickens were roosting in their boxes for the night, and Andrew noticed they now had a new one. One of Freemont's sons must have brought her over. He patted Fred's flank, made a mental note to purchase hay for the winter soon, then started to go inside. He paused. It was dark now, but a sliver of moonlight shone on the property. He surveyed the backyard and thought about the addition he'd told Joanna he would build on the house. Maybe he could hire

Asa to help him until his friend found a job. He'd have to start soon if he was going to have the place ready in two weeks. He rubbed the back of his neck, wishing he had more time. Then he halted his thoughts. He couldn't keep second-guessing himself. He'd work around the clock if he had to.

His mind full of building plans, Andrew walked into the house. His mother was sitting in the living room, hand sewing the edges of a small lap quilt. She removed her reading glasses as he shut the door. "How is Asa?" she asked.

"He's doing well." Andrew would keep his promise to Asa and not reveal his secret. "I invited him for supper on Monday."

"Why not tomorrow?"

He took off his hat. For some reason his nerves twanged as she looked at him expectantly. "I'm bringing Joanna by in the morning. We, uh . . . we have something to tell you."

"Oh." His mother didn't move, and Andrew noticed an unusual wariness in her eyes. She looked at him for a long moment before finally speaking. "It will be nice to see Joanna."

His brow furrowed. Strange. He hadn't expected that response. Surely she knew they were going to tell her they were engaged. Why else would he bring her over to make an announcement? Yet she seemed more unsettled than happy.

She placed the folded quilt in a large basket on the floor next to her chair. "Andrew, whatever decision you and Joanna have made, I hope you have both prayed about it and thought it through."

He hesitated. "We have." Not exactly the truth, but he had prayed he'd have the chance to make up for hurting her. And God had given him that chance.

"Andrew, marriage is a serious responsibility. You have to make sure you're making the right decision."

"Like *Daed* did with you?" He squeezed his hands into fists, then quickly unfurled them. The accusation wasn't fair. His mother wasn't to blame for his father leaving them. "I'm sorry. I shouldn't have said that."

Mamm rose, her back straight, her chin lifted. "*Yer vatter* and I have both made mistakes. Neither of us would want you to repeat them."

Andrew clamped his mouth shut before he said something else he would regret. Bartholomew Beiler had made his choice, and it wasn't his family. Wondering why his mother wasn't bitter stumped Andrew.

The hurt and defiance still in her eyes, *Mamm* said, "*Gute nacht*, Andrew." She went upstairs, not waiting for him to answer.

He dropped onto the hickory rocking chair. He should go after her and apologize again. She didn't deserve his anger. His father did. Of course the man wasn't here to face his broken family. Coward.

His hands clenched the arms of the chair. Most of the time he was able to keep his resentment toward his father hidden, buried away so he didn't have to feel the anger or betrayal. But every once in a while those emotions vaulted to the surface. He forced them down again.

Once he and Joanna were married, he would be devoted to her. He would never hurt her. Never leave her. He would be the man his father should have been.

Naomi shut the door to her bedroom, then placed her hand over her chest. Andrew's words had stung, but that wasn't what upset

94

her. She understood his and Irene's pain. Both her children kept their feelings about their father bottled tight. But sometimes they leaked out, like they had with Andrew tonight. Over the years she wondered if she had made the right decision, if she had handled their father's departure correctly. She would probably second-guess herself for the rest of her life.

She couldn't focus on her doubts now. She had something more pressing to deal with. Andrew and Joanna were getting married. She couldn't have picked a better wife for Andrew. He and Joanna were perfect together, but not now. This was the worst possible time for them to get married. What was either of them thinking?

They weren't thinking, and that was the problem. As for Joanna . . . The poor girl had been through so much. Marriage wouldn't heal the wound her parents' deaths had left. And Naomi knew there was nothing she could say that would change Andrew's mind. If anything, he would dig his heels in harder, insisting he was right and she was wrong. He was following his heart, something Andrew didn't give easily, and when he did, it was thoroughly. *Just like Bartholomew . . .*

She closed her eyes, a distant memory breaking through the worry. It had happened six years ago. After Andrew and Irene were asleep, she was in her bedroom taking the bobby pins out of her hair before getting ready for bed. Suddenly, she heard a tap on her bedroom window.

She froze for a moment, then slowly crouched and reached underneath her bed for the baseball bat she kept there. As she pulled it out, the window jiggled. She never left it or any door or window in the house unlocked. She lifted the bat but couldn't move any farther, frozen in fear. When she saw a face in the window, she jumped. Then the bat hit the floor. She rushed to the window, unlocked it, and threw it open. "Bartholomew?"

He grabbed her face and kissed her. "Sorry," he said, pulling back. "I couldn't help myself."

She could barely breathe as she stepped back to give him room to climb into the bedroom. He shut the window and locked it, then took her into his arms.

"I can't believe you're here." She rested her cheek against his chest. How many times had she longed to be in his embrace like this again, only to know it was impossible? But there she was, being held by her husband, feeling his heart pounding in his chest in rhythm with her own.

He released her and gazed at her face, as if drinking her in. "Still so beautiful." He took out the last bobby pin, the final lock of her hair cascading down her back. "It's been too long since I've done this," he said, running his fingers through her hair.

She blushed at his words, his attention, her lips still tingling from his kiss. Then reality struck. "You're not supposed to be here."

"You couldn't expect me to stay away forever."

Her heart did a backflip. "Does this mean—"

He put his finger against her lips. "*Nee*. I can't come back. Not yet."

"Then when?"

He sighed. "I don't know."

She moved away from him. He was dressed like an *Englisch* man now, his blond hair cut short in the back, his strong, stocky body clad in a plain black T-shirt, dark blue jeans, and black sneakers. He also looked older than his thirty-five years. While Naomi's life had been difficult, her husband's had been worse.

She sat on the edge of the bed, more confused than excited now. "Do they know you left?"

He shook his head and sat down next to her. "*Nee*. And I have to *geh* back. If I don't, they'll come after me."

She sighed, pain lancing her heart. She'd have to tell him good-bye again. She took off her glasses and wiped her eyes. "Then maybe you should have stayed away."

"I couldn't. I had to see you and the *kinner*."

Naomi shook her head. "They can't know you were here."

"Naomi—"

She turned to him and took his hands in hers. Despite the strange clothing and haircut, he still looked handsome. He still made her pulse thrum and her heart sing. They had been separated for most of their marriage, yet she didn't love him any less. But when it came to Andrew and Irene, she had to put them first. "They'll ask too many questions."

His blue eyes were wide with pleading. "They're asleep, aren't they? I'll just take a peek at them."

She shook her head. "What if they wake up? How will you tell them you have to leave again?"

Bartholomew turned from her. "You're right," he said quietly, pulling his hands from hers.

Cupping his rough cheek with her hand, she guided his gaze to hers. "I want you to come home and live with us again." She started to cry. "I want you to be *mei* husband again."

"Oh, Naomi." He leaned over and kissed her. Tenderly, softly, then drew away too soon. "I want that more than anything. And someday, God willing, I'll return to you and *mei kinner*."

She closed her eyes as he pulled her toward him and kissed her forehead. "I pray for that every *daag*."

"I don't deserve you," he whispered roughly.

Lifting her head, she said, "*Ya.* You do." She leaned against him, and they didn't say anything for a few moments. "When do you have to *geh* back?" she finally asked, her voice catching in her throat.

"In a few minutes."

"You can't stay until morning?"

He shook his head, sorrow and regret filling his eyes. "I wish I could." He stood, bringing her up with him. "Just know that I think of you every moment of the *daag.*" He stroked her hair with both hands this time. "I'm counting the seconds until I can be with you again. When I can hug *mei sohn* and *dochder* again." He squeezed his eyes shut. "When I can be the husband and father you all deserve." He hugged her close, released her, then disappeared through the window.

Naomi opened her eyes, blinking until she realized she was in the present again. Her heart pounded in her chest. She hadn't seen Bartholomew since that day. But she knew he'd been faithful. She had the letters—and her faith in him—to prove it. Writing to him over the years had been risky. She knew that. But this wasn't the first time she'd sent him a letter, and it wouldn't be the last. Over the years she had kept him updated on the various milestones in Andrew and Irene's lives—when they finished school, when they were baptized, when Andrew's farrier business had become successful. Bartholomew had written her in return—short, terse notes that didn't give away much information. But he had always signed them the same way each time: BB + NB. Their initials, which on their second date he had carved into a palm tree right outside her childhood home in Florida.

She went to her desk and sat down. She understood more than anyone the pull of deep, abiding love. She also knew about the folly of youth and how following your heart could not only bring you great joy but also intense pain. Over the years she had thought about telling her children the truth. She was tired of living a lie. But she couldn't, not without hurting them more than they already were. Even though they were adults now, she continued to cling tightly to her secret. And she also held on to the hope that someday Bartholomew would return and explain everything. It was his story to tell, not hers.

Naomi closed her eyes against a fresh set of tears. *How long will we have to wait, Lord?* She didn't know. All she could do was put her family's future into God's hands—and that included Andrew and Joanna's marriage.

She pulled out a piece of paper from her desk. Andrew was facing the biggest milestone of his life, and like every major event in his young life, he had to do it without his father. Bartholomew should know about it.

The paper blurred in front of her. She'd had to do so many things without her husband. Raising two children alone, even with the support of the Birch Creek community, had been difficult. More guilt lay at Naomi's feet because Irene and Andrew weren't the only ones who didn't know the truth about Bartholomew. Despite the lies and the circumstances, Irene and Andrew had turned out to be wonderful, God-loving adults. Yet there was a hole in their lives—just as there was a hole in Naomi's heart.

She wiped her eyes, picked up the pencil, and began to write.

CHAPTER 8

The next morning Joanna managed to get out of bed, still sore from yesterday. Andrew would be picking her up in a couple of hours. Her nerves frazzled, she busied herself with making a quick Sunday morning breakfast—homemade bread, butter, strawberry preserves, boiled eggs, and applesauce. The rich scent of coffee had filled the kitchen when Sadie and Abigail walked in.

"Where's Aden?" Joanna asked, trying to keep the worry out of her voice.

"He's sleeping in this morning," Sadie said.

"You two stay up late last night?" Abigail said with a saucy grin.

Sadie's face turned bright red as she poured a mug of coffee. "That's none of *yer* business, Abigail."

"I know. But I'm ready to become an aunt." Abigail sat at the table. "'*Aenti* Abby' has a nice ring to it. Don't you think so, Joanna?"

Joanna glanced at Sadie, unsure what to say. Then Sadie smiled. "Abigail told me about the wedding."

"I'm sorry." Abigail threw up her hands. "It slipped out." She looked contrite. "Forgive me for spoiling *yer* news?"

Joanna nodded, oddly relieved that she didn't have to tell Sadie about her engagement. In fact, Abigail seemed to be more excited about the upcoming wedding than Joanna. Another warning bell went off in Joanna's head.

"And," Sadie added, joining Abigail and Joanna at the table, "you shouldn't put pressure on either of us. You'll be an *aenti* in God's timing."

"I know. I'm impatient, that's all."

Sadie nodded. "What else is new?" Ignoring Abigail's cutting look, Sadie said, "Let's say grace."

Joanna bowed her head, but she didn't focus on prayer. She'd always wanted children. Andrew's children, to be precise. They hadn't talked about it, but she assumed he wanted *kinner* too. Those thoughts led to what would happen on their wedding night, which amped up her anxiety even more. At one time all she craved was a little physical attention from Andrew. Not much, and certainly not anything that should happen after marriage. But a kiss or three would have been more than welcome. Now when she thought about intimacy with him, she didn't get familiar butterflies pleasantly flitting around in her stomach. It felt more like bats were battering her insides.

"When is Andrew coming to pick you up?" Abigail asked.

Joanna opened her eyes. She hadn't realized the prayer was over. Knowing that Abigail was watching, she took a slice of bread, even though she wasn't hungry. "Around nine."

"I'm happy for you both," Sadie said. "Aden is too."

"We're due for some happiness." Abigail slathered her bread with the preserves. "And on that note, we need to get serious about planning the wedding."

Joanna froze. They wanted to talk about wedding plans now? "I think we have plenty of time for that."

"Are you *ab im kopp*?" Abigail fumbled with her bread slice. "We have two weeks. Make that sixteen *daags*. Either way, we have almost *nee* time to plan. And since we both missed out on Sadie's wedding, *yers* needs to be extra special."

Sadie set down her mug. "Aden and I should have waited to get married. We just . . . couldn't."

Abigail frowned for a moment. Joanna thought that was a strange answer too.

"You don't regret marrying Aden, do you?" Abigail's humor had disappeared, replaced with concern.

Sadie looked at them with absolute seriousness. *"Nee."*

Joanna leaned back in her chair. At least she wasn't the only one who was rushing into marriage. And, she reminded herself, Aden and Sadie were very happy. There was no reason why she and Andrew wouldn't be happy too.

Sadie glanced at Joanna and smiled. "I'm not saying you and Andrew should wait. Everyone's wedding, and the circumstances surrounding it, is different."

Abigail blew out a breath. *"Gut.* I was only joking about not being there for *yer* ceremony. You had a *gut* reason for marrying quickly. And it all worked out as it should, just like Joanna and Andrew's marriage will." She paused. "Life is short. We know that more than anyone." Pushing the butter plate toward Joanna, Abigail asked, "Should we have it here or at the Beilers'?"

"Our *haus* is bigger." Sadie picked up her coffee and took

a sip. She turned to Joanna. "Would you like to get married in *Mamm*'s wedding dress? I did."

A lump appeared in Joanna's throat. "Did it make you feel closer to *Mamm*?" she asked softly.

"The *daag* was a blur for me." Sadie gripped the coffee mug, averting her gaze. "But *ya*. I think it did."

"We might have to take the dress in a little." Abigail sighed. "I have the opposite problem—I've been having to take out my dresses." A cloud passed over her eyes before she reverted back to her good mood. "But that's only temporary. "I'm going to lose this extra weight before the wedding. I don't want to look like a cow."

"You don't look like a cow," Sadie said.

Abigail rolled her eyes. "Stop being nice. I know I've gained weight. I'll admit I've been overindulging lately."

"But you're still beautiful," Joanna said. Abigail's face was a little plumper and her hips a bit wider, but she was just as pretty as ever.

"And you're very sweet as usual." She pushed the rest of her bread away. "I'm going to see Joel this afternoon. He didn't stop by yesterday. I'm a little put out with him."

Sadie stood and picked up the dishes, including Abigail's half-eaten piece of bread. She left Joanna's bread on the napkin. "You're waiting until afternoon?"

"I don't want to interrupt his family devotion time. I can wait a little longer to see him. But not much longer." She wiggled her eyebrows. "Now, back to the wedding." She grinned at Joanna. "We'll have it here, and you're wearing *Mamm*'s dress. I'm assuming we're going to invite the entire district."

Nodding, Joanna took a bite of her bread. If Abigail could be disciplined enough to lose weight, Joanna could at least eat what was offered to her.

Sadie came back to the table. "We should also decide on food."

"*Ya,*" Abigail said, "because after two weeks of dieting I'm going to be hungry!"

Sadie laughed, and even Joanna joined in. It had been so long since the three of them had been happy together. She loved her sisters so much.

Aden entered the room, Homer on his heels. The dog hadn't slept with Joanna last night, but now he went straight to her. She reached down to pet his soft head. While Sadie gave Aden his breakfast, Abigail found a piece of paper and a pencil and started to make a list of food for the wedding. Joanna let Homer lick the bread crumbs off her fingers. Then he sat and looked up at her, his pink tongue sliding out of the side of his mouth as he panted.

In that moment, surrounded by her sisters, Aden, and Homer, peace finally cut through her fear. She could marry Andrew. Even with her scar and her limp she would give him her best. That included not using her crutches at the ceremony. It would take extra work on her part, but she would prove to Andrew and everyone else that she could be a good and capable wife.

Later that morning Joanna's peace quickly dissipated. She nearly had a panic attack when Andrew picked her up. Her stomach lurched as they neared his buggy, and her face broke out in a sweat although her body felt cold. She stiffened beside him.

"Joanna?" His brow furrowed with concern. What's wrong?"

"I . . . I don't know." She looked at the buggy, and the thought of getting inside petrified her. Flashes of the accident went through her mind—the buggy being struck, her body flying through the air—

"Joanna."

Andrew's low, soothing voice brought her out of the nightmarish memory.

"Talk to me," he said with quiet tenderness. "What's going on?"

"I haven't been in a buggy since the accident," she whispered.

He rubbed the back of his neck. "I should have thought about that. I'll be right beside you, though. We'll *geh* slow. If you want me to stop or turn around and *geh* back, I will."

She wanted to tell him to forget about everything—the buggy ride, seeing Naomi and Irene, the wedding. Her confidence had dwindled to almost nothing. But she couldn't say any of that to him. She had vowed to be strong, and somehow she would be. "I'm ready to get in now." She handed him the crutches.

"Do you want me to pick you up?"

Balking at the shameful image of him lifting her into the buggy, she shook her head. "*Nee*. I can get in myself."

"At least let me help you."

He was so eager to assist her, so kind and patient with her, she didn't protest when he put his arm around her waist and half-lifted her into the buggy. During the drive he kept his word, driving slow, sitting closer to her than he ever had before, and checking on her so much that by the time they got to his house she was on the verge of being smothered. At least she didn't feel panicked anymore.

A short time later, when Andrew told Irene about the engagement, his sister was thrilled. She hugged Joanna and grinned. "I always wanted a sister. Now I have the nicest one in Birch Creek."

But Naomi was more reserved. "You'll make *mei sohn* very happy," she'd said in her soft voice.

"She already has."

They spent a couple of hours at the Beilers' before Andrew took her back home. He pulled the buggy to a stop in her driveway, then got out and met her on the other side. Before she could say anything he put both hands on her waist and lifted her out of the buggy. To her surprise, he lingered for a moment. She glanced down at his hands. They nearly spanned her ever-thinning waist, and she could feel the warmth of his touch through her dress. A tiny spark alit within her, only to die when he abruptly dropped his hands and stepped away, then hurriedly retrieved her crutches and handed them to her. "I'll be by later this week."

She put the crutches under her arms. He had been considerate enough to pull close to her house so she didn't have far to walk. "Okay."

He looked at her for a moment, as if he wanted to say something else. Instead he nodded and went back to his buggy.

She frowned. Earlier that morning she'd been worried about physical intimacy with Andrew. But when he held her waist as he helped her from the buggy and stood close enough that she could hear what she thought was some pretty heavy breathing considering she didn't weigh much, the longing for him to kiss her returned. But perhaps that desire was wrong. Maybe Andrew keeping his distance was how courting should be. She really didn't know. It all added to her confusion.

For the rest of the week Joanna continued to double up on her exercises. This left her tired at night, but she was making progress. She was also being more efficient in the kitchen and had started baking again, much to Abigail's dismay.

"How am I supposed to lose weight if you keep making all these tasty treats?" She looked at two peanut butter pies on the table.

Joanna faltered. "I'm sorry," she said, holding out her hands. "I can stop baking—"

"*Nee.*" Abigail shook her head. "Aden loves *yer* desserts. Even Sol has said they were *gut*, and you know he says hardly anything when he's over here." She lifted her chin. "I'll have to find the willpower"—she looked at the pies longingly—"somehow."

But despite Abigail's protestations, Joanna made a small, low-fat apple cake the next day. "No butter, just apples and applesauce."

Abigail's face lit up. "*Danki*, Joanna. That's so sweet of you." She smiled as she looked at the miniature cake. "Literally."

Joanna grinned and went back to making peanut butter cookies, one of Andrew's favorites. But when Andrew hadn't come over to see her by Saturday morning, she told Sadie to give the cookies to Aden and Sol. "I don't want them to *geh* to waste." She managed a smile, in spite of her disappointment that Andrew hadn't shown up.

"I'm sure he had a *gut* reason," Sadie said. Then she took the plate of cookies outside where Aden and Sol were working on more bee frames.

Joanna wasn't so sure. She hadn't been very good company lately, and things were still weird between her and Andrew. There was also something else going on, something she hadn't revealed to anyone, including her sisters. During the past week she'd been having nightmares. Most of the time she woke up before she could remember them. The only clues she'd had about them was the dread and foreboding that filled her when she awakened. As usual she chalked it up to nerves. What bride wasn't anxious before her wedding? Especially if everything was off-kilter between her and the groom?

Shortly after supper, Andrew finally arrived, looking tired and filled with apologies.

"I've been working on the addition," he explained as they sat outside on the back patio. The evening was cool, the sun almost hidden behind the horizon. Sadie, Aden, and Abigail had conveniently made themselves scarce. Homer ran around the backyard, pausing to roll in the grass, then sprinting into the woods and back until he finally settled at Joanna's feet.

She gripped the mug of hot chocolate she'd made right before he arrived. Andrew had declined her offer to make him some. "Sounds like you've been very busy."

"I have. Asa's been helping me."

Joanna nodded. When Andrew picked her up last Sunday to take him to his house, he had told her about Asa's return.

Andrew slumped slightly in the chair. "He's been work-ing on it during the *daag* while I'm at work. Right now he's on the waiting list at Barton Plastics. Some guy just put in his two weeks' notice, so Asa thinks he'll be hired on soon."

"*Gut.*"

"It won't be much of an addition, considering the time crunch. But it will be enough for us in the beginning. We can always add on later. At least we'll have some privacy."

Joanna looked up from her lap to Andrew. He was gazing at

her intently but then pulled his eyes away. He ran his hand over the back of his neck. "I figured you'd want that," he said, not looking at her. "Privacy."

There he was, being accommodating again. She thought about all the work he was doing, basically two full-time jobs for them to have a place to live. *"Danki,"* she said, battling another wave of guilt, feeling more inadequate than ever before. He was doing all this for her. *What if I disappoint him?* She didn't know how she'd live with herself if she couldn't make him happy.

Consumed with her thoughts, she didn't say anything else. Andrew also remained silent. They were surrounded by the sound of the breeze lifting the tree limbs and shaking off the brown leaves. During the day the maples and oaks burned vibrant orange, red, and yellow. In the dusk the colors were almost indistinguishable. A stronger breeze kicked up and she shivered.

"Are you cold?" he asked, turning toward her in the chair. He looked at his short sleeves. "If I had *mei* coat, I'd give it to you."

"I have one inside."

"I can get it for you if you want. Or we can *geh* inside and talk some more."

We're not even talking now. He also sounded strained, as if they had only known each other a few days instead of most of their lives. She decided to put both of them out of their misery. "I probably should get to bed early since we have church in the morning." Tomorrow would be her first time back at church since the accident, and she was both anticipating and dreading seeing everyone at the service.

He quickly rose to his feet. "You should have said something if you were tired. I can help you up." He reached out his hand.

She started to accept it, then reminded herself that she had a little more than a week before they were married, and she needed to be as independent as possible. She put down the mug and grabbed her crutches. Standing up was still a little awkward, but she was getting stronger. The extra exercises were helping.

If he was bothered by her rebuff of his offer, he didn't show it. "Can I pick you up in the morning?" he asked.

In the dim light of dusk she couldn't make out his expression. But his body language said it all—both hands in his pockets, maintaining a respectable distance, and sounding more than a little uneasy.

"I'd like to *geh* with *mei familye*," she said. Which was true. She wanted to be with her sisters before church—the first service the three of them would attend together without their parents. She was about to explain that to him when he nodded and spoke.

"I understand. I'll see you at church, then."

"I'll show you out."

"That's okay. I don't want you to get too tired." He walked a few steps away, as if he was going around the house to the driveway where his buggy was parked. Then he made a sharp turn and went back to her. "Could I take you home, at least? We can stop by *mei haus* on the way and I can show you the addition."

He was so kind. And she was so . . . Joanna. Ugh. All her shortcomings slammed into her brain at the same time. *"Ya,"* she said, not wanting to keep him waiting on an answer.

"Gut. I hope you'll like it, Joanna."

"I'm sure I will." She leaned on her crutches. "I better get inside."

"Okay. Wait, you forgot this." He picked up her mug and handed it to her. "Or should I take it inside for you?"

Was this how their marriage was going to be, him doing

everything for her? Nee, *it won't.* "*Danki,* but I can manage." She took the mug from him.

"All right. *Gute nacht,* Joanna."

"*Gut nacht,* Andrew."

She waited outside until he disappeared around the corner of the house. She sighed and leaned against her crutches. It had to get easier between them. Didn't it?

CHAPTER 9

The next morning Joanna prepared for church. As she looked in the bathroom mirror, her expression tightened. The redness of her scar had faded a bit, but the ridge remained prominent. She still had to use both crutches, especially since she would be navigating around a large group of people. She would be stared at. Questioned. All with curiosity and good intentions. Then she would listen as the bishop announced her engagement to Andrew. She forced a smile at her reflection, trying to look enthusiastic. She looked deranged instead. She sighed and leaned against the sink.

A knock sounded on the door. "Joanna?" Sadie was on the other side. "Are you ready? Aden and Abigail are in the buggy."

She fixed another smile on her pale, thin face, this one seemingly a bit more genuine. "*Ya*. I'm ready."

It was easier for Joanna to get into the front seat of the buggy, so she sat next to Aden as they made their way to church, and her sisters sat in the back. Abigail and Sadie kept up a steady stream of chatter about the wedding preparations. Joanna knew she should be participating, but she wasn't in the mood to discuss it right now. She folded her hands together in her lap and glanced at Aden, who had been quiet since they left the house. As if he sensed her gaze on him, he turned and smiled.

"I didn't realize there was so much involved in planning a wedding." He tilted his head toward Sadie and Abigail. His smile dulled a little. "Our wedding was different. It was much smaller."

"I wouldn't mind a small wedding," Joanna said, mostly to herself.

He leaned toward her a bit. "I think Sadie and Abigail are looking forward to having everyone over. That hasn't happened since . . ." He cleared his throat. "This time it's for a happy occasion."

Joanna nodded. Her parents had always enjoyed having people over. Because their district was small, the Schrocks had held church services in their home at least three times a year, sometimes four. Her mother had been a wonderful host.

She remained silent the rest of the ride to the Zooks'. Aden maneuvered the buggy next to a long row of identical black buggies. As soon as she turned to climb out, she saw Andrew striding toward her. His friend Asa walked slightly behind him.

"Hey," he said, his smile a little shy. Was he nervous about today too? He held out his hand.

She stared at his work-roughened palm. She wanted to get out on her own. But what if she fell in front of everyone? She didn't need to start the morning off with a disaster, so she handed him her crutches. He held them with one hand while helping her out of the buggy. *"Danki,"* she said as he gave them back to her. Then she looked at Asa, pretending he hadn't witnessed her struggling to get out of the buggy. "It's *gut* to see you again, Asa."

"You too."

Joanna thought Asa looked a little worse for wear since the last time she'd seen him. That had been several years ago, though. He'd always been a good-looking boy and had always been meticulously groomed. He definitely wasn't a boy anymore. But right now, although he was still handsome, he also seemed haggard. Even his smile seemed a little weighed down.

"I hear there's a big announcement this morning," he said in a low voice.

She gripped the crutches. *"Ya."*

Asa opened his mouth as if to speak again, but his jaw went slack. No words came out of his mouth. Then he quickly clamped his lips shut as Abigail moved to stand next to Joanna.

"Asa." She gave him one of her pretty smiles. Joanna wished she had a sliver of Abigail's confidence. "I heard you were back in Birch Creek. Welcome home."

But he didn't respond. Instead he stared at her, his gray eyes not moving from her face.

Abigail's smile faded, and she lifted one questioning eyebrow at Joanna. "Um, I better get inside," she said, giving Joanna's arm a squeeze. "I'll see you all later."

Joanna watched as Abigail made a quick beeline to Joel, who was standing near the barn. It was only when she looked at Asa that she realized he was watching her sister too.

"I'm going inside," he said suddenly. Without another word he hurried toward the barn.

"Is something wrong with Asa?"

Andrew shrugged. "Not that I know of. He was acting a little *seltsam*, though. He's had a lot on his mind."

Joanna was about to say something else when she saw a couple of her girlfriends coming over to her. So was Sadie's friend, Patience Glick. Patience had been by the Schrocks' a few times during the week to help with the wedding preparations. As the girls neared, Andrew mouthed, "See you later," and headed for the barn.

"Wait up, Andrew." Aden, who had been talking quietly with Sadie, hurried to join him. Together they made their way to the barn.

Moments later Patience reached Joanna and Sadie first. "It's *gut* to see you this morning," Patience said to Joanna. "I'm glad you're able to come to the service." Then she looked at Sadie, her cheeks flushed and her face beaming. "I need to talk to you later. I have some news."

Sadie returned her smile with a wide one of her own. Patience's news obviously wasn't that much of a secret. Even Joanna could tell by the glow of her skin and the sparkle in her eyes that she was expecting. She was happy for her.

The rest of the women joined them. As they talked, Joanna felt the tension ease from her body.

"I've missed you," Karen Yoder said. She was Bishop Yoder's second-eldest child and one of Joanna's lifelong friends. "I'm sorry I haven't been by before, but I thought you needed time to settle in after . . ." Her gaze softened. "I'd like to come visit next week if that's all right."

Joanna was touched by her friend's thoughtfulness. "I'm sure we'll get together soon." She didn't want to say anything more specific because, once Bishop Yoder made the announcement, Karen and some of Joanna's other friends would offer to help with the wedding preparations. Her friend would be seeing Joanna sooner than she thought, and for a reason she did not suspect. None of her friends did. Again, the ease she'd briefly felt was displaced by apprehension. Now she just wanted the announcement over with.

"The service is starting soon," Karen said. "We should find our seats."

"You *geh* on ahead." Joanna didn't want Karen and her other friends to be late because she walked so slow. "I'll be right behind you."

"Are you sure? We don't mind walking with you." The other women in the group nodded their agreement.

"I promised Joanna we would sit together," Sadie interjected. "We'll be there in a minute."

Karen nodded, and the women left. Joanna turned to Sadie, relieved that her sister understood. Sadie smiled in return, and she and Joanna walked at a slow pace to the Zooks' barn.

The barn was almost full by the time they got there. Abigail turned around and waved to them. She had saved her and Sadie a seat. When Joanna sat down she looked around for Andrew. She found him sitting on the other side of the room with the rest of the men, two bench rows closer to the front than she was. He and Asa were talking while they waited for Bishop Yoder to start the service.

She started to rub her nose, then caught herself, hoping no one had noticed. Her former schoolteacher, Julia Miller, and her two small children sat next to her. When the youngest daughter began to stare at Joanna, she tried to keep her gaze forward. Out of the corner of her eye, she saw the little girl climb into Julia's lap and whisper in her ear.

"She was in a terrible accident," Julia said quietly. Then she added, "It's not polite to stare."

The little girl turned away, and Joanna felt self-conscious again. She tried to focus on the hymns, then on Freemont's sermon, which, while heartfelt, didn't have the polish or power she'd been used to from Aden's father. As the new bishop rambled about God's goodness to those who were obedient, she glanced down at her hands. They were shaking. Was she being obedient by marrying Andrew and ignoring her doubts? Yet God wouldn't want her to hurt Andrew. She dipped her head, praying for God to give her a clear answer.

Instead she heard Bishop Yoder announce her engagement.

Joanna heard a few quiet voices congratulating her and Andrew. They would be more outspoken once the service was over, but right now there was soft murmuring throughout the Zook barn.

After the service Karen came up to her and gave her a hug. "I'm so excited for you! And surprised. I had *nee* idea you and Andrew were a couple. I can't wait to help with the wedding preparations."

Joanna hugged her back, catching some of her friend's enthusiasm. For the hundredth time she told herself that everything would be all right. But as she peered over Karen's shoulder, she saw several of the older women looking at her and shaking their heads. She froze in Karen's embrace, unable to keep her thoughts from taking a dark turn. Did they think Andrew was making a mistake? That because she was scarred and crippled she wasn't worthy of him?

She pulled out of Karen's embrace, the urge to flee building inside her, along with unwanted tears. This was not how she wanted her first Sunday among the congregation to go—with her running away and crying. But she couldn't help herself. She wanted to go to the sanctuary of her home, where no one judged her or stared at her or felt sorry for her. "I'll see you later, Karen," she managed to say, her voice sounding like a nail scratching against rusty metal. Turning away from her friend, she started for Aden's buggy, only to slam straight into Andrew.

"Whoa," Andrew said, holding out his hands to steady Joanna as she plowed right into him. "Are you okay?" She looked up at him, her chestnut-brown eyes filled with fear. What happened to make her so afraid?

She stepped back and leaned on her crutches. "I'm sorry I bumped into you."

"You don't have to apologize—"

"I was trying to get to Aden's buggy."

"But Joanna," he said, puzzled. He sensed something was wrong. "I'm taking you to *mei haus*, remember?"

"Oh, that's right." She let out an awkward laugh. "I wasn't thinking clearly."

"It's okay. Been a lot of excitement this morning."

"*Ya.*" She let out a breath. "So we should *geh, ya?*"

Andrew wanted to stay and talk to a couple more of his friends, but Joanna seemed to be in a hurry. "Sure."

She looked upset as he helped her into his buggy. A little angry, even, as he put his hand at her waist. He wanted to keep it there and savor the contact for a few moments, like he had last week when he took her home from his house. It was getting harder to resist putting his arms around her. But now wasn't the time, and it definitely wasn't the place in front of the congregation. She also didn't seem open to an affectionate gesture from him. In fact, she seemed very closed, staring at her lap while he got into the buggy and then gathered Fred's reins.

As they made their way back to his house, he thought about his conversation with Joanna last night—or rather, the lack of conversation. He felt bad for not visiting her earlier in the week like he'd promised, but he'd been too tired after working on the addition. He was pushing himself. Even during the church service he had trouble staying awake, despite the anticipation of Freemont announcing his engagement. He would have tried harder to talk to Joanna last night, but he couldn't make the effort.

He was also a little bothered that she hadn't made much of an effort, either. Maybe she'd been mad at him for not keeping his word. Or maybe she was truly tired, like she'd said. He didn't know because she wouldn't tell him anything. She didn't confide in him the way she used to before they were dating. And she was especially reticent since the accident.

If he hadn't been confused about how to handle his relationship before, he was definitely baffled now. All he could do was try to do right by her and pray that after the wedding she would be more at ease. *I could use some ease, too, Lord. Help me out here.*

Fortunately he didn't live too far from the Zooks', so he and Joanna didn't have to endure the awkward silence in the buggy for very long. He pulled into the driveway and to the barn. "It will only take me a second to put Fred up. If you need help getting out, I can do that first."

She looked at him. "I need to do it myself, Andrew. The more I do, the faster I'll get better."

"You don't have to rush, though."

"I'm not." She smiled, and this time he saw a little sparkle in her eyes. "I'm okay, Andrew. I promise."

He nodded, her words encouraging him and also making him think his worries about their relationship might be for nothing.

After he stabled Fred he walked out of the barn and saw Joanna limping to the back of the house where the addition was. He moved beside her, slowing his steps until they were in front of the structure. Thanks to Asa, they'd made a lot of progress. The foundation, walls, and roof were finished, including the drywall, which Asa knew how to do. He led her to the door. It still needed staining. He also wanted to add a screen door, but he would do that after the wedding. He opened the door and stood behind her, clasping his hands behind his back as she navigated the two steps to get into the house. *Please, Lord, let her like it. It's not much, but I hope it's enough to make her happy.*

"It's nice," she said when they were inside.

Nice. He wasn't sure how to take that. "It will look better once we paint it." Andrew walked to the kitchen area, which led into a cozy living space. At least he'd tried to make it cozy. It was definitely meager, like every room in the addition. "I know the kitchen's small, but we can make it bigger later. The cabinets are arriving tomorrow." He paused and cleared his throat. "Do you, uh, want to see the bedroom?"

She paused, then nodded shyly. He walked through the small living area to a door and opened it. The room wasn't very big, but it was enough for the two of them. "You can bring whatever furniture you want," he said, holding the door open for her.

She hobbled inside and looked around the bare room. The scent of sawdust and drywall still permeated the space. A small smile formed on her lips. "*Danki*, Andrew. This is nice."

That word again. Was that all she could say? He'd hoped for more enthusiasm. His gut churned. "You don't like it?"

"I do. I like it a lot. It will be a nice home."

He hid his disappointment at her lackluster reaction. After a long moment of silence, he said, "*Mamm* and Irene are probably home by now. Are you hungry?"

"Not really."

He looked at her, and for the first time he noticed the shadows under her eyes. He mentally kicked himself. Here he was upset with her underwhelming response to his hard work, and it was clear she was exhausted. "Do you want to *geh* home?"

"Andrew, I—"

"It's okay if you do." He stepped toward her, wanting to run the back of his hand across her pale cheek. She'd lost quite a bit of weight since the accident, and she hadn't had much to spare to begin with. But as usual, he kept his hands in his pockets. "I don't want you to get too tired."

She opened her mouth as if to protest, then nodded. "I am tired."

"I'll hitch up Fred, then."

A short while later he pulled into the Schrocks' driveway. On the way to her house, he had thought about asking her what was really wrong. Did she want to postpone the wedding? Or call it off completely? If she did, he wanted to let her know he understood. That he was sorry he was pressuring her. He brought Fred to a stop and turned to her. "Joanna, I—"

She was asleep.

He watched her for a moment, his shoulders relaxing. She looked beautiful with her long eyelashes resting against the tops of her cheeks. Soon he would awaken every morning to her lovely face. The thought chased away his doubts and made his heart squeeze with happiness. He also reminded himself that she was still healing. *Patience. I've got to have patience.*

He was about to wake her up and tell her she was home when he had an idea. He climbed out of the buggy and went to her. Gently, he put his arms around her and lifted her from the seat. She didn't open her eyes, just snuggled her cheek against his shoulder. His heartbeat tripled as he carried her to the house. She was light in his arms and felt like she belonged there.

Not wanting to disrupt her sleep, he opened the kitchen door and walked in. Sadie and Aden were at the table eating lunch. Sadie opened her mouth to say something, but Aden touched her arm. He put his finger to his lips. Andrew was about to mouth the word *bedroom* when Sadie gestured to a room off the kitchen.

He laid Joanna down on the bed, careful not to disturb her sleep. Then he stood back and surveyed the room. He'd never been in Joanna's bedroom before, and he was surprised at how sparse it was. There was nothing here that seemed to reflect Joanna's personality, except for a pink-and-gray woven rug on the floor. Then he realized this wasn't her room, only a temporary one. She couldn't navigate the stairs, not with any ease. *She can't even sleep in her own room.* Another reminder of how much she'd lost and how difficult her life had been after the accident.

He tarried a few minutes and watched her sleep, relieved to see the strain and tension on her face had disappeared. Unable to resist, he bent down and kissed her cheek, his lips lingering for a moment. She didn't stir as he finally pulled away. He looked at her for a long moment, thinking about how much he loved her. All he wanted was for her to be happy, to feel as peaceful as she looked right now. He would do anything to make that happen.

CHAPTER 10

"A ndrew's taking Joanna home," Irene said, looking out the window as her brother guided his buggy onto the street.

"Already?" *Mamm* said. "I thought she might stay for lunch."

"Maybe she was tired."

"I think she was definitely tired."

Irene sat at the table and worked on her grocery list. Plenty of food still needed to be prepared for the wedding. As she perused her list, she sighed. She was happy for Andrew and Joanna, but she couldn't shake the feeling that something was wrong.

"More shopping?" her mother asked as she set a chicken salad sandwich in front of Irene.

"*Ya.* I'll *geh* to the Schrocks' in the morning and purchase what I need."

"I'll *geh* with you. I'm sure those *maeds* are getting overwhelmed with the planning, plus still running the store." She started to peel a boiled egg.

Irene tried to work on the list, but she couldn't focus. Finally she put down her pencil. "*Mamm*, do you think Andrew and Joanna are doing the right thing?"

Mamm paused mid-peel. "Why do you ask that?"

"I know they love each other. And I do think they should get married. But I'm wondering if it's the right time."

Mamm set the half-peeled egg on her plate. "I can't tell Andrew what to do. Joanna said yes to his proposal. If she didn't want to marry him, she wouldn't have agreed to."

"But so soon?"

Her mother put her hand on Irene's. "It's not our business. I know you care about *yer bruder* and Joanna. But they've made their decision. We can only pray it's the right one for them, even if we might disagree with the timing."

"Maybe we should let them have some time together after the wedding. You know, without us around."

"What do you mean?"

"I thought we might take a trip to Shipshewana. Except for moving to Birch Creek, we haven't been anywhere since . . . since *Daed* left."

Rubbing her forehead, *Mamm* looked down at her plate. "I'm not sure we should leave right now."

"Why? You could see Asa's *mudder* while we're there. I know you've missed her since the Bontragers moved." Irene still didn't know what was going on with Asa. With Andrew being so busy with work and building the addition—not to mention being moody lately—she hadn't had a chance to talk to him. Asa came over during the day, but he kept to himself. He brought his own water and food and refused Irene's invitations to come inside for lunch. It seemed that everyone was acting *seltsam* lately.

"We'll see." *Mamm* went back to peeling her egg, but she didn't look at Irene.

"We would only be gone for a week or so. It would be fun. An adventure. It would also be nice to get out of Birch Creek for a while—"

"I said we'll see. Let's get through the wedding first, *ya*?"

Irene picked up her pencil, feeling thoroughly chastised. Her mother rarely raised her voice. *Add* mei *mother to the list of people acting out of character.*

"Irene?"

She looked up and saw the sadness in her mother's eyes.

"I'm sorry. I promise we'll talk about taking a vacation once the wedding is done." She cupped Irene's cheek, something she hadn't done since Irene was a child. "You're a lot like *yer vatter*," she said, her tone wistful. "He was always looking for adventure. I see a lot of him in you."

Irene swallowed. "Does it bother you?"

"*Nee*. I just wish—" *Mamm* paused. "I wish he was here to see what a wonderful woman you've become."

Irene was close to tears. Her mother never mentioned *Daed*, and Irene never asked about him. She had been angry with him for leaving, but slowly over the years she'd tried to set that aside. Now she realized that eventually her mother would be alone. Andrew was getting married, and Irene still held out hope that she would marry, too, even though the prospects in Birch Creek were limited.

Not to mention that for some bizarre reason she couldn't keep her gaze or mind off Sol Troyer at church this morning. Part of it was that every time she attended service, she remembered his confession and the raw honesty he'd displayed that day.

The other part . . . Well, she couldn't explain that. The more she told herself not to think about Sol, the more she thought about him. But she had to keep the reminder of her father foremost in her mind. She didn't want to end up like her mother—alone.

"Why aren't you mad at him?" Irene asked. She'd never voiced the question to her mother, not wanting to upset her or dredge up painful memories. But lately she wasn't in control of her thoughts, or her mouth.

Mamm hesitated before answering. "I was angry when he first left." She looked away. "But I forgave him. I had to."

"Because of our faith."

"*Ya*. And because with forgiveness comes freedom."

"But you're not free. You're not able to date or remarry—"

"And I'm fine with that. God has given me peace about what happened with *yer daed*. I'm glad Andrew hasn't let his anger keep him from falling in love." She tilted her head, a partial smile on her lips. "God will bring love to you too."

"I wasn't really thinking about that," she lied, her cheeks heating a bit.

"Weren't you?" Her mother's smile widened, her eyes softening with understanding. "You'll be surprised how God puts a couple together."

"Like he did for you?" Irene hoped her words didn't cause her mother pain, but she had to ask.

The kettle started to whistle, and *Mamm* quickly rose from her chair. She turned off the burner. "I loved *yer vatter*. I still do."

That was something Irene never understood. In all the years since he'd left, *Mamm* hadn't said an ill word about *Daed*. She never talked about him at all. "How can you love him after he left us?"

Mamm turned to her, her hazel eyes moist behind her glasses. "How can I stop?"

"He did." Irene crossed her arms, the taste of bitter bile coating her mouth. She thought she'd dealt with this. Now she was upset on her mother's behalf.

Mamm folded her lips inward.

Irene went to her, regretting that she'd brought up the topic. "I'm sorry. I shouldn't have said that."

"It's okay." *Mamm* poured the hot water into a ceramic pitcher before dropping several tea bags inside. Curls of steam rose from the pitcher's opening. "I've come to terms with what happened to *yer vatter.*" She looked at Irene. "I hope you and Andrew eventually will too."

Irene wasn't so sure. How could children truly forgive a father who cast them aside, who hadn't even tried to make contact for over a decade? *He never even said good-bye.* One morning she and Andrew woke up and *Mamm* told them their father was gone. Later, when they were teenagers, she said he'd left them for another life. Andrew had always said it was another woman, although *Mamm* had never confirmed it. Irene didn't dare ask details. Someday she would find out what really happened. But that wouldn't be today.

For her mother's sake, she dropped the subject, and neither one of them talked about it further. But as she ate her lunch, she vowed that her future husband—if she had one—would have integrity, a strong faith, and devotion to his family. That man wouldn't be like her father. *And he won't be Sol Troyer.* She'd find someone else, even if she had to leave Birch Creek to do so. The only alternative was being alone—and unlike her mother, the thought of that kind of future did not give her peace.

Lack of sleep was taking its toll on Joanna. While she'd taken a decent nap Sunday afternoon—and didn't remember Andrew bringing her home or putting her in bed, which apparently he did according to Sadie—on Monday night she could barely keep her eyes open as she washed the supper dishes. She'd had another nightmare Sunday night and hadn't been able to fall back asleep. Like the other ones, it had been vague but terrifying. Since she was so tired tonight, she prayed she would have a couple of hours of dreamless sleep—if she didn't conk out at the kitchen sink first.

Abigail was gone, having left for Joel's before supper. Joanna rinsed off a plate as she recalled the smile on her sister's face after Joel stopped by the store earlier in the day and invited her over. "Finally we're going to have some time together," she'd said. When she left, her round cheeks had been rosy with excitement. Joanna smiled as she put the dish in the drainer, happy that her sister was going to see the man she loved.

Sadie came up behind Joanna. Without asking she grabbed a towel and started drying the dishes. Aden was doing a little more work on the beehives while there was still some daylight left. Joanna had never met anyone who was so singularly devoted to his work. It also made him happy, and that was the important thing. Homer was under the kitchen table sniffing for leftover crumbs. He was another happy camper in the Schrock household.

"I can finish the rest of the dishes," Sadie said. "You seem tired."

Joanna was about to take her sister up on her offer without arguing for once. She started to nod her agreement when Abigail burst into the kitchen. Both Joanna and Sadie whirled around in surprise. That surprise turned to concern when Joanna saw tears streaming down their sister's cheeks.

"Abigail?" Sadie dropped the towel and rushed to her. "What's wrong?"

She didn't reply, only sat down at the table. She stared straight ahead, as if in shock.

Forgetting her own fatigue, Joanna limped to her. She sat down on the other side of Abigail. "What happened?" she asked, putting her hand on her sister's arm.

Abigail's beautiful eyes swam with tears. "Joel broke up with me."

The kitchen door opened again. Abigail didn't turn around when Aden walked in. He met Sadie's gaze with a troubled one of his own, then whistled to Homer and took the dog outside.

"I can't believe I was so stupid." Abigail wiped her cheek with the back of her hand.

"You're not stupid," Sadie said.

Joanna got up for a dry kitchen towel, handed it to Abigail, and sat back down. Her sister took it and blew her nose. "*Ya*, I am," Abigail said. "I thought he invited me over to ask me to marry him. Instead, he dumped me."

Joanna gaped. Joel had broken up with Abigail? That didn't seem possible. At a loss for words, she rubbed Abigail's arm. "I'm sure you two will work it out."

"*Nee*, we won't. He's seeing someone else." She tossed the towel on the table. "While I was in Middlefield, he started dating Rebecca Chupp and didn't tell me. Then tonight he had the nerve to say we were never that serious to begin with." Her head fell forward. "I thought he loved me like I loved him."

Sadie's lips pressed tightly together, and Joanna understood her anger. Abigail didn't deserve such treatment. After being at Joanna's bedside for weeks, thinking her boyfriend was being faithful to her? Joanna couldn't understand how Joel could be so cruel. She never would have suspected it, either. He seemed like such a nice guy, always polite, always willing to lend someone a hand if they needed him. *How could he break Abigail's heart like this?*

Abigail continued to sniffle. Joanna was almost in tears herself. Then she remembered the wedding. Her eyes grew round. She couldn't possibly get married now, not while her sister was so miserable. "I'll postpone the wedding."

"Nee!" Abigail and Sadie said at the same time.

"You're not going to postpone anything." Abigail gave her a stern look. "I'm not going to let my problems—*nee*, I'm not going to let *Joel* ruin *yer* important *daag.*" She stood, her eyes now dry. "I'll handle this myself. I just need to be alone for a little while."

Sadie started to get up. "Maybe that's not such a *gut* idea."

"Don't," Abigail said, holding up her hand and backing away. "I just need . . ." She turned and ran out of the kitchen.

Sadie leaned back in the chair. "I feel so bad for her."

"Did you have any idea he was seeing anyone else?"

Sadie shook her head. "While you and Abigail were gone, I was trying to piece everything back together here. Then Aden and I got married . . . I should have paid more attention. Then again, he probably kept his relationship with Rebecca a secret." She scowled. "I have half a notion to give him a piece of *mei* mind. But I doubt Abigail would want that."

"Nee, she wouldn't."

Sadie stood. "I should tell Aden it's okay to come inside now."

As Sadie went outside to find Aden, Joanna drummed her fingers against the table, her heart aching for her sister. If Abigail hadn't been in Middlefield with Joanna, maybe she and Joel would still be together. Despite Abigail's insistence that the wedding continue, Joanna still wanted to cancel. She couldn't see how she could be happy while her sister's heart was broken.

Or was she looking for another excuse?

She rose from the table and finished the dishes, her fatigue compounded with worry, but not only for Abigail. For more than a fleeting moment, she'd been willing to use her sister's pain to postpone her wedding to Andrew. She assumed she had her seesawing emotions under control. She thought she was over her doubts about the wedding. But every time she thought she was in command of her life, something knocked her back—usually her own qualms.

As much as she tried to tell herself she was healing, that after she and Andrew were married their relationship would be back to normal, she didn't truly believe it. But what other choice did she have? It was too late to back out now. And all her prayers for help and understanding were going unanswered. As the date of the wedding neared, the distance between her and God became greater. She didn't understand any of it.

After the kitchen was clean, Joanna took up her crutches and went to her room. Sadie and Aden had stayed outside, probably discussing Abigail and Joel. Her exhaustion had increased over the past hour, but when she turned out her light and lay in her bed, her eyes remained wide open. She couldn't sleep while Abigail was hurting, or when she was racked with uncertainty about marriage, or when she was afraid that when she closed her eyes she'd have another nightmare. *Be strong and courageous.* A verse from Deuteronomy . . . or was it Joshua? She could never seem to remember whole scripture verses, only snippets and pieces. Hopefully it was enough for her prayers. *Be strong and courageous . . . Be strong and courageous . . .*

"Abigail? Sadie?" Joanna found herself in the middle of the kitchen. How did she get here? She looked down at her dress. She was fully clothed, as if she'd never gone to bed. She waited for one of her sisters to answer her. When she didn't hear anything, she continued to call their names. "Sadie? Abigail?"

She searched downstairs, then upstairs, then downstairs again. She went outside. The store was closed for the night. When she called for Aden, he didn't answer either. Homer also wasn't around. Where did everyone go?

Joanna walked back into the kitchen, barely aware that she wasn't using her crutches. Her family had to be here somewhere. She searched for a note, some kind of clue to where they would have gone. She found nothing.

Then she heard the lock on the kitchen door click. She whirled around, frightened by the sound. "Sadie?" She went to the door and tried to unlock it. The lock wouldn't budge. She heard clicks all through the house. The windows and doors were all locking on their own. She started to panic . . . to scream . . .

"Joanna!"

She bolted upright at the sound of her name. The light was on in her room, and Sadie stood over her bed. Without thinking she grabbed Sadie's hand. "Thank God! You're here!"

"It's okay, Joanna." Sadie sat down next to her on the bed, not letting go of her sister's hand. Homer nudged his nose between her and Joanna, but Sadie ignored him. "You were having a nightmare."

Joanna's breathing slowed. This time she remembered what happened. This nightmare had seemed real. With a shaky hand she pushed her long braid over her shoulder. "I woke you up?"

"*Nee.* I wasn't asleep yet. But you were crying out. You sounded terrified." Sadie brushed a stray lock of damp hair away from Joanna's face. "Do you have these often?"

"*Nee,*" she said, lying, almost in tears from the nightmare and her sister's gentle, maternal gesture. She couldn't admit to Sadie that not only was she having nightmares, but they were getting worse. *Be strong and courageous . . . What a joke.*

Sadie squeezed Joanna's hand. "Do you want me to stay with you?"

She shook her head. Somehow she'd find a way to deal with this on her own. She had to before she got married. Andrew would think she'd lost her mind if she woke up screaming in the middle of the night. "I'll be all right."

"I don't mind staying."

She let go of Sadie's hand. "Everyone has nightmares every once in a while, *ya?*"

"*Ya.*"

"See? So I'm normal, like everyone else." She was normal, wasn't she? She was starting to doubt even that.

"I never said you weren't, Joanna." Sadie turned off the lamp on Joanna's bedside table, but not before Joanna saw her frown. "See you in the morning."

Joanna lay in the dark, terrified to close her eyes. Eventually she couldn't stay awake. One minute she was drifting off, the next minute her alarm clock rang. When she sat up her nightgown was dry, her sleep dreamless. She breathed out a huge sigh of relief. *Lord, please let that be the last nightmare.*

~

The rest of the days leading up to the wedding went by without incident. Andrew hadn't stopped by, but Joanna knew he was busy with the addition. Abigail was quiet as she continued to help with the wedding preparations. Other than being more reserved than usual, she acted as if nothing had happened between her and Joel. Karen Yoder and a couple more of Joanna's friends came over to help make the house spotless for the ceremony and fellowship afterward. She had to admit it was nice to be around her friends. They were a welcome distraction. The company and activity must have relaxed her nerves, too, because the nightmares had stopped.

The night before the wedding, Abigail asked Joanna to try on the wedding dress for one last fitting.

Joanna slipped on the dark blue dress. Although she'd tried to eat more the past several days, she was still thin. But Abigail was an excellent seamstress, and the dress fit perfectly.

Joanna looked at her crutches leaning against the end of her bed. She was strong enough now to walk a decent distance without them, but she continued to use them. She planned to surprise everyone tomorrow when she walked down the aisle unaided.

A knock sounded on the door. "Is it okay to come in?" Abigail asked.

"*Ya*," Joanna replied, smoothing the skirt of the dress.

Abigail entered, Sadie directly behind her. They both looked at Joanna for a long moment.

"You look lovely," Sadie whispered.

"*Ya*. You do." Abigail's lower lip trembled. "You're a beautiful bride."

Joanna blushed at the compliments. Her sisters were going overboard. They all knew it. Yet something about wearing her mother's dress with her sisters' approval made her feel warm inside. It also triggered her grief. "*Danki* for everything," she said, her throat tightening with gratitude. "I'm not talking about just the wedding."

Abigail gave Joanna a quick hug. "I've got to put away *mei* sewing supplies." She hurried out of the room.

Joanna turned to Sadie. "I'm worried about her."

"Don't be. Abigail's strong. Just like you."

But Joanna didn't feel strong, not compared to her sisters. They didn't know what a coward she truly was.

"I was going to wait for tomorrow to give you *yer* wedding gift, but I think now would be a better time." She grinned, then whistled. Homer bounded into the room and went straight to Joanna. "Here he is."

Joanna's eyes widened. "You're giving me Homer?"

"He's been *yer* dog since you came home. It's only right he lives with you and Andrew. Although I guess I should have asked Andrew if it was okay."

"It will be. He loves all animals, not just horses." She leaned on her crutches as she reached to pet the top of Homer's head. Sadie's gift lifted her spirits. "This is perfect. I was going to miss him so much."

"And now you don't have to." Sadie hugged her. "Now, *geh* upstairs and get some sleep. You need to be rested for *yer* wedding."

Later that night, Joanna sat at the edge of her bed. The wedding dress hung on a hanger over the back of the bedroom door. Homer snuggled against her, as if he knew he was going to have a new home and was happy about it. Joanna glanced at the crutches. Touched her scar. And vowed to stop feeling sorry for herself. She was marrying a wonderful man whom she loved. She didn't want him to see her looking less than happy. *Tomorrow is going to be perfect.* She kept saying it to herself until she almost believed it.

Andrew hefted another pile of hay with his pitchfork and put it in Fred's stall. The horses' stalls were already clean, but he couldn't sit in the house with nothing to do, even though it was well past dark. Usually being around the horses calmed him, but his nerves were more ramped up than ever. He spread out the hay, his arms and shoulders aching from working during the day and finishing up the addition until late at night. It wasn't perfect and would definitely need a woman's touch, but it was as complete as it was going to get. He couldn't wait for Joanna to see it. He even had a surprise for her in their bedroom. He smiled as he thought about it.

When he looked up from his work, he saw Asa standing in the barn doorway. "Hey," he said, stepping out of Fred's stall. "I didn't hear you come in."

"You were pretty involved in cleaning."

Andrew looked around at the spotless barn. "*Ya*, I guess I was."

"I figured I'd find you here." He walked farther into the barn. "Just checking to see how you're doing."

"I'm *gut*."

"Oh, that's obvious." He looked around the barn. "Never seen this place so clean." He grinned. "Nerves getting to you?" When Andrew didn't reply Asa said, "If they weren't, then something would be wrong. Every guy is jumpy before his wedding."

"I want everything to be perfect for her."

"Of course you do. You love her."

Andrew set his pitchfork aside and walked over to his friend. "I can't thank you enough for all *yer* help with the *haus*. I'll give you a hand with *yer* place once Joanna and I are settled in."

"Nope. I've got it taken care of, remember?"

"I can't even return the favor?"

Asa shook his head.

"All right." He had to respect Asa's position, even if he didn't comprehend it. "If you change *yer* mind, I'm here."

"I know." His mouth lifted in a half-grin. "I may not have much time to work on the *haus* anyway. Heard from Barton— they're going to hire me on, starting Thursday."

"That's *gut* news. I'm glad it worked out for you."

"So far everything is. It helps me to feel more at peace about being back here. I'm still not sure what God's up to, but I'm trusting that he knows what he's doing." He clapped Andrew on the back. "Are you all set for tomorrow?"

"*Ya*. Everything's ready. It's the waiting that's doing me in."

Asa chuckled. "Again, that sounds normal." He grew serious. "I'll pray everything goes well for you both tomorrow."

"I'll take those prayers. A little extra help from the Lord is always a *gut* thing."

After Asa left, Andrew finished spreading the hay in Fred's stall. His thoughts turned to his father again. He'd had his *daed* on his mind a lot lately, which was weird. He'd spent the majority of his life trying to forget his father. Often he was successful. But every once in a while, like now, he would think about him and remember what their life had been like in Florida before he left their family. His *daed* used to charter a boat with a few other Amish men and their sons, and they would fish in the ocean. Andrew could still remember the smell of the salt water, the way the spray felt against his cheek, his excitement over reeling in a large grouper or orange roughy. Then they would take the fish home, clean them, and his mother would fry them until they were golden brown.

He stopped spreading the hay and straightened, gripping the pitchfork handle. Why was he thinking about fishing now? Or his father? Sure, his *daed* would be a missing part of the biggest day of his life. But what else was new? He'd missed everything else important.

Realizing he was driving himself crazy with his thoughts, he put up the pitchfork and headed to the house. He should be focusing on Joanna, not *Daed*.

Andrew stopped in front of the addition, opened the door, and walked inside. One last check to make sure everything was ready for Joanna. He took a quick look around the living room, then went into the bedroom. His surprise for Joanna was on the bed—a pink-and-white-patterned quilt. Very girly for his tastes, but he knew she would love it. He couldn't wait to see the spark of happiness in her eyes. He smiled, backed out of the room, then closed the door. *Tomorrow, Joanna, you'll be* mei *wife.* Despite his nerves, he was ready to become a married man.

CHAPTER 11

Happiness filled Joanna's soul. After two weeks of doubting herself and her decisions, she was now Andrew's wife. She couldn't have been more thrilled, or more in love.

As he drove their buggy down the road, she snuggled against him. A perfect wedding day. No crutches. No pain. And right before Bishop Yoder had asked them to say their vows, Andrew had leaned forward and kissed her scarred cheek in front of everyone.

Her stomach fluttered as she took in his handsome profile. How could she ever have been anxious about marrying him? He took her hand and kissed her fingers. "I love you so much, Joanna."

"And I love you."

She leaned her head against his shoulder. There was only one thing missing from today—her parents. *Mamm's* doubts would have disappeared if she could have seen what a perfect couple they were.

"Joanna?"

She lifted her head and looked at her new husband, basking in the loving smile he gave her. *"Ya?"*

"I can't wait to spend the rest of *mei* life with you."

Suddenly she lurched in the seat as something slammed into the buggy. But instead of hurtling through the air, she somehow remained in her seat. The buggy shuddered to a halt. The horse! She looked up, but she didn't see the animal. She let out a relieved breath when she saw the empty harness. Somehow the horse had escaped. She turned to Andrew, the perfect sunny day instantly shrouded in gray storm clouds. Terror filled her.

Andrew wasn't there.

"Andrew?" She scrambled out of the buggy. The fields surrounding her were empty. There was no one in sight, no sound other than her desperate calls to her new husband. He didn't answer.

She searched through the tall grass. With each step her legs ached. Her hips stiffened. Pain she'd never felt before dragged at her. By the time she saw Andrew's black hat lying on the ground, she had stumbled to her knees, unable to walk, the agony in her hips, legs, and face almost unbearable.

"Andrew?" she rasped, crawling forward, her hands sinking into grass that had suddenly turned into thick, sucking mud.

Then she saw him. The man she had loved for almost half of her life was lying in a crumpled heap. She started to cry as she reached him, turning his lifeless body into her arms, his blood covering the front of her mother's wedding dress . . .

Joanna shot up to a sitting position, the heel of her hand pressed against the scream trying to escape her lips. After she'd swallowed her terrified cries, she put her hand on her pounding heart, sweat drenching her nightgown. With trembling fingers she flipped on the battery-powered lamp beside her bed. Her gaze darted around the room, making sure she wasn't in the empty field cradling Andrew's dead body.

This nightmare had been the worst one yet. She was so paralyzed with fear she could barely move. Even when Homer nudged his cold nose under her elbow, she couldn't respond. She pulled her knees to her chest, ignoring the pain the movement caused, and rocked back and forth on the bed. The nightmare wasn't real. It didn't mean anything. Still, she gasped for air, streams of tears wetting her face.

A different and more frightening fear took hold. Would she still have nightmares after she married Andrew? What would he think of her waking up in the middle of the night, dripping with sweat and unable to stop crying? How could she tell him she dreamed about him dying?

She put her damp face in her hands. When she was finally able to stop shaking, she glanced at the small clock on her nightstand. Five in the morning. The wedding would be starting in a few hours. Soon they would be husband and wife. She had to get her emotions under control.

When the last trace of fear refused to leave her, she went to her knees. Only God could quash her fear. She couldn't do it on her own. Her hips ached in this position, but she needed to pray. *Why, Lord? Why am I dreaming about losing everything? Haven't I lost enough? Don't I deserve some happiness?*

She opened her eyes. Did she deserve happiness? Did she really deserve to get married when her parents had been dead for only two months? When Abigail's heart was broken? *When I can't be a whole wife to Andrew?* She waited for God to answer, for the fear to subside. Finally she couldn't handle being on her knees any longer, especially since God remained silent.

She grabbed her crutches and went to the bathroom. She couldn't give in to the fear. Somehow she had to deal with it. Today was supposed to be the happiest day of her life. And it would be, if she could get herself together. She washed her face, splashed some extra cold water on her swollen eyelids, pinned up her hair, and put on a kerchief. The guests wouldn't be arriving until around one. In the meantime she wasn't going to sit around stewing in her fear. She headed for the kitchen to make breakfast, Homer on her heels.

When she walked into the kitchen she could already smell coffee percolating and pancakes and bacon cooking. Abigail manned the stove while Sadie set the table.

"What are you doing?" Joanna asked, surprised. She'd expected—and wanted—the kitchen to herself. She needed all the time she could get to gather her wits.

"Making breakfast," Abigail said, her tone breezy, even though Joanna saw the sadness in her eyes that had been present since her breakup with Joel. "And don't say you can do this." She held up her spatula. "I know *mei* pancakes aren't as *gut* as *yers*—"

"That's not true—"

"It is and you know it. It's about time we made breakfast for you."

"You don't have to."

"We know," Sadie said. "But this will be our last breakfast together. We want it to be special."

Joanna noticed the bright pink carnation in a small vase on the table. It was a simple, lovely centerpiece. She leaned against her crutches, overcome with emotion. *"Danki,"* she said, trying not to choke on the word.

"Now, *geh* sit down. When Aden gets back from the barn, we'll start eating." Sadie went to a cabinet and took down several mugs, then began pouring coffee into them. "Naomi and Irene will be here shortly. They said they would come early to help with setup."

"What do I need to do?" Joanna propped her crutches against the table.

"Nix. Except to relax and let us take care of you." Sadie put the coffee in front of Joanna as she sat down. "Today is *yer daag.*"

A small part of her enjoyed this special attention. It distracted her from her anxiety. They were celebrating her wedding as they would have if the accident had never happened. She would have done the same if she had been here for Sadie's wedding.

The thought short-circuited her moment of happiness. Everything in her life was tinged with gray, even the small pleasures like her favorite buckwheat pancakes and extra-crispy bacon. She made sure she smiled, made sure they knew how much she appreciated them. How much she loved them. All the while feeling as if her world was closing in and slowly suffocating her.

At loose ends, Joanna returned to her room. She read her Bible for a little while, hoping the words would give her mind and heart peace. But the letters blurred on the page and she shut the book. Sitting on the edge of her bed, she fidgeted, twisting her fingers together and rubbing her palms. How was she supposed to relax when she was so on edge? She needed something to do, yet no one would let her do anything. Even Homer was busy outside, greeting with an excited bark everyone who arrived to assist with wedding preparations.

Desperate to keep her hands busy, she took off her *kapp* and brushed her hair. A thick lock fell against the scar on her cheek. She froze. Touched the scar with her fingers. Set her hairbrush next to her on the side of the bed and let out a heavy sigh. Last night she'd tried to convince herself that today would be perfect. How could it be when she was so imperfect? Not just her scar, but her limp. Most of all, the painful emptiness in her heart that she feared Andrew wouldn't be able to fill. Not that she doubted him. She doubted herself.

She wasn't strong. She wasn't courageous. She was afraid, and none of her thoughts and prayers changed that.

Frustrated, she grabbed the brush and yanked it through her hair, welcoming the pain. At least she was feeling something other than fear. She didn't know how long she sat there, brushing her hair, tugging at her scalp, trying to collect herself. Finally she had to stop brushing or she would pull out too much hair. She plaited the tresses into a single braid and coiled it in a bun at the crown of her sore head. Then she pinned her *kapp* in place, took her crutches, and left the room. She couldn't stay here anymore.

When Naomi and Irene arrived, Joanna offered to help again, only to get shooed out into the backyard. She sat on one of the plastic chairs on the back patio and watched as Aden, Sol, and Asa set up long tables and chairs. She wasn't any more settled inside, but at least she was distracted by the flurry of activity around her. Asa looked her way and waved. She waved back. Forced another smile. And desperately wished she was somewhere else.

She glanced at the thick copse of trees that bordered the backyard. Homer had already run into the woods, something he did almost every day. She wanted to follow him, to disappear into the trees and escape everything. She used to love to take walks—in the woods, at the nearby park, even down the road to get ice from the ice machine. It was something she and Andrew used to do when they were friends. The walks had stopped when they started dating. Why? Why had so much changed between them? She closed her eyes. She'd give anything to turn back the clock. To have her parents here, to feel confident and excited about her wedding and marriage.

She heard the back door open and looked over her shoulder. Sadie handed her a glass of lemonade.

"They're almost finished setting up, I see." Sadie gestured to Aden and Sol. They were putting chairs around the last table. Armed with the white tablecloths they'd brought, Naomi and Irene started covering the tables, securing the cloths at the corners so they wouldn't flap in the intermittent fall breeze. Although Aden had mowed and raked the lawn yesterday, more than a few brown leaves now dotted the green grass, and the scent of burning wood from nearby stoves and fireplaces filled the crisp air. The sun shone brightly in the clear sky.

"It's a lovely *daag* for a wedding," Sadie added. "Not a cloud to be seen."

Joanna looked up at Sadie. "Am I . . ." She couldn't bring herself to ask her sister if she was doing the right thing.

"Are you what?"

She took a deep breath. She should tell Sadie about the dreams. Maybe she would have some insight. If anything, she would tell Joanna she was being foolish, that dreams were dreams and nothing more. They didn't mean anything. "Never mind," was all she could say.

Sadie frowned and Joanna turned away just as Abigail came outside. "What are you two doing out here? Joanna, why aren't you dressed? Sadie, I thought you came out here to get her." Abigail put her hands on her plump hips. "You're going to be late for *yer* own wedding."

"She'll be fine," Sadie said. "We have plenty of time."

Abigail threw up her hands. "How can you two be so calm? The wedding is in little more than an hour. People are already starting to show up. If I was getting married . . ." She huffed out a breath and went back in the house.

A short while later Sadie and Abigail were helping Joanna get dressed. Joanna didn't protest when Sadie brushed out Joanna's waist-long hair, not telling her that she didn't need to. There wasn't a single tangle thanks to Joanna's brushing abuse earlier that morning. Sadie then carefully pinned her hair into a bun before fastening on her *kapp*. Abigail stood back and looked at Joanna's dress, armed with a pincushion just in case, even though Joanna had tried on the dress the night before. Her sisters were doing everything they could to make her feel special and loved. But in the back of her mind, all she could think about was how she was being dishonest—with them, with Andrew, and with herself.

"*Mamm* would have loved to see this," Sadie said.

"*Daed* too," Abigail added. "I don't care if it's prideful to say, Joanna. You're beautiful." She pulled away. "I can't wait to see the look on Andrew's face when he sees you."

Sadie touched Joanna's shoulder. "Don't be nervous. Even though I know it's hard not to be."

Right before they left, Abigail said, "The living room is already packed with people. Everyone's excited to see you get married, Joanna."

Swallowing, Joanna nodded. She didn't trust herself to say anything.

"See you downstairs." Abigail smiled, and she and Sadie left the room.

Once again she was alone in her room. She was starting to hate the small space. Without the buoyant energy of her sisters, Joanna's fears returned, this time more powerful than ever. She didn't bother praying. It hadn't done her any good this morning. She looked at her crutches. Her unsteady legs told her she should pick them up and use them. But she would be a pitiful sight limping to her soon-to-be husband, unable to walk under her own steam. She straightened, then slowly put one foot in front of the other. After a few hesitant steps, she opened her bedroom door and headed for the living room.

When she reached the doorway, she saw that Sadie, Abigail, and Aden were all standing there waiting for her. Aden offered her his arm, but Joanna refused to lean on him. She saw the flash of hurt in her brother-in-law's eyes, but she wanted to do this on her own. Everyone was standing, obscuring her view of Andrew. She did see Bishop Yoder, red-faced and looking like he was ready to bolt at any second. This was his first wedding as the bishop. He tugged on the front of his shirt, but when he met her eyes, he gave her an encouraging smile.

The kind gesture didn't help. With each step she made toward Andrew, she felt like she was slogging through a thick swamp. She searched for him but still couldn't see him. Every terrifying thought and nightmare she'd had the past two weeks slammed into her. She'd thought he would be her anchor once she saw him. But he seemed as adrift as she felt.

Her legs buckled and she crumpled to the ground, hitting the side of her head on the wood floor.

"Joanna!"

Andrew sounded far away. She felt a hand on her shoulder, felt the crush of people crowding around her. She was conscious, but she couldn't open her eyes. She couldn't face her family and friends. She couldn't face Andrew. Her wedding wasn't supposed to be like this. She wasn't supposed to be cowering in a lump on the floor.

"Joanna." Andrew's worried voice reached her ears, and she opened her eyes. He was kneeling in front of her, shielding her from the crowd with his strong, compact body.

"I can't do this," she whispered.

"What? Joanna, I can't hear you." He bent down until his head was near hers.

All she could see was him. All she could hear was her own breathing, mixed with his. She looked him directly in the eyes. "I can't marry you."

He froze, holding her there with a desperate gaze. "Joanna, you must have hit *yer* head—"

Somehow she managed to get to her feet. She stumbled away, ignoring him as he called out her name.

CHAPTER 12

"Joanna!"

Andrew pushed through the crowd of people that had surrounded Joanna the moment she fell. She couldn't marry him? He had to have heard her wrong. Although he'd tried not to, before he saw her he thought of his father again. Not pleasant memories, but resentment that he wasn't here. He fought to control his spontaneous anger. The emotion had been unexpected and unwelcome, coming at the worst possible time. His father had managed to spoil what was supposed to be the happiest day of his life, and he wasn't even there.

Then he saw Joanna. She looked beautiful, and he felt his anger fade just as she collapsed to the floor. Then she'd left. No, not left—run away, like something terrifying was chasing her. Abigail went after her, and he propelled himself forward to follow, only to be stopped short by Sadie.

"*Nee*, Andrew."

The quiet yet forceful words somehow pierced through the

questioning murmurs of the wedding guests. His gut ached, like he'd been sucker punched. "She said she couldn't marry me."

"I know. I heard her. Let us talk to her, Andrew. Give us a little space." She turned and hurried to Joanna's room.

"All right everyone," Bishop Yoder said above the din of the crowd. He sounded more confident and in control than Andrew had ever heard him. "Why don't we all *geh* outside for a bit?" The crowd started to disperse as he put his hand on Andrew's shoulder. "I'm sure it's just nerves," he said, opening the door and letting the fall breeze enter the stuffy living room.

Andrew didn't move. His thoughts darted back and forth, torn between going after Joanna and respecting Sadie's wishes.

Asa appeared in front of him. "Are you okay?"

Andrew shook his head. "*Nee* . . . I don't understand . . ."

"She's probably getting ready to come out even as we speak. She did take a pretty hard fall."

That had to be it. She wasn't thinking straight. Now a new emotion thrummed through him—alarm. What if she was seriously hurt? "I need to see her."

Asa shook his head. "Wait until she's ready to see you. Do you want a drink?"

"I want to see Joanna."

Asa held up his hands in surrender, then went outside with the rest of the guests.

Now the living room was empty. Andrew could hear voices outside, punctuated by Homer's barking. She would come out any second. He would see her smiling, and all the guests would come back, and he and Joanna would finish the ceremony. She wouldn't leave him at the proverbial altar. She wouldn't abandon him. *We aren't making a mistake.*

But as the minutes ticked by, he was losing patience and losing hope. "I can't wait anymore," he muttered and started for her room.

"Andrew."

He turned around. He hadn't heard his mother come in. "What?" He sounded sharper than he'd intended to, but all he wanted was to get to Joanna.

"Maybe . . . maybe this is for the best."

Why would she say that? "I don't believe that. I *refuse* to believe it. Do you know something I don't?" By this time it was clear to him that Joanna wasn't coming back. "Because I'm confused about why my fiancée just told me she can't marry me."

"If you'll sit down—"

"Nee." He held up his hand. "I will not sit down. I want to see Joanna. She hit her head on the floor. She could be injured. She needs me right now."

"I don't think she does."

Andrew had never felt more on the verge of punching something in his life. When he was a kid, he would take his anger out on a nearby tree, although he'd learned the hard way that punching an oak wasn't the best way to defuse his temper. As he'd grown older, he'd become more adept at tempering his emotions. But this . . . betrayal . . . He couldn't handle this. "I need *her*," he said, surprised at the choke in his voice.

"I know you do." Naomi went to him and put her palm against his cheek. "You love her. And she loves you. But right now she needs her family."

"I'm her family," he rasped.

"Not yet." She dropped her hand. "One *daag* you might be. But I'm sorry, Andrew. I don't think it will be today."

Irene stood at the edge of the Schrocks' property, away from the house and the tables and decorations, away from all the people who had expected to see her brother get married and were now waiting outside for . . . for what? Twenty minutes had passed and no one except Aden and Asa had come out of the house. Aden was talking to Bishop Yoder, but so far the bishop hadn't signaled for everyone to go back inside. What was going on? Surely her brother wouldn't be abandoned on his wedding day.

She began to pace, hugging her arms to her chest against the wind that was growing stronger and colder. When she saw a few of the women start to clear the tables, her stomach lurched. *Oh, Andrew.* Her brother didn't deserve this kind of pain. And she never would have guessed in a million years that Joanna would be the one to inflict it on him.

"Are you okay?"

She halted her steps and looked up. A shocked shiver ran through her as she saw Sol standing in front of her. What was he doing here? *Why is he concerned about me?*

She'd seen him among the guests, of course. It was hard not to notice Sol. Tall and broad-shouldered, but not stocky like her brother or as lean as Aden. He'd taken off his black hat, and his reddish hair, which was in need of a cut, flipped up at the ends and moved with the breeze. But it was his eyes that were affecting her more than anything. Usually they had a gleam of mischievous defiance in their green depths. Now they were softer, filled with gentle curiosity.

Irene turned from him. She didn't need this . . . whatever it was she was feeling for Sol right now. She'd vowed to stay away from him. For some unknown reason he'd decided to make that difficult for her.

"Irene," he said, his voice hesitant. "I . . ." He sighed. "Never mind. I'll leave you alone."

She closed her eyes. Despite everything, she couldn't be rude. He had made amends with the church, after all. And out of everyone attending Andrew's wedding, he was the only one who had reached out to her. "Wait," she said, facing him again. "I'm fine. Thank you for asking."

He ran his large hand through his thick mass of hair. In the afternoon sun it rivaled the shades of red and orange on the maple trees behind him. He looked at her for a moment, his gaze locking with hers, causing a jolt to run through her. "I saw you alone over here, and I wanted to make sure you were all right."

She crossed her arms more tightly against her chest. "I am."

"*Gut.*" He glanced over his shoulder as if he were checking something in the woods. There was nothing there, and she realized he was restless . . . or nervous. Why he would feel that way around her, she had no idea. Then he turned to her again. "If you, uh, need anything, let me know."

She wanted to say no. She should say no. "I will," were the words that came out of her mouth.

He gave her a short nod, then walked away.

What was that about? She frowned, irritated that she'd responded to Sol at all. Yet he had seemed genuine. And different. Definitely different. She shook her head at her own foolishness as she saw him walk toward the barn instead of joining the rest of the crowd. When they were growing up, Sol had never lacked for friends. Unlike Aden, he'd been more social, but Irene had always suspected it was superficial. Since his return he had kept to himself and stayed at his mother's side, as if he were protecting her from something. Or he was being a good son and making sure she was taken care of after his father left. That was something the two of them had in common now—absent fathers.

The wind blew against her face, making her eyes water. She didn't want to have anything in common with Sol. And she shouldn't be thinking about him anyway, not while her brother was in turmoil. Yet she didn't know what to do. She even felt guilty for being upset with Joanna. But if she called off the wedding, clearly she hadn't been ready to get married. Andrew, however, had been.

A few moments later she joined the other ladies and helped fold up the tables. Her worst fear was realized. The wedding was canceled. What would Andrew do now? *Lord, help my brother. He doesn't deserve a broken heart.*

Her mother came out of the house. Irene hurried toward her. "Andrew?" she asked when they were away from prying ears.

Naomi's eyes were full of unshed tears. "He'll be all right . . . eventually."

"He's not getting married." Irene already knew it, but she said the words out loud, a tiny part of her hoping it wasn't true, that this was all a big mistake.

"*Nee.* Not today."

"So it's postponed?"

Naomi shook her head, lines of worry and sadness creasing her forehead. "Andrew left a little while ago. I'm not sure where he's going, but he needs some time alone."

Irene nodded, tears welling in her eyes. Not just for Andrew, but for Joanna too. What she'd done was horrible, but there had to be a good reason she'd ended things with Andrew this way, if it *was* the end. *There had better be a good reason.* "What about Joanna?"

Mamm clasped Irene's hands. "We need to pray for them both."

⁓

"Take a few deep breaths." Sadie placed the cold washcloth Abigail had brought on Joanna's forehead. "It was hot in the living room. We probably should have kept the front door open."

"We just didn't want Homer coming in." Abigail crouched in front of her. "He gets too excited around so many people."

Joanna didn't look at her or at Sadie. She barely felt the coolness of the damp washcloth on her hot forehead. All she could do was stare straight ahead. She'd done the unthinkable. She had hurt Andrew. She had humiliated herself and him in front of the entire district. The exact things she hadn't wanted to do, she ended up doing to him anyway, only in the most painful way possible.

She had to apologize. But she couldn't move, and it wasn't because of her pain or unsteady legs. She couldn't make herself go to him because she knew she had done the right thing. That knowledge didn't make her feel any better. In fact, her heart was filled with pain, the way it had been in the hospital after she'd heard about her parents' deaths. Now something else had died, this time inside her.

"Joanna?" Sadie's gentle voice pierced through the haze.

"I can't marry him." She kept her gaze straight ahead. "I won't marry him."

Abigail got up and sat down on the other side of the bed.

"Okay, we don't have to do this today. It won't be a problem to wait until tomorrow—"

"*Nee.*" Joanna's voice was firmer, and she took the washcloth from Sadie and tossed it on the floor. "I can't marry him at all."

"For goodness' sake, why not?" Abigail's voice rose. "Why would you do this, Joanna? Andrew loves you. Do you know how special that is? How precious it is to be loved so deeply that everyone can see it?"

"Abigail—" Sadie said.

"*Nee*, I won't be quiet." She popped up from the bed. "I can't believe you would do this to him." She started to cry. "I know how much Joel hurt me. I can't imagine what Andrew's going through right now."

Joanna didn't say anything. She didn't shed a tear.

"How can you sit there like stone? Don't you love him, Joanna?"

She slowly turned and looked up at Abigail, her eyes still dry. "*Ya,*" she said truthfully. "I love him."

"Then why can't you marry him?"

Joanna looked away. Abigail huffed and stormed out of the room.

Sadie got up from the bed and picked up the washcloth. She folded it in half, then in quarters. "What should I tell him?" she asked quietly.

"To leave." Joanna looked up at her sister. "Tell him to leave."

Sadie opened her mouth to say something but only shook her head. She walked out of the room and shut the door.

Joanna lay on the bed, curling up on her side, her mother's wedding dress wrinkling beneath her. She kept staring at the wall in front of her. Her mind, which had been racing for so long, finally quieted, until she wasn't thinking about anything. Gray haze covered her thoughts until her eyes closed and she fell asleep.

For the first time since the accident, she slept in complete peace.

Andrew lifted the square hay bales in the corner of the barn and tossed them up into the loft. Normally he did this job using a ladder and situated the bales in a way that he could pack most of them in. But he didn't care. He'd spent the last several hours in here, throwing up hay bales, scattering straw all over until his church clothes were covered in it and he was bathed in sweat. After his non-wedding he had driven to Birch Creek, tethered Fred and the buggy, and walked along the creek bank, trying to collect his senses and dispel his anger. When that hadn't worked he'd gone home and started stacking bales. His horses had been startled. They could sense something was wrong, but they eventually settled down. Andrew couldn't say the same for himself.

"You're going to run yourself into the ground," Asa said, walking up to him.

Andrew hurled the bale at the loft. It hit another bale and landed on the barn floor. Andrew stormed past Asa and grabbed the bale and flung it back up again.

"Have you been here all night?" Asa asked.

Breathing heavily, Andrew glared at him. He didn't want to talk, not even to Asa. "*Geh* away," he said, looking around for another bale. But that was the last one. Seeing that seemed to strip him of his energy, and he leaned his back against the barn wall. "I'm not in the mood for a pep talk."

"I didn't come to give you one." Asa shoved his hands into the pockets of his pegged jeans. Not his Sunday clothes, which he'd been wearing at the wedding.

"What time is it?" Andrew asked dully.

"Just past dawn."

"Then, yeah. I've been here all night."

Asa shuffled his feet against the straw strewn on the floor. "You gonna be okay?"

He narrowed his eyes at Asa. "My fiancée dumped me. She won't see me. What do you think?"

"Sorry. Dumb question."

Andrew pressed the bottom of his palm to his forehead. "I don't mean to take it out on you, Asa."

"Hey, I don't mind. That's why I'm here."

"I can't believe she did this." He dropped his hand and started to pace.

"I'm sure she didn't mean to—"

"*Ya*, she meant to." He clenched his lips together before speaking again. "She could have told me she was having second thoughts. I knew something was wrong. But she kept telling me everything was fine."

"Andrew, give her a break."

"I tried!" He shoved his hands through his hair and started pacing. "She's the one shutting me out. I wanted to be there for her after the accident. She wouldn't take my calls, didn't want me to visit. But I understood. Then when we were finally able to talk, I thought I'd convinced her she could trust me. That we would be better together than apart." He crouched to the floor, holding his head in his hands. "Now she doesn't want to have anything to do with me."

"I'm sure that's not the case. Give her a little while. She'll come around."

Andrew looked up at his friend. "I don't care if she does." Which wasn't completely true. If he had a lick of sense, he wouldn't care anything about her after her desertion, yet he still did. *I still love her.* But he wouldn't let her into his heart again. He couldn't afford another emotional blow. He looked down again and heard Asa's heavy sigh.

"If you need anything, let me know."

Andrew didn't look up, didn't acknowledge his friend's offer. He stared at the dirty, straw-laden floor in front of him as he heard Asa leave. After a long moment, he stood, the ache in his chest so acute he didn't think he could bear it. He'd given Joanna his heart, and she'd shredded it. In front of everyone. How could he recover from that?

He didn't know what time it was when he finished in the barn. He headed for the house and stopped when he saw the addition bathed in the cool light of dawn. His teeth ground together. He should be inside with his bride right now, not out here alone and hurting. He stormed to the addition and kicked down the door, anger and pain pulsing through him. He stood in the tiny living room, his chest heaving as he looked around at the home he'd worked so hard to make for Joanna. Just the sight of the closed bedroom door made him want to throw up. He ran out of the addition and back into the barn, grabbed a sledgehammer, and went back inside the new part of the house. He'd tear the place down to studs. He couldn't bear to look at the monument to his pain.

He lifted the hammer to plant the heavy sledge into the freshly painted drywall . . . and stopped. Every ounce of energy drained from him. Dropping the sledgehammer, he staggered to the couch and collapsed. He put his head in his hands and sobbed.

~~~~~

Joanna awakened the next morning, still wearing her mother's wedding dress. Sunlight bathed her room, and she rubbed her eyes and stretched. Her hips ached a little less this morning. She briefly wondered why but didn't dwell on it. When she was completely awake, she sat up, and the previous day's event hit her in the chest like a brick.

What had she done? She covered her face with her hands, shame filling her. She'd hurt the man she loved. Abigail was furious with her. Sadie was confused. And the entire district had seen her run away from Andrew. What did she do after that? Slept like a baby.

She dropped her hands and looked at the end of the bed for Homer, but he wasn't there. Great. He was probably mad at her too. How could she face anyone? They probably all thought she was crazy. Right now, she thought she was crazy.

But she was compelled to get out of bed. Hiding wouldn't solve anything. She eventually had to face what she'd done, and she'd start with her family. She quickly dressed and started for the kitchen. She was partway out of her room when she realized she had forgotten her crutches. She looked down at her legs. They were steadier than they had been since the accident. As she put one foot in front of the other, she felt balanced. She still hurt, and she stumbled a bit, but the difference from how she was yesterday was astonishing.

She was about to enter the kitchen when she heard Sadie's and Aden's voices. They were speaking in low tones, and she could tell it was a private conversation. She didn't want to intrude and was about to turn and go back to her room when Sadie mentioned Joanna's name.

"I should *geh* and check on Joanna," Sadie said.

Joanna stilled as she heard the chair scrape against the floor. Although she didn't need her crutches right now, she wasn't agile enough to rush back to her room.

"Let her sleep," Aden said. "She obviously needs it."

"But I'm worried about her. Aren't you?"

Aden didn't respond right away. Finally, he said, "*Ya*. I'm worried about Andrew too. But we can't interfere."

"I don't think making sure *mei schwester* is all right is interfering."

Sadie sounded sharp and angry. Joanna peeked around the doorjamb. She and Aden were sitting next to each other at the kitchen table. Sadie was rubbing her palm against the tabletop while Aden remained still beside her.

"I should have done something," Sadie said, her tone abating a bit.

"Like what?"

"I don't know!" She pressed her fingers against her temples. "There were . . . signs."

Aden tilted his head. "What kind of signs?"

Sadie looked at him. "She's been losing weight. She's been anxious. She works too hard. Then there are the nightmares." She shook her head. "It was too soon for her to get married. I didn't even know she and Andrew were that serious until Abigail told me about their engagement."

"I guess you and I aren't the only ones who can keep a secret." Aden said the words without a hint of humor.

Joanna's brow lifted, Aden's words cutting through her growing guilt. *What secret?*

"I don't understand why they didn't wait. If they had, we'd be celebrating after their wedding, not worrying." She clasped her hands together so tightly her knuckles turned white. "Then there's Abigail. She's hurt because of Joel, and she's upset with Joanna."

She saw Aden get up from the table and kneel in front of Sadie. He took her hands in his. "I think you've had some happiness, *ya?*"

Sadie looked down at her lap. *"Ya,"* she said softly. "I want that happiness for *mei schwesters* too."

Aden touched Sadie's chin so tenderly a lump formed in Joanna's throat. "You're worrying too much, *lieb.*"

"I have a right to worry, don't you think?"

"Sadie, you need to trust that God is in control. Like he was with us." Aden rose, bringing Sadie up with him. "Joanna is an adult. You can't control her or Andrew. You can't fix their relationship or take away Abigail's pain. You can only love and pray for them. Let God do the rest." He held out his arms. *"Kumme* here," he said.

Sadie leaned against him, her cheek resting on his chest as he ran his hand up and down her back. "It's so hard. They're all I have left."

He rested his chin on her head. "You'll always have me."

She pulled away and looked up at him. When Aden dipped his head toward Sadie's, Joanna stepped away from the kitchen.

Unsure where to go, she made her way to the living room and leaned against the sage-green armchair where her mother used to sit. Amid the guilt and remorse she felt for causing everyone so much trouble, seeing Aden comfort Sadie, witnessing the love between them, made her long for Andrew. *I could be with him right now.*

No, she couldn't. Calling off the wedding had been the right thing to do. She wasn't ready to be a wife. But she shouldn't have been a coward about it. *Be strong and courageous . . .* It was about time she started living that way.

She went back to the kitchen with the intent of telling Sadie not to worry about her anymore, but she found the kitchen empty. She glanced at the clock on the wall and saw that it was past eight. Sadie must have gone to the store. Aden was either with her or working on his new project, now that he and Sol had finished the bee frames. He'd started to replace the roof on the barn, then stopped to help out with the wedding.

Now that she was standing in the kitchen, she saw signs of the wedding celebration everywhere—the countertops and table were covered with desserts and food that didn't need to be kept in the ice cooler. She looked at the delicious array, and her stomach growled. She sat down, pulled the plastic wrap off a plate of brownies, and shoved one in her mouth. It tasted delicious. She closed her eyes, reveling in the taste of chocolate and only slightly wondering how she could enjoy it so much when everything in her life was more upside down than ever. When she heard the outside door to the kitchen open, she stopped chewing. Naomi walked inside.

"Sadie said not to bother knocking. She thought you'd be

up by now." Naomi shut the door behind her. "I was hoping we could talk."

Joanna swallowed the rest of the brownie. She looked down at her hands and was surprised to see they weren't shaking. She wasn't rubbing her nose, either. Still, she steeled herself for the berating she deserved as she sat down. Naomi sat beside her but didn't say anything for a moment. She simply moved a couple of the pies out of the way so she could put her hands on the table. She clasped them together.

"How is Andrew?" Joanna couldn't believe she asked the question, but she genuinely wanted to know.

"That's a *gut* sign."

"What is?"

To Joanna's surprise, Naomi smiled. "You're asking about *mei sohn*."

Tears filled Joanna's eyes as she looked at Andrew's mother. "I'm sorry," she said, her vocal cords drawing tight. "For everything."

"I know you are. This isn't all *yer* fault, so don't blame yourself."

"*Ya*, it's *mei* fault. I called off the wedding."

"There never should have been a wedding in the first place." Naomi sighed. "I know *mei* son. He can be persistent. Pushy, even, when he wants something."

"He wasn't pushing me."

"Wasn't he?"

Joanna picked at a brownie crumb. "I wanted to make him happy."

"And he wanted more than anything to marry you."

Joanna felt a tear slip down her cheek, followed by another one. "I thought I wanted to marry him too. Before the accident—"

"Everything was different before the accident." Naomi covered Joanna's hand with her own. "Including Andrew. When we were told what happened, and how you were in surgery with serious injuries, we didn't know if you were going to live. That devastated him. I'd never seen him so worried or upset. That's when I knew he loved you. When Andrew gives his heart, he gives it fully. But that doesn't mean he's always right."

"I love him. Despite what I did to him yesterday, I love him."

"And despite what you did yesterday, I believe he still loves you."

"I don't see how that's possible."

"Then you need to take some steps to rectify *yer* situation. Apologizing to him would be a *gut* start."

Joanna swallowed. "I doubt he'll even see me."

"You won't know until you try." Naomi released her hand. "*Kumme* by tonight and talk to him."

"I . . ." Yesterday she couldn't bring herself to face Andrew. Now she was desperate to see him. "I will."

Naomi stood. "Supper is at six. Stay if you'd like to eat with us." She put her hand on Joanna's shoulder. "I believe you two will find *yer* way back to each other. And when you do get married, both of you will be ready."

Joanna wished she had Naomi's confidence. What she had done to Andrew was unforgivable. Yet she had to ask for forgiveness, even if he wouldn't give it to her.

That evening Sadie drove Joanna to the Beilers'. Abigail was still upset with her, and she hadn't said more than a few words to her the entire day. Before Joanna and Sadie left, Abigail went back to the store after closing time, something she rarely did.

"Are you sure you want to do this?" Sadie asked as she guided the buggy toward Andrew's house.

Joanna thought about the conversation she had witnessed between Sadie and Aden that morning. If her sister was upset with her, she was hiding it well. Sadie seemed as steady and supportive as ever. Joanna also wondered about the secret Aden mentioned. She was curious, but Joanna wouldn't pry. Whatever her brother-in-law was referring to was none of her business, and if Sadie wanted her to know, she would tell her. Joanna had to respect that.

"Joanna?"

Sadie's voice brought Joanna out of her thoughts. "Sorry. *Ya*, I want to do this. I have to tell him I'm sorry." She looked out the buggy's opening. "I have so many people to apologize to."

"*Nee*, you don't. We all understand."

"Abigail doesn't. And I doubt Andrew will."

"Abigail is fighting her own battles, Joanna. I believe she loved Joel more than we thought. He hurt her deeply. Her anger toward you might be displaced."

"She would probably still be with him if she hadn't had to stay with me in Middlefield."

"If their relationship couldn't stand a few weeks of distance, then it wouldn't withstand a marriage. It's *gut* that Joel was honest with her now, even though she's hurting from it."

"Like I should have been honest with Andrew."

"*Yer* situation is different. The accident—"

"I know I messed up, Sadie. You don't have to make excuses for me."

"I'm not. Joanna, I love you. I know you're hurting, both physically and emotionally. But we've all been affected by what happened to you." She huffed out a breath. "None of us has talked about it. Abigail hasn't, and I've been afraid to bring it up with you. I didn't want to cause you more pain. But maybe if we had talked about the accident before the wedding, you would have been able to *geh* through with it."

Joanna sat back in her seat, letting Sadie's words soak in. She was right. They hadn't talked about the accident. They talked about missing their parents, and they had become closer as sisters recently. But they hadn't discussed the actual incident. "I don't remember much of what happened."

Sadie glanced at her. "I'm sorry. I shouldn't have brought this up now."

"*Nee*, you're right. I do need to talk about it." She twisted one of the folds of her dress. "Right before the car hit us, I told *Mamm* and *Daed* I wanted to marry Andrew." She didn't reveal that Andrew had rebuffed her proposal. She remembered how hurt she'd been when he'd done that. How angry she was. But the way she had rejected Andrew was ten times worse.

"What did they say?"

"They weren't happy. Especially *Mamm*. She said we weren't ready, and she was right. *Mamm* knew more about me than I did." She paused. "I haven't told anyone that. Not even Andrew. I wanted to prove to everyone that I was ready to get married. That I could be a *gut* wife."

"You will be."

"Maybe. Someday." *If Andrew ever forgives me.* "When I was

about to walk down the aisle, I realized I didn't want a one-sided marriage. That's why I couldn't *geh* through with it."

"You're doubting he loves you?"

"*Nee.* That's not what I mean." She paused, struggling to admit how weak she felt, how weak she really was. But if she wanted to be strong, she needed to be honest. "I don't want Andrew to have to take care of me."

Sadie guided the buggy down Andrew's road. "He wouldn't. Right now you're a little bit limited, but it wouldn't always be that way."

"I'm not talking about that, either." Joanna sighed. Sadie wouldn't understand. She had always been independent. Her goal had been to run the store, and now she was doing it, and she would have accomplished that even if their parents were alive. Abigail was witty and gregarious, and she loved fiercely. What was Joanna? A mouse. A coward. She wasn't truthful with Andrew or herself. Now they were both paying the consequences.

Andrew's house was a short distance away. Sadie didn't respond until she pulled the buggy into the driveway. She turned to Joanna. "We can talk about this later if you want. Just know that keeping everything bottled inside isn't *gut*. Trust me, I know from firsthand experience." She gestured to the house. "Do you want me to stay out here and wait for you?"

"Please, come inside with me?" Now that she was here she was afraid to see Andrew alone. She reached for her crutches and used them to get out of the buggy. She didn't trust herself without them when she wasn't at home. She and Sadie walked to Andrew's front door, her stomach a knot of dread. What could she say that would convince him how sorry she was?

Sadie knocked on the door, and it opened immediately. It

was Irene. Her lips pressed together for a moment, and Joanna felt her disapproval. Naomi might easily forgive, but Irene wouldn't. Joanna wasn't surprised. The Beiler siblings looked out for each other.

"*Mamm* said you'd be stopping by to talk to Andrew. He's out back, near the garden. Sadie, *kumme* in. *Mamm* and I have almost finished making supper." She looked at Joanna, her sharp gaze mellowing slightly. "Will you let Andrew know?"

"*Ya.*"

Sadie gave Joanna an encouraging smile, then joined Irene and went inside. Joanna stood alone on the porch, leaning on her crutches. It was a fairly far walk to the back of the Beilers' property. She removed the crutches from underneath her arms and looked at them. She was so tired of depending on them. She leaned them against the porch railing. Maybe not using them was a mistake. Maybe she'd fall flat on her face in front of Andrew. But she had to try to walk to him without them. *I can do this.*

It took twice as long for her to reach the garden than it would have if she wasn't limping. But she felt some freedom without the crutches, her legs strengthening a little with each step as her nerves tightened. She found Andrew where she expected him to be, at one of his favorite spots overlooking the sweeping pasture behind his property, which gave a gorgeous view of the sunset. Today it was cloudy, and there would be no beautiful, colorful display.

He stood there, his back to her, his hands in his pockets. He'd always been so strong, and not just physically. But now his wide shoulders were slumped, his head hanging slightly. As she neared him her palms grew slick. She nearly tripped but managed to regain her balance. He must have heard her, because he turned around. He didn't move toward her. When she got close enough to see the hard set of his jaw, she gulped.

"What are you doing here?" His blue eyes were icy.

"I . . ." Her voice stuck in her throat. "I came to apologize."

"Fine. I forgive you." He turned around, giving her his back.

"Andrew—"

"There's nothing else to say." He crossed his arms but didn't turn around. "You made *yer* feelings perfectly clear yesterday."

She moved to stand in front of him. "I don't want to leave things like this between us—"

"There is *nee us*." He scowled and dropped his arms. "Not anymore. *Geh* home, Joanna. You got what you came for."

"I love you. Despite everything, I do."

"You have a strange way of showing it." His voice sounded strained, as if his vocal cords were going to snap. "Was this *yer* plan to get me back for hurting you? I didn't know you were vindictive. Then again," he sneered, "I don't think I know you at all."

"Andrew, please. I can explain."

"I don't want to hear it." He started to walk away, then turned and stalked back to her. "You had the most important part of me—*mei* heart. If you loved me, you would have been honest with me. If you didn't want to get married, you should have told me."

She flinched against his verbal onslaught, but she held her ground. "I didn't want to disappoint you."

"You don't think yesterday was a disappointment?" He slammed his fist against his chest. "You don't think you hurt me?"

She could feel the pain radiating off him in waves. "I know I hurt you." Her voice rose. "I should have said something sooner."

He narrowed his eyes. "Why didn't you? Why did you agree to marry me when you didn't want to?"

"I . . ." She had to tell him the truth. "I didn't want you to take care of me anymore."

He ran his hand over his face. "That's what a husband does. He takes care of his *frau* and *familye*. That would have been *mei* job."

"I know. That's the problem."

Andrew crossed his arms again. "Here's what I think the problem is. *Yer* feelings have changed, and you were too scared to tell me you didn't love me anymore."

She had been scared, but not about that. "That's not true. I said I love you."

"And you expect me to believe it?" He shook his head. "Maybe you can't admit it to yourself. All I know is that you realized you don't want to be stuck with me for the rest of *yer* life."

Joanna went to him, his words slicing her. "How can you even think such a thing?"

"What else am I supposed to think?" He turned away. "Leave me alone," he said in a thick, pain-filled voice.

"I can't do that, Andrew. I want to fix this. I want us to be together again."

"But I don't want to be with you." He shoved past her and headed for the house.

Her toes dug into her shoes so she wouldn't fall. There was no mending this. She could see that now. She'd hurt him too deeply. But one thing would never change. She would love him for the rest of her life.

CHAPTER 13

On Thursday morning the sun was well past the horizon by the time Cameron was on the road. It was tough to say good-bye to Mrs. Rodriguez, but Cameron knew the faster he put the miles between him and Langdon, the better for him and Lacy. He should reach the West Virginia border by lunchtime, and then he would be outside of Charleston by late afternoon. Last night after Lacy was asleep, he searched on his phone for jobs around the Charleston area. He was qualified for several, and he was able to apply online for one of them.

He wasn't too far from Langdon when he ran into a detour. He groaned as he followed the signs for the next fifteen minutes. What kind of backward detour was this? All he wanted was to get to the freeway, but the signs kept taking him farther away. He seized the steering wheel when he realized he was in Birch Creek.

His stomach knotted as he saw a black buggy, and he took special care to drive around it, not just because Lacy was in the car. Making sure he was doing the speed limit, he glanced in the rearview mirror at her car seat, which was facing backward. His truck was small and old, but it was a king cab and had a backseat. He couldn't see her face, but she'd been sound asleep when he put her in the seat earlier that morning. He'd fed and diapered her, dressing her in a pink one-piece fleece outfit, a gift from Mrs. Rodriguez.

The truck suddenly lurched, and he heard a loud popping sound. Lacy started to cry as Cameron gripped the steering wheel. "It's all right, sweetheart," he ground out, guiding the vehicle to the side of the road. He turned off the ignition and leaned over to check on her. She had settled back down again, her eyes drifting shut. "Good girl," he whispered, then pocketed his keys. He climbed out of the car, closing the door quietly. When he saw what happened, he swore under his breath.

A flat tire. And he didn't have a spare.

Great. Just great. He thought about his low reserves. He needed a tow and a tire, and he could barely afford either one of them.

Cameron cursed again and pulled out his cell phone, staring at the screen. No bars. He held up the phone and pivoted, trying to find a signal. Nothing. He glanced around and saw a few white houses without shutters spaced out along the street. What he didn't see were cars parked in the driveways. If that hadn't clued him in that he was on a predominantly Amish road, the lines of wash hanging and swaying in the fall breeze did.

He tried to stem his panic. He was stuck in the last place he wanted to be. He had two choices—he could backtrack on the road on foot until he had a signal, or he could knock on one of the doors and see if he could borrow their phone. He knew enough about the Amish from working at Barton Plastics to know they used phones sometimes. Some of the Amish guys even carried around cells, although he'd never seen them chatting on them.

He shoved his useless phone into the pocket of his jeans, went to the truck, and opened the back door. He took Lacy from the car seat and headed for the nearest house, cradling her tiny body against his shoulder. Somehow she remained asleep.

As he walked up the gravel driveway to a small, simple house, a calico cat fell into step beside him. His sneakers ground against the small stones. The sound seemed to echo in the quiet of his surroundings. Instead of the thrum of traffic, he heard the soft lowing of a cow. He saw two horses in a small corral, munching on stubbly grass. He heard birds twittering, smelled the scent of burning wood in the air from nearby chimneys. Everything seemed to reach his senses in a way he'd never experienced before. Living in the city all his life, even a small one like Langdon, had numbed him to nature.

He tried to steady his nerves as he climbed up the steps to the wooden front porch. A planter filled with orange and purple mums was near the door. Otherwise the porch was cleared off, without a speck of dirt or a stray leaf. Cameron knocked on the screen door and waited. No answer. He knocked again. Lacy rubbed her cheek against his shoulder. She would be waking up any moment now.

He was about to leave when the door opened. An Amish woman looked at him, her light blue eyes wide and wary. She was young, possibly his age, wearing a white bonnet-looking hat and a light blue, long-sleeved dress, which was typical of what Amish women wore around here. He couldn't help but give her a once-over, her odd way of dressing making him curious, and noticed that she was barefoot. Realizing he was staring, he lifted up his head and met her questioning gaze. "Hi. I've got a flat tire and my cell isn't working." The words came out in a rush, and she started to frown at the same time Lacy began to fuss. He rubbed his daughter's back and continued. "Do you have a phone I could use? I need to call for a tow."

She regarded him for a moment as Lacy continued to squirm. Patting her back wasn't working, so he shifted her to the crook of his left arm, his hand on her tiny bottom. She couldn't be wet again, could she? Or hungry? Was she cold? At this point he had no idea. The little mewling cries she let out were different from the usual ones.

"A tow?" the woman asked.

He nodded, trying to pay attention to both her and his daughter. "I don't have a spare tire, so I need a tow truck. And a new tire. Lacy, shhh." He bounced her gently in his arms, and that seemed to calm her for a moment.

"Our phone is in the shanty." She pointed to a small wooden structure at the end of the driveway. "You're welcome to use it."

"Thanks." Lacy's cries turned into high-pitched screams. Yep, she was hungry. "I have to feed my daughter first," he said over the noise. *Why did I tell her that?* It wasn't as if the woman needed to know or was even interested. "I'll use the phone when I'm done." He started down the steps. He didn't realize the woman was following him until she tapped him on the shoulder.

"Your wife can come inside and feed the baby." She hugged her arms. "It's a little chilly out today. It's much warmer in the house."

Maybe being cold and hungry was what had Lacy in a snit.

She'd been warm and cozy in the truck, and he hadn't put a jacket on her. The familiar feeling of being out of his element rose within him. "It's just me and Lacy. I can feed her in the truck." *And find her jacket while I'm at it.*

"I'm sure that wouldn't be comfortable for either of you."

She moved to stand in front of him, her expression filled with kindness and concern. Nice, but not what he needed right now. If she didn't get out of his way, he'd have to sidestep her. With every second she delayed him, Lacy's cries grew louder, and with every second he was delayed, he was forced to stay in Birch Creek.

"Why don't I feed her while you make the phone call? I'm pretty good with babies."

Cameron hesitated, thinking of the foolishness of handing his baby girl over to a complete stranger. But she was Amish, which meant she was religious and Lacy would probably be fine. Right now he'd do anything to get to West Virginia faster. "I'll run and get her bottle out of the truck."

"I can hold her while you do."

He paused, still uncertain, then decided to chance it. "I'll be right back." He put Lacy in the woman's arms and ran to his truck, looking over his shoulder several times. The woman didn't move, just rocked Lacy in her arms. From this distance he could hear Lacy's cries growing in intensity. He grabbed her diaper bag and tiny jacket and sprinted back to the woman. She was singing to Lacy, the words in a language he didn't understand. It calmed Lacy a little bit, but she was still crying.

"She's cute." She looked at Cameron. "So sweet."

"She is, except when she's hungry."

"Oh, babies are sweet even when they're hungry. I'm Irene, by the way."

"Cameron Crawford." As soon as he said his name, he wanted to kick himself. Then he calmed down. No one would be looking for him here on a back road in Birch Creek. He didn't have to worry about her knowing his real name. "Nice to meet you."

She held out her hand, and Cameron was about to shake it when he realized she was gesturing to the diaper bag. "Don't worry. I'll take good care of your little one. You make your phone call."

For some bizarre reason, Cameron felt a sudden calm come over him. He trusted Irene, which was weird because he didn't trust strangers easily. It had taken him a good week to trust Mrs. Rodriguez to watch Lacy after Mackenzie died, and he had known her for a few months. But Irene had a peaceful disposition, she seemed like a natural with babies, and he had to get that tow as quickly as possible. He handed the bag to her, hoping he wasn't making a huge mistake.

Irene slipped it over her shoulder and nodded at the shanty. "Take your time. When you're done, come inside. I'll be in the living room with . . . Lacy? Is that her name?"

Cameron nodded. He rushed to the shanty, then came to a skidding stop at the end of the driveway. He called to Irene, "Is there a phone book in there?"

"Ya. It's from last year, but you should be able to find the number you need. I think you will, anyway—I've never called a tow truck before."

But Cameron was already opening the shanty door, grateful for a fairly up-to-date phone book. He glanced over his shoulder one more time to see Irene head for the house with Lacy. This was going to be the quickest phone call he ever made.

Cameron squeezed inside the shanty, which had one small window that let in cloudy light from outside. A stronger breeze kicked up, shaking the small booth as he thumbed through the phone book. He hadn't used one of these since he was a little kid. He searched through the yellow pages for towing services, found the biggest ad, and looked at the phone. He couldn't believe they still had a rotary phone, something else he hadn't seen since he was a little kid. He dialed the number, then tapped his fingers against the wood-planked wall and waited for someone to answer. The number was out of order.

He hung up and dialed the next number. This time he got a recorded message. The next number he chose was also out of order. And the next. He looked at the front of the book. Eight years out of date. Irene was a little off on the date. Could his luck be any worse? He dialed the last number and held his breath. Finally, someone answered.

"Connor's Towing," the gruff voice on the other end said. Static crackled through the line, and Cameron could tell the guy was on a cell phone.

He explained the situation. "So I'll need a spare too," he told him.

"You don't have one in your truck? Not too smart of you."

Cameron grit his teeth, his patience as thin as paper right now. "Can you give me a tow or not?"

"Son, you don't have to be rude about it." A pause. "But since I can tell you're desperate, I'll try to fit you in. It will be a while, though. Got two people in front of you. Business is busy today."

Relief flowed through him. "Thanks. What time do you think you can be here?"

"Oh . . ." A long pause, and Cameron thought he was going to lose it. "Three hours. Maybe four?"

Cameron groaned and leaned his head against the shanty. "Not any sooner?"

"Nope. And I've got another call coming in, so you better let me know now if you want me to come out."

Cameron gave the guy the address. Four hours? What was he going to do during that time?

"I'll call you when I'm on my way," the guy said.

Cameron frowned. "I'm, uh, using a phone in a shanty."

"Ah. You're in Birch Creek, then? I didn't recognize the street name. Then again, I don't get too many calls from the Amish. Just look for me around one o'clock."

After Cameron thanked the guy and hung up the phone, he ran back to Irene's house. He knocked on the door first before walking in, not wanting to barge into her house. His body tensed as worst-case scenarios fleeted through his mind, but then he felt ridiculous when he saw Lacy contentedly sucking on a bottle while Irene held her.

"Did you find someone to come get your car?"

He nodded, not bothering to correct her that he had a truck, not a car. "They can't come out until early afternoon." He looked at Lacy. His hands itched to hold his daughter again, but she seemed fine with Irene. Interrupting her feeding would just upset Lacy and make Irene think he didn't trust her.

"You can stay here and wait," she said.

Cameron shook his head. "Uh, you don't know me from Adam."

"Who's Adam?"

He couldn't help but chuckle. "What I mean is that I could be an ax murderer or something."

"But you're not."

"Are you always this trusting?"

Lacy slowed down her sucking, and Irene pulled the bottle out of the baby's mouth. She leaned Lacy against her shoulder and patted her back. His daughter burped. Irene was right. She was good with babies.

"No. But I can tell you're harmless."

He crossed his arms, intrigued. "How so?"

"You're too comfortable with Lacy, for one thing. And you were worried about leaving her with me. Oh, I think she's done." The bottle drooped in Lacy's mouth, and her long-lashed eyes drifted closed.

"Maybe I'm using her as a way to get into your house."

Irene met his gaze, unflinching. "But you aren't, are you?"

He shook his head. "I'm just trying to get to West—uh, get to the freeway with my daughter." His stomach growled. In his hurry to get on the road, he had skipped breakfast.

Irene rose from the chair, carefully cradling Lacy. "Here." She gestured with a tilt of her head. "Have a seat. I'll fix you something to eat."

He was about to protest. He didn't want a handout or to be beholden to anyone, especially an Amish woman in Birch Creek. But what choice did he have, other than to sit in the truck with Lacy for the next four hours? Irene held Lacy out to him. He took his daughter and sat in the hickory rocking chair.

"Do you like ham and cheese?"

Right now he'd eat the sole off his sneaker. "Sounds good."

"I'll be back in a minute." Then she paused. "Do you need to use the phone again to call your wife?" At his frown she added, "To tell her about the flat tire."

"My wife . . . passed away."

Irene's mouth dropped open. "I'm so sorry. I didn't mean to—"

"It's all right." Eventually he would get used to the awkward pain that occurred when he had to explain that he was a single father. But not today. "I'm used to the question," he said, lying. He glanced at Lacy. "It's . . . hard, you know?"

"Yes." Her voice was nearly a whisper. "It's always hard to lose someone you love."

He looked at her, the pain in her eyes so stark it had him wondering whom she had lost. Then she brightened, the moment passing so quickly he might have imagined it. "How old is Lacy?"

"Two months." He kissed the top of his baby girl's head and held her close.

After a pause she said, "I'll get that sandwich."

He glanced around the living room, which was sparse but cozy. Heat emanated from a wood-burning stove in the corner. But the last place he wanted to be was in an Amish home. The reminder of what he had done bubbled to the surface. Although he came from a broken home, he'd never broken the law in his life, and now he was running from it. *I'm doing this for Lacy. I can't raise her from a prison cell.* He had to keep reminding himself that the end justified the means. It was the only thing that kept him from strangling on the guilt.

Lacy rubbed her cheek against his shoulder and let out a tiny sigh. He pressed his toe against the floor and started tipping the chair back and forth, letting the heat from the woodstove envelop him. He closed his eyes, and for a few moments he allowed himself to relax, to enjoy holding Lacy in the silence that surrounded them, to forget about everything he was doing wrong and how desperate he was to do right by his daughter.

Irene ran a large knife through a juicy Honeycrisp apple, cutting the fruit into wedges. She placed them on the plate next to the ham and cheddar cheese sandwich she'd made for Cameron. She had no idea if he liked apples, but giving him only a sandwich seemed pitiful. Her mother had left that morning to go shopping at the Schrocks' to resupply the pantry. They had spent so much time preparing food for Andrew's wedding that they had failed to realize their own supplies were running low.

She put the knife in the sink, then leaned against the counter, her head pounding. She still couldn't believe what Joanna had done. Andrew was a wreck, even more so since Joanna had stopped by to apologize. She assumed he had gone to work today, but she really didn't know. He wasn't talking to her or to *Mamm*. She had never seen him so upset.

Mamm had said he needed time, and Irene understood that. Still, her heart went out to her brother, and she wished there was something she could do to help him. When their father left, they leaned on each other to try to understand his abandonment. Over the years they'd had their fair share of arguments. What siblings didn't? But she loved him. He didn't deserve to be hurt so deeply.

She rubbed the center of her temples. Her brother was miserable, her mother was worried even though she was trying to hide it, and now there was an *Englisch* stranger in her living room. Andrew would be livid if he knew she'd let a man in the house while she was alone.

But from the moment she saw Cameron holding his baby daughter, she knew she had to help him. He didn't look like any *Englisch* man she'd seen before. He was tall and thin. Too thin, she thought. His black hair was slicked back and tied at the neck in a long ponytail that hung between his shoulders. His jaw was covered with dark stubble, and thick black eyebrows rested above his eyes. There were dark shadows beneath them, as if he hadn't slept in a month. There was also something desperate about him, but not dangerous. Now that she knew his wife had died, she understood.

She picked up the plate of food along with a glass of tea and carried it into the living room. She slowed her steps, then stopped completely and leaned against the door frame. Both father and daughter were asleep. His brow, deeply furrowed before, was now relaxed, along with the rest of his face and body, as he slept in the rocking chair. She tiptoed into the room and set the food on the coffee table, then snuck back into the kitchen.

～ン

Andrew gripped Fred's reins as he turned into his driveway. He'd tried to work today, but he couldn't focus. Not wanting to hurt the horses or himself, he rescheduled his appointments and went back home. He didn't know what he was going to do there, either, but at least he wouldn't accidentally injure one of his clients' animals.

He pulled up to the barn, purposely ignoring the addition. He still intended to take it down. He would have gotten partway through the demolition last night if Joanna hadn't come over. He'd been so angry with her he went back to the addition, only to fall asleep on the couch again. When he woke up to sunlight streaming through the pristine glass of a brand-new window, fresh pain washed over him as he remembered everything he'd lost.

As he put Fred back in his stall, he thought about Joanna's visit again. He hadn't realized it at the time, but she wasn't using her crutches. Good for her. And he realized he meant it. He was furious with her, but he wanted her to heal.

I love you.

Her words and the tearful passion with which she'd spoken them still resonated in his heart. But his feelings were the last thing he trusted. Despite himself, he still loved her. He always would. But he refused to be hurt by her again. He would continue with his life the way it had been before they dated. He'd work hard at his job. Take care of his mother and sister. Everything would go back to being the same as it had been when he and Joanna weren't romantically involved.

He accidentally jerked Fred's reins. "Sorry, *bu*," he said to the horse. Who was he fooling? Nothing would be the same—or right—again.

He started for the house, saw the addition, and went around to the front door. He'd spend the rest of the afternoon taking the addition apart. Maybe Asa could use the materials for his house. He opened the front door and his jaw dropped. There in his living room was an *Englisch* man sitting in the hickory rocking chair, holding a baby.

⁓

At the sound of the front door opening, Cameron's eyes flew open. He bolted upright in the chair, startling Lacy. His daughter started to cry as he turned to see a broad-chested Amish man walk into the living room, his eyes wide with surprise, then narrowing with suspicion.

"Who are you?" he asked. He was shorter than Cameron, but his chest was twice as wide and his thick arms had to be three times as strong as Cameron's. "What are you doing in my house?"

Cameron rose and stood near the woodstove, rubbing Lacy's back to soothe her. "Cameron Crawford," he said, immediately wanting to kick himself for giving his full name. Then again, it wasn't like the police would be looking for him in an Amish home. It would be the last place they would search. "I had a flat tire a little while ago and I'm waiting for a tow."

The man strode toward him, his hands fisted at his sides. "Where's my sister?"

"I'm right here, Andrew." Irene walked into the living room. "And before you get any more upset, everything is fine."

Andrew went to her. They spoke to each other in a language Cameron didn't understand, but from the turbulent look on Andrew's face and the irritated one on Irene's, he could tell they were arguing. Irene caught Cameron's gaze and suddenly brushed past Andrew.

"Sorry for my brother's rudeness." She glared at Andrew, whose icy blue eyes snapped right back.

The peace he'd felt moments ago evaporated. "We should leave." He scooped Lacy's diaper bag off the floor.

"You don't have to go," Irene said. "Lacy doesn't need to be out in the chilly air."

"But—"

"Irene's right." Andrew stepped forward, looking a little less upset. "Why don't you show me what happened to your car?"

"Truck," Irene said, correcting him.

That drew an irritated look from Andrew, and Irene gave him one right back. Oh yeah, they were siblings. Cameron didn't have any brothers and sisters of his own, except for dozens of foster siblings, none he had ever kept in touch with. He'd regretted that since Mackenzie died. But like him, they had been eager to turn their backs on their former lives and cut ties with everyone. Sometimes that was the only way to break free of a past no one wanted to acknowledge or remember.

"You can show me what happened to your truck," Andrew said. "Maybe I can help you fix it."

Cameron was about to tell him there was nothing Andrew could do, but then he caught the man's meaning. He wanted to talk to Cameron alone. Cameron handed Lacy to Irene. His daughter murmured a little bit, then settled against Irene's shoulder.

Andrew opened the door, and a cool blast of air hit Cameron as he stepped out onto the front porch. He followed Andrew down the porch steps. When they were a few feet away from the house, Andrew turned around and crossed his thick arms across his chest.

Cameron held up his hands, palms facing outward. "Dude, I'm sorry. I didn't mean to bother your sister. I swear, my tire went flat, I don't have a spare, and I can't get cell service. I was gonna wait in the truck until the tow arrived, but she insisted I come inside."

"Sounds like Irene."

"Then I fell asleep and . . ." He stopped talking as Andrew continued to study him. Cameron shoved his hands into the pockets of his jeans. "Lacy and I can wait in the truck. It's not a big deal."

"When is the tow supposed to arrive?"

"Around one, hopefully." Cameron pulled out his phone and checked the time. He grimaced. "At least three more hours."

Andrew gave him another long look, sizing him up. "I don't mean to be rude," he said, dropping his defensive stance and relaxing a little bit. "I'm surprised, that's all. We don't get many *Englisch* around here. Especially an *Englisch* man with a baby."

"I totally get it. If I came home and found a strange man in my apartment . . ." Cameron shook his head. "You're a lot calmer about it than I would have been." He paused, an idea occurring to him. Maybe he wouldn't have to wait for the tow truck after all. "You got a spare tire? I just need something to get me to the nearest service station. I'd pay you for it, of course."

Andrew shook his head. "Don't have much use for tires around here. Not ones for trucks, anyway."

It had been a long shot, so Cameron wasn't surprised by Andrew's answer. He was disappointed, though. "Guess you wouldn't."

"Where are you from?" Andrew asked.

"Langdon. But I'm in the middle of moving," he added quickly. "Heading south."

"Taking the back roads?"

"Yeah." Cameron nodded. "There was a detour from the freeway. Construction or something."

Andrew started for the house. "We should go back inside

before my sister comes out here. I'm sure she's standing at the window watching us. She can't mind her own business sometimes."

"I've got to say, for my daughter's sake, I'm glad she didn't this time." He glanced over his shoulder at the house in time to see the white curtain fall across it. He smirked. Andrew was right. "Your sister is nice," he said. He turned back to Andrew and saw the man's gaze narrowing. "I don't mean anything by it. I'm not interested in her like that." Great. Now he sounded like he was insulting her. "Look, my wife died a couple of months ago . . ." A lump lodged in his throat.

"I'm sorry," Andrew said.

"Yeah." Cameron rubbed the back of his neck, pushing aside his ponytail. He was so tired of hearing everyone's apologies. They meant well, but the words wouldn't bring Mackenzie back. "Thanks."

Andrew frowned. "It's not easy."

Cameron put his hand back in his pocket. "Sounds like you understand."

"Sort of." Andrew sighed. "Love hurts," he muttered, looking down at the ground.

"Yeah. It does. But it's worth it. I wouldn't trade the time I had with Mackenzie for anything. She was my world, and she gave me my daughter. That's worth a dozen broken hearts in my book." He cleared his throat, feeling weird that he was getting so personal with a complete stranger. Yet he couldn't stop himself from saying his next words. "I'd do anything to have her back."

Andrew stared at him, but it seemed like he was seeing right through him. Then with a shake of his head he said, "Let's go inside."

For the next two hours Irene took care of Lacy, changing her, rocking her, and holding her while she took another short nap. "Eat and get some rest," Irene said. "You look like you need it."

That was blunt but accurate. He practically inhaled the sandwich and apple slices, then stretched out on the couch, too tired to protest anymore. Besides, he didn't need to fall asleep at the wheel and cause another accident. He clenched his hands together, then relaxed enough to close his eyes.

Andrew woke him up when the tow guy arrived. Cameron took Lacy from Irene. She handed him the diaper bag.

"I can't thank you enough for letting us hang out here," he said.

She touched Lacy's little arm and took a step back. "I hope you find the peace you're looking for, Cameron."

He hadn't said anything about looking for peace. Little did she know he would never find it. Not lasting peace, anyway.

"I'll be praying for you and Lacy."

"Uh, thanks."

Cameron and Lacy left the house and headed for the tow truck. Now he had both Mrs. Rodriguez and Irene praying for him. He didn't ask for their prayers. They were pointless, anyway. God wouldn't listen. Not after what Cameron had done. Once he crossed the Ohio state line, he wasn't looking back.

⌒

"I'll be right back," Naomi told the taxi driver as she opened the car door in front of the post office in Cuyahoga Falls. She used an actual taxi service and not one of the drivers in the Birch

190

Creek area. It was expensive, and also necessary. No one could know she went twice a month to this post office to send mail, and hopefully get a letter in exchange.

She'd written Bartholomew right after the wedding fell apart and had tucked the letter into her purse. Usually she waited until Andrew was at work and Irene went out for the day to go to Cuyahoga Falls, but with Andrew's unpredictable behavior and Irene sticking close to home, she had taken her buggy and horse and tethered them at Asa's, knowing he started his new job at Barton Plastics that morning.

As she opened the door to the post office and headed for the private box she'd rented years ago, she thought about the lie she'd told Irene. Only half a lie, since she planned to go to the Schrocks' after she returned to Birch Creek. But she still lied, as she had been doing for so many years. The guilt was wearing her down, but she didn't have a choice.

Naomi pulled the key out of her purse and inserted it into the lock. The door swung open and her heart skipped at the sight of a letter. She took it out, holding it in her hands like the precious document it was. Bartholomew wrote as often as he could, but it wasn't enough. She treasured each letter.

But as she looked at the familiar handwriting on the envelope, she frowned. It wasn't addressed to her. The letter was for Andrew.

She looked inside the box again. There was nothing else there. The return address in the corner was fake, the one Bartholomew always used when he corresponded with her. Why was he writing to Andrew? She locked the box, put Andrew's letter in her purse, then slipped her own letter to her husband in the mail slot and left the post office.

It was nearly a forty-minute drive back to Asa's house. Naomi's mind was whirling with questions. She wished Bartholomew had at least written her a note telling her why he was sending Andrew a letter. She should have at least had some warning. They had decided together not to tell Andrew and Irene about the past and why he had left. Why was Bartholomew breaking that promise now? And what was in his letter?

Several times she was tempted to open the envelope, despite knowing she would be betraying both her husband and her son. But she couldn't do it. She had to trust that Bartholomew had a good reason, and an urgent one, for writing to Andrew. She also had to respect Andrew's privacy.

The drive seemed longer than usual as she struggled with her thoughts. The cab pulled into Asa's drive. Naomi paid the driver, untethered her horse and buggy, and went to the Schrocks' to pick up groceries. She didn't linger, and other than exchanging a few polite pleasantries with Sadie, who was operating the cash register, she didn't say much. She hurried home, only to stand in the barn, unsure what to do. Should she hand the letter to Andrew? Of course he would ask questions if she did, questions she wasn't prepared to answer.

She left the barn, and her gaze landed on the addition. For some reason Andrew had spent the last two nights inside the new construction, which she thought was strange. But she wouldn't question him about it. He had been silent and surly since Joanna's visit the day before, and she didn't want to meddle any more than she already had. She still believed they would find their way back to each other, but they would have to do it on their own and according to God's will.

Naomi started for the house, then changed her mind and

went into the addition. "Andrew?" she called out, in case he was there. He wasn't. She saw the coffee table in the middle of the living room and set Bartholomew's letter on it. Giving the letter one last look, she turned and left.

CHAPTER 14

Thursday evening Joanna sat on the back patio. She'd watched the sun set over an hour ago, and the air had turned cold. It was nearing the end of October, and she should have on a jacket instead of the light sweater. But she couldn't be bothered to get up and get one. Her cheeks were cold, her hands like ice. Homer lay at her feet, his head lifting every once in a while at the stray sound of a dog barking in the distance or a horse whinnying.

She stared at the leaves strewn across the yard, the moon casting a silvery and almost eerie glow in the night sky, going over her visit with Andrew. Last night she didn't have a nightmare, but she didn't sleep well, either. She tossed and turned, thinking about Andrew's pained expression, the harshness in his voice that she'd never heard before as he sent her away. Had she expected anything else, though? *You got what you deserved.*

The back door opened and Abigail came outside. She draped

a jacket over Joanna's shoulders and sat down in the chair next to her. "Thought you might be getting cold."

Joann looked at her sister in surprise. Abigail had been giving her the silent treatment ever since Joanna called off the wedding. Was this an olive branch? "I am a bit chilly."

"Why didn't you come inside?"

Joanna shrugged. She wouldn't tell Abigail that she couldn't stand the strain between them. She was doing what Sadie said—giving her sister time.

"I'm sorry, Joanna. I know I've been terrible to you since the wedding. I shouldn't have gotten so angry."

"I don't blame you. I disappointed everyone."

"For goodness' sake, stop it."

Joanna jerked her head toward Abigail. The moon was full tonight, and she could see the shadow of irritation on her sister's face.

"Joanna, what's done is done. You told Andrew you were sorry, and he's the only one who needs *yer* apology. The rest of us should be apologizing to you for pushing you into something you weren't ready for. But we thought marrying Andrew would make you happy."

"It would have." Joanna turned to Abigail, her throat tightening. "I've made so many mistakes since I've been home. I don't know what to do to fix them."

"Maybe you don't have to do anything. How have you felt since you talked to him?"

"Horrible." She sighed. "But not completely. I'm upset that he's angry with me. But I don't regret calling off the wedding. I only regret hurting him."

Abigail leaned back in her chair. "Then I think there's hope for the two of you."

"If you had seen Andrew, heard what he said . . ." She shook her head. "It's over. I have to accept that." Somehow.

Abigail didn't say anything for a long time. "I know what you mean. How do you stop loving someone?"

Joanna reached for her sister's hand. "I don't know."

"You do have one thing in *yer* favor. Andrew isn't like Joel. He's not fickle with his feelings." She tapped the heel of her shoe against the concrete patio. "He still loves you, despite *yer* physical changes. I know you've been self-conscious about the crutches and the scar. But Andrew doesn't care about that. He wanted to marry you anyway." She released Joanna's hand. "Joel dumped me because I gained a few pounds."

"Did he say that to you?"

"*Nee*, but look at who he's dating right now. Rebecca Chupp. She's very pretty."

"So are you."

"Clearly Joel doesn't think so."

"Looks don't matter—"

"Aha! See." Abigail faced her. "To Andrew, you're beautiful. Crutches or no crutches, scar or no scar."

"How do you know?"

"Because we see the way he looks at you." Abigail's voice sounded thick. "Joel never looked at me that way. I think he liked when I flirted with him. When I . . ." She paused. "Joanna, for some reason you've always focused on what you think you lack. You don't realize how strong you are. You survived the accident. You fought back the pain of surgery, and you're free of the crutches. You still see the good in people and you always have, even when the rest of us are cynical. You are beautifully and wonderfully made. The only person who doesn't see it is you." She stood. "I've got to finish up a rug tonight. Sadie's going to sell it in the store tomorrow. If someone buys it, I might make more. Looks like I'll have some extra free time now. Are you coming inside?"

"In a minute. Abigail?"

"*Ya?*"

"Joel doesn't deserve you. You'll find someone who does."

"Right, because there are *so* many single men in Birch Creek. Maybe if we lived in a larger settlement—"

"You're not thinking of leaving, are you?" Joanna panicked. Abigail couldn't leave. She needed her and Sadie. Aden too. They were the only family she had.

Abigail didn't say anything for a long moment. "*Nee.* I'm not going anywhere. I couldn't leave you and Sadie, even if that means being single for the rest of *mei* life."

"We'll both be."

"*Nee*, not you. You and Andrew will find *yer* way back. I truly believe that." She went inside.

Joanna tapped her hand against the arm of the chair. Abigail had uncovered one of Joanna's insecurities when it came to Andrew. Her physicality was part of her weakness, but not all of it. Like she told Sadie, she didn't want a lopsided marriage. When it came to Andrew, she didn't feel on equal ground. *I never felt on equal ground with him.*

Her eyes widened. Since that day in sixth grade when he stood up for her, he'd been her savior. She felt safe with him, but she never felt *enough*. If she were, he wouldn't hesitate to show her affection. He would have been eager to marry her when she proposed, not after the accident. It wouldn't have taken her almost dying to gain his love.

But why did she need Andrew to prove his love? Why couldn't she accept it from him on his own terms? Why didn't she tell him what she needed instead of making him guess?

Because I never felt worthy. That wasn't a new feeling born out of the accident. She had always felt as if she were lacking something. She'd been racked with self-doubt for as long as she could remember. Her perception of herself was the reason her relationship with Andrew was unbalanced. *I am beautifully and wonderfully made.* On her own, she was enough.

But with Andrew she was better.

She stood up, her legs feeling stronger than ever before. She still wanted Andrew. Now she knew she could—and would—fight for him.

⟳

After Cameron left, Andrew was at loose ends. He thought about lecturing Irene on the foolishness of letting strange men into the house when she was alone—or at any time—but after talking to the guy, he realized Irene had done the right thing. He also couldn't get what Cameron had said about his wife off his mind. *I'd do anything to have her back.* But there was nothing he could do to get her back. Andrew remembered how terrified he'd been when Joanna was in the hospital. He couldn't imagine the grief and pain Cameron was going through. Joanna was alive. She was a buggy ride away. All he had to do was drive to her house if he wanted to see her. But as long as he was on this earth, Cameron would never see his wife again. That fact did give Andrew pause, but it didn't fix the break between him and Joanna.

He spent the rest of the day stacking firewood, even though it was already stacked. He needed something physical to do that didn't require him using tools. He couldn't hurt himself with firewood—at least he thought so, until he dropped a large piece on the toe of his boot as Joanna's rejection played over in his mind again. By the time it was dark he was physically exhausted and mentally drained. He walked past the addition, intending to go to the main house, take a shower, and hopefully get a decent night's sleep for once. The only way he'd be able to do that was if he could get Joanna out of his mind. So far he hadn't been able to.

He passed by the addition door. His feet stopped on their own accord, as if something was pulling him toward the structure. Although he didn't want to, he opened the door and walked into the living room. What was this, his mind playing some kind of torture game with him that he couldn't stay away from what was supposed to be his and Joanna's home? It made no sense. Yet there he was, opening the door and stepping inside the living area, breathing in the still-fresh scent of paint and wood flooring. *What am I doing here?*

Then he saw a letter on the coffee table. It hadn't been there this morning when he woke up. Why would his mother or Irene put his mail in here instead of giving it to him directly? Then again, he hadn't been the friendliest person to be around lately. He strode to the table and snatched up the letter.

He didn't recognize the handwriting or the return address. He almost tossed it back on the table, sure it was an advertisement of some sort, probably some timber company offering money to clear the trees off his land. He was getting more and more of those notices lately, and he wasn't interested. But he opened the envelope anyway.

After he read the first few sentences, he dropped onto the couch.

Dear Andrew,

I know you must be shocked to hear from me. I also know I don't have the right to contact you after all these years. But when your mother wrote and told me you were getting married, I had to write to you.

I wish I could be there for your big day. A man needs his father, even when he's grown. I haven't been the father you needed me to be. For that I am truly sorry. I hope one day to make it up to you.

Andrew stopped reading. He clenched the paper in his hand. Make it up to him? Did he really think a letter would be the way to restart their relationship? He started to crumple the paper in his fist, but he stopped, flattened it against his thigh, and continued to read.

You probably don't want to hear any advice I have, especially when it comes to marriage. I've made so many mistakes in that department. But I want you to remember this—love Joanna as you would love yourself. Not because God commands it, but because your wife deserves the best from you. Joanna Schrock must be a very special woman for you to be in love with her. Treat her with kindness, gentleness, and love. That is what a real man—a real husband—must do.

Your mother doesn't know I'm contacting you. She also doesn't know I'm going to tell you the truth. All these years we needed you and Irene to believe I left because of someone else. That's not the reason. It never was. I love your mother. She is my wife, and always will be. Someday I hope to tell you the whole story, but I can't right now. Just know that I didn't want to leave my wife and children. I had to leave.

I'll always love you and Irene, even if you can never forgive me for what I've done. God willing, one day I'll be able to tell you in person. I won't write to you again. Don't tell anyone you heard from me, including your sister. It's important that things stay exactly the way they are, at least for now.

God bless your wedding and your marriage.

Love,

Dad

Andrew slumped in his seat. He stared at the words on the page. Was this a joke? It didn't make any sense. He picked up the envelope again and looked at the return address. It was a town he'd never heard of in California.

He dropped the letter, jumped up from the couch, and thrust his hands through his hair. The letter couldn't be real. Someone was playing a cruel prank on him, hitting him where and when he was most vulnerable. But who would do that? He never talked about his father to anyone in Birch Creek, including Joanna. He wanted to excise the man out of his life. So no one in the district would know enough about what had happened back in Florida. He also knew deep down that no one in Birch Creek would be that cruel.

The letter was real. The lump forming in his throat felt like a boulder. What his father didn't know was that he had tried to give Joanna his best. It wasn't good enough.

And whatever had driven his father away . . . He shook his head. All the wounds he'd tried to patch up over the years started opening. He sat back down on the couch and hung his head. His throat ached, his nose stung, and he couldn't believe he was close to tears. He'd thought his heart had turned to stone when it came to his father. But after reading that he still loved his mother . . . that he hadn't left because he wanted to . . .

Andrew looked up at the ceiling. *What do I do now, Lord?*

After having his truck towed to the nearest service station and being told it would take them several hours to get to it, Cameron found a motel within walking distance. He planned to lay low for a few hours until his truck was ready. So far nothing had gone according to plan. In fact, everything seemed to be against him. But that would change once he was on the road again.

He'd stayed in some dumps before as a kid when his mother was using, and she would take him with her to score drugs, often spending the night at the dealer's dilapidated house, apartment, or trailer. But this was possibly the worst—and cheapest—place he'd ever stayed. He could do anything for a few hours, he figured.

His cell phone rang. He reached for it and answered. "Hello?"

"Cameron Crawford?"

His guard went up at the unfamiliar voice. "Speaking."

"Yeah, we've got your truck here. You wanted a new tire?"

This was a different guy than he'd talked to earlier. Cameron glanced at Lacy, who was still awake but watching his movements. "Yeah. Is the truck done?"

"Not yet." He paused. "We're not going to get to it today. Sorry."

"What?"

"We've been backed up. I had a guy go home with the flu. It's been crazy around here. But we'll have it done first thing in the morning."

Great. So now he and Lacy were stuck here? He wanted to throw the phone against the wall. "What time?" he said through gritted teeth.

"Eight thirty. Also, you picked out a cheap tire. I'd recommend something a little better if you're planning to drive a lot. We've got a medium-priced tire that would save you money in the long run—"

"I'll take the cheap one."

"Seriously, you'll be better off with—"

"Just put the tire on the truck!"

"All right." The man paused, his next words sounding more tentative. "We do body work. Do you want us to fix the damage to the front?"

The phone nearly slid out of Cameron's hand. He'd forgotten about the dent on the right side of the front of the truck. After the accident he'd tried to pound it out himself. Apparently he hadn't done that good of a job. "No," he said, then swallowed.

"You sure? It won't take long to do."

"I'm sure." Cameron forced his tone to be steady.

"We'll call you in the morning when we've got the tire put on."

"Thanks."

An hour later Lacy started screaming. Over the next few hours, he tried everything to calm her down. He fed her, changed her, gave her a sponge bath because he didn't trust the cleanliness of the moldy tub in the bathroom, dressed her, undressed her, and finally set her in her carry seat and let her squall. When he couldn't stand it anymore, he picked her up and walked around with her. She had started to settle down when the hotel phone rang, triggering another crying jag. He picked up the receiver.

"Hello?"

"We're getting complaints," the scratchy, cigarette-tinged voice of the front desk guy admonished.

Cameron didn't need to ask him what the complaints were about. "I'm trying to get her settled. She doesn't feel good." He had no idea if that was Lacy's problem, but he had to say something.

"If you don't keep the noise down, you'll have to leave." *Click.*

Cameron set the receiver back in the cradle. Lacy was still crying. "Shhh. Daddy's got you. It will be all right."

He found that walking up and down the width of the room and holding her flat on her stomach over his forearm seemed to help. After almost an hour she quieted, and he set her on top of her blanket on the bed. He lay down next to her, not bothering to change out of his clothes. He was exhausted and thankful she had finally gone to sleep. As he lay on his side and stared at her sweet, peaceful face, he could hardly believe that minutes before it had been scrunched up into a red, squalling ball.

He continued to look at her, his eyelids growing heavy. For some reason he remembered what Irene had said before he left. *"I'll be praying for you and Lacy."* So far her and Mrs. Rodriguez's prayers weren't working.

Yet a tiny part of him felt something he couldn't define. It wasn't peace or happiness or even a steadying of his nerves. But something was stirring inside him, just beyond his reach and understanding. It was enough to allow him to close his eyes for a moment, to catch a few winks before Lacy woke up again wanting a bottle or a fresh diaper or something he couldn't figure out.

His cell phone rang again. His eyes flew open. How long had he been asleep? He looked at Lacy, who was wide awake but quiet. She stared at him, her round blue eyes studying his face as if she'd never seen him before. Then she smiled, and his heart soared. Her first smile. He was on the run and stuck in a roach motel, but it was the most beautiful thing he'd ever seen.

He pulled out his phone and looked at the number. The service station. He sat up and answered. "Hello?"

"Mr. Crawford? Your truck is ready."

Cameron checked on Lacy one more time before getting up and pulling back the green window curtain. Daylight hit his eyes. "What time is it?"

"Eight thirty."

He looked back at the bed. Lacy had slept through the night? He smiled at her. "Good girl."

"What?"

"Sorry." Cameron let the curtain fall. "I'll be there as soon as I can." He hung up the phone and went to Lacy, who was now starting to fuss. He changed her diaper, fed her a bottle, then gathered their things and walked to the station.

The guy was behind the counter, already writing up Cameron's ticket with greasy fingers. A white oval name tag with the name Karl was stitched on his dark blue shirt. "Sure we can't fix that dent for you?"

"Yeah. A friend of mine said he'd take care of it for me."

Cameron didn't blink as he told the lie. Somehow he'd have to get that dent fixed, but he couldn't afford it right now.

The guy peeled the ticket off the pad and handed it to Cameron.

Cameron pulled out his wallet, which was thick with money. Before he left Langdon he had closed out his account. It pained him to part with $120, but he had no choice. He thumbed through the bills, glancing up when he realized Karl was staring at his wallet. Cameron quickly took out the money and handed it to him.

Karl seemed to be taking his time punching in the amount and sliding the bills into the cash drawer. Cameron tapped his foot as he held on to Lacy's carry seat. He snatched the key out of Karl's hand when the guy finally handed it over to him.

Cameron put Lacy in the backseat of the king cab, then got into the driver's seat. He touched his forehead to the steering wheel. They were getting out of here. When he hit the freeway thirty minutes later, he felt like he could finally breathe.

CHAPTER 15

By Saturday Joanna couldn't stand it anymore. She'd spent the past couple of days trying to figure out how to reach out to Andrew, praying that God would show her what to do. She still didn't have a clear idea. However, she knew her prayers weren't in vain. Although she was still confused about making things right with Andrew, the rest of her life was moving more smoothly. She didn't need the crutches anymore. She was finding joy in cooking and baking again. She had even worked one day in the store. Not for very long and she hadn't done much, but it was good to do something different. When she caught a young *Englisch* girl staring, she assumed it was because of her dress and *kapp* and not her face. It was the first time she hadn't been self-conscious about the scar.

"You seem to be feeling better," Sadie had said when Joanna helped her close the store that night.

"I am." She smiled, and this time it wasn't for the benefit of her sister or because she was trying to convince anyone she was okay. She really was okay. She still grieved her parents, and she and her sisters had a couple of crying sessions together as they talked about the memories. But overall she was in a much better place than she had been for months. The only thing missing was Andrew. And with each passing day the hole his absence left in her heart grew.

During breakfast that morning Joanna had said, "I'd like to move to my bedroom upstairs."

Sadie sprinkled cinnamon sugar on a piece of freshly buttered bread. "Are you sure? You can stay downstairs as long as you want."

Joanna shook her head. "I don't have trouble with the stairs anymore. I want to be in *mei* old room."

After breakfast, Aden and her sisters helped Joanna move her belongings back to her bedroom, Homer trailing behind. When they left she sat down on the edge of the bed. Being in the room gave her a sense of normalcy. She looked at the light pink curtains covering the window, then shifted her gaze to her bureau. She smiled. It was good to be truly home.

She patted Homer on the head and stood. It was time to prepare lunch for Sadie, Abigail, and Aden, who was outside splitting firewood. The nights had turned cold, and they used the woodstove in the living room every evening now. Soon it would be November. Her heart grew heavy. They would be facing the upcoming holidays without their parents.

Joanna left her room and started to head for the stairs, but she paused. She stared at the door of her parents' bedroom. She hadn't been in the room except the day she had returned from Middlefield. With her heart and mind filled with memories and grief, she went to the door, held her breath, and opened it. The room had remained untouched since Joanna's return. It was also stuffy. Clearly Sadie and Abigail hadn't been in here either. She opened the window to let in the cold, fresh air. She turned and saw a box on the floor. She and Abigail had looked through the contents right after Joanna had come home. She crossed the room and sat on the floor. A dull pain twinged in her hips, but she ignored it. She opened the box and went through the contents again.

She pulled out a half-knitted sock. A ball of yarn and knitting needles. She had already taken the cookbook that had been in the box and had used some of the recipes. As she dug through scraps of fabric, another set of knitting needles, and several spools of thread, she saw a small stack of recipe cards held together with a rubber band. At the top of the first one was written "Matthew's Favorites."

Tears brimmed as she read through the cards. Some of the corners were bent and food spots and splashes were on all of them. She also saw small notes written in tiny letters next to the recipes.

Coleslaw: use less vinegar next time
Sugar cookies: need to bake longer
Chicken and noodles: he loved this. Will make more often.

Ever since Joanna could remember, her mother would make chicken and noodles every week. She hadn't thought about it until now, but her father's eyes had always lit up when she put a heaping serving on his plate. As she looked through the rest of the recipes, she realized why they were in the box and not in the kitchen. Her mother had made them often enough that she didn't need the cards anymore. Yet she had kept them.

Memories washed over her. Her parents weren't demonstrative with their affection in front of her, Sadie, and Abigail. But they showed their love to each other in other ways. *Mamm* made *Daed's* favorite foods. *Daed* always brought her a mug of hot tea in the evenings. They had probably done dozens of things Joanna never noticed.

How had she shown Andrew her love since she'd been back to Middlefield? She hadn't. Even agreeing to marry him hadn't been out of love but out of fear she would be alone. In her heart she had accused Andrew of rushing the wedding out of guilt or pity. But her motives for marriage hadn't been pure, either. In fact, they had been even more selfish.

She put everything back in the box, giving the recipe cards one last look. "You were right, *Mamm*," she whispered. "I wasn't ready to marry Andrew. But I am now."

By Saturday Andrew was finally able to put in a full day's work, but that didn't give him any satisfaction. About mid-afternoon his throat had become scratchy, and as he pulled into his driveway he started to cough. He'd avoided his mother and sister, this time for reasons other than he didn't want to talk about his failed wedding. He'd spent the nights alone in the addition, trying to puzzle out what to do about Joanna and the letter. Eventually he gave up trying to figure it out. He was tired. Exhausted, actually. When he arrived home from his last job of the day, he decided he'd ignored his family enough. He was also done with sleeping on the couch, having been unable to bring himself to sleep in the bedroom in the addition.

After stabling Fred he went into the house, expecting supper. He found a note from Irene instead:

We went to visit Rhoda Troyer for the afternoon. Will be back in time for supper.

He glanced at the clock. It was past suppertime, but he didn't care. This wouldn't be the first time he'd fended for himself. But he wasn't really hungry. He coughed again and got a glass of water. Although he wanted to turn in early, he knew he'd probably lie awake and think of Joanna and his father for hours until he'd fall asleep. He set the glass down on the counter and went outside.

The sun was halfway past the horizon and nearly obscured by clouds. He hadn't taken his jacket off, but he was still cold. The wind had been brutal today but had died down in the past hour. He looked at the addition again. He promised himself he would dismantle it after work on Monday. He coughed again and was about to go inside when he noticed a couple of shingles on the ground. Great. Even though he was taking the structure apart, he couldn't leave the roof exposed with the threat of rain. He picked up the shingles, collected his tool belt and a ladder from the barn, and went back to the addition. He leaned the ladder against the house. As he climbed the first couple of steps, fatigue dogged at him. As soon as he secured the shingles, he would go back inside and straight to bed—insomnia or no.

He had a longer coughing fit when he reached the top of the roof. Drops of rain hit his back as he bent to nail down one of the shingles. He glanced up as he heard a buggy coming down the driveway. Expecting it to be his mother and Irene, he started on another shingle. But instead of their buggy stopping close to the barn, it stopped beside the addition. He looked up as he brought the hammer down and saw Joanna getting out of the buggy. The head of the hammer smashed the back of his hand. He yelped as he dropped the hammer and grabbed his hand in pain.

"Andrew?" She looked up at him, shielding her eyes from the rain that was coming down harder now. "What are you doing up there?"

"Trying to fix the roof," he ground out.

"In the rain?"

His hand throbbed, his throat was on fire, and he was getting wet. To top it off, he started to cough.

"Are you sick?" she asked. She was getting wet, too, but she didn't seem to notice.

"*Nee.*" It felt like he was swallowing razor blades. "What do you want, Joanna?"

"To see you."

He started to shiver. "Th-there's n-othing more to s-ay."

"Andrew, please come inside. We both need to get out of the rain."

"I have to fix these shingles." If they had a heavy rain and the roof was exposed, it would lead to a bigger problem and possibly a leak. "Then I'll be inside."

"All right. I'll meet you there."

He thought she was going to go to the main house. But she took a large basket out of her buggy and went into the addition. As if she lived here. He gave his head a shake, coughed again, then finished nailing the other three shingles in place. By the time he was done, rain was dripping from the brim of his hat and he was soaked even through his coat. He carefully made his way down the ladder. He saw that Joanna's horse wasn't attached to the buggy. At some point she must have put her horse in his barn. He opened the door and walked into the addition, gripping his wet coat to his chest.

When he walked inside, he noticed the gas lamp was on in the living room. He slipped off his work boots and shivered again. Joanna was putting out food on the second-hand coffee table he'd picked up at a yard sale on his way home from work three days before the wedding. The array of food was odd—some kind of stuffed bread, red-skinned potato salad, macaroni salad, peanut butter cookies, peanut brittle, and a jar of peanuts. When she pulled out a two-liter of his favorite soft drink, he walked over to her. "What are you doing?" he asked, crossing his arms in more of an effort to warm up than be defensive.

"Making you a picnic." She gestured to the food on the table. "I brought *yer* favorites."

They were. On closer inspection he saw that the stuffed bread was actually a big pepperoni roll, which he loved. The macaroni salad had tuna in it, another favorite. And he never turned down peanuts or anything peanut-flavored.

"I hope you don't mind that I stabled my horse. I didn't know how long the rain would last."

"Joanna—"

"I'll *geh* in the kitchen and get some cups. Irene and *yer mamm* can join us if they want to. I made plenty."

And she had, more than two people could eat, especially someone like Joanna who didn't each much in the first place. "They're not here," he said, then coughed again, more violently than before.

She frowned, moved around the table, and went to him. "I

thought you said you weren't sick." She put the back of her hand on his forehead. "Andrew, you feel hot."

"I'm fine. You can *geh* back home." His head started to pound. When she tried to remove his jacket, he resisted. "I can do it," he said, shrugging out of the coat.

"I know," she said softly, looking directly in his eyes. "But let me help you. It's *mei* turn to show you how I feel," she added in a whisper.

He wasn't sure what she was talking about, and at that moment he didn't care. His body shook uncontrollably as she took his wet coat. She disappeared into what was supposed to be their bedroom, then came out carrying the quilt that had been on the bed. She wrapped it around him. "Stay here. I'll be right back."

As if he could go anywhere. He could barely remain upright. Whatever bug he had, it was hitting him hard and fast. He was grateful for the warmth of the quilt.

When he thought he'd have to sit down, she came into the room carrying a shirt and pants. "You need to get out of *yer* wet clothes." She laid the dry clothes on a nearby chair, removed the quilt from his shoulders, and turned around. "Let me know when you're dressed again."

The situation would have struck him as bizarre if he hadn't felt so bad. He took off his wet clothes and put on the dry ones. His bare feet were pressed against the cold wood floor and his teeth started to chatter. "I-I'm d-done."

She led him to the couch, and he lay down, closing his eyes. All he wanted to do was sleep, but he was too hot and cold and sore all over.

"Drink some of this."

He opened his eyes. Joanna was seated at the edge of the

couch, holding a mug, steam rising from the top. "I don't want *kaffee*," he said, wondering how she managed to make it so fast. He also felt warmth from the small woodstove in the corner of the room. She'd started a fire too?

"It's not *kaffee*. It's tea. I found some feverfew in *yer mamm's* kitchen. It will help."

Andrew took a few sips and lay down. He closed his eyes and a few moments later Joanna nudged him again.

"You need to drink all of it."

He didn't have the strength to argue with her. When he finished the tea, he fell back on the couch. It was only then that he noticed she had brought him a pillow from his bed. Their bed.

"Why are you here?" he said in a raspy voice.

"Because I want to be." Her fingertips brushed against his forehead.

His eyes drifted closed. Only when he was on the brink of sleep did he realize she didn't have her crutches.

~⌐

Cameron had driven halfway through West Virginia when he'd panicked. West Virginia wasn't far enough. He kept driving through West Virginia, Virginia, and then Tennessee, stopping only to take care of Lacy. When he was near Chattanooga, she started to fuss. He pulled over at a rest stop and tried to feed her, but she refused her bottle. The last two feedings she had only eaten a couple of ounces. Now she didn't want any of it. He'd checked her diaper, but it was dry. When he reached back to feel her tiny hand, it was hot. He stopped at a drugstore right before closing, bought a thermometer and pain and fever reliever, then checked in to another cheap motel. Despite giving her the medicine, her fever had climbed to 105. How could she have gotten so sick so fast?

Soon he knew he couldn't wait any longer—he had to take her to the emergency room. He called the front office to save on cell phone minutes. The woman who answered the phone gave him directions to the local hospital. He put Lacy in the truck and rushed her there.

Lacy had grown still and quiet when he arrived, and her skin was taut and hot. So very hot. He picked up her carry seat and ran into the ER. "My baby is sick," he exclaimed. "She's got a high fever—"

The woman behind the glass windows opened it. "Can I help you?" she said, her voice irritatingly calm.

"My baby," he struggled to catch his breath. "She's got a high fever, and everything I've tried isn't working."

"Just a moment." She closed the glass, and Cameron wanted to put his fist through it and shake her. Just as he was about to yell out in frustration, she opened the window again. "Bring her back. A nurse will take her while I get your information."

"Thank God." The doors opened and he went inside. A nurse in white scrubs took the baby from him. "What was her temperature?"

"A hundred five an hour ago."

"And how old is she?"

"Two months."

"I'll take her to a room." He started to follow, but she held him back. "You need to give your information to the front desk. Then you can come back."

"I'm not leaving my daughter."

"I can come get the information," the woman behind the counter said. She lowered her voice. "She's new to this ER. She doesn't know the procedure yet."

Just what he needed, a newbie nurse. He calmed himself and nodded to the clerk, then went to the room, where the nurse was already taking Lacy's temperature. "It's 105," she said, with no emotion in her voice.

"Like I said," he mumbled.

"How long has she been ill?"

"A few hours. It came on really quick."

"Is she taking her bottle?"

"Not really."

"What about her diapers? Has she had several wet ones today?"

He shook his head.

"I'll have to get an IV started." She went to a cabinet as Cameron stood by Lacy.

"An IV?"

"She's dehydrated." She put on gloves and got out her supplies. "You're her father, right?"

"Yes."

"It won't take me long to get the fluids going. By that time the doctor will be here." She looked at him. "Sorry to give you a hard time earlier."

"It's okay." But he wasn't focused on her. He was focused on Lacy.

"Is there anyone else you need to call?" the nurse asked as she hung a bottle of clear fluid on a hook.

"No. It's just me and Lacy."

She arched a brow but didn't say anything.

Cameron watched, pain lashing through him as his daughter cried during the IV procedure. Just being at the hospital brought back memories of Mackenzie, but he squashed those as he focused on his daughter. Lacy settled down as Cameron stroked her fevered brow.

The clerk came into the room with a computer on a rolling stand. The nurse checked the IV again. "The doctor should be here any minute." Then she left.

The clerk started typing. "What's the patient's name?"

"Lacy Crawford."

She asked a few more questions about Lacy's vitals, then said, "I'll need your insurance card."

"I . . . I don't have one."

She looked at him for a moment, still tapping on the keyboard. "Then you'll be responsible for the bill yourself?"

"Yes." He pushed back the loose strands of his long hair.

"I'll need to get a copy of your driver's license."

"Why?"

"I need a form of identification."

He paused, and he could feel the eyes of the clerk on him. He dug out his wallet and handed her his license. She put the information into her computer. "I'll make a copy of this and bring it back to you."

He looked at Lacy again, who was now drifting off to sleep. He touched her forehead, which was still burning hot. "Where's the doctor?" he asked, his tone harsh.

"He'll be here in a few minutes."

The clerk left. Cameron stared down at Lacy, his eyes taking in the large bandage that covered her tiny hand where the nurse had inserted the IV. He wiped at his eyes. Would he lose Lacy in a hospital, the same way he'd lost Mackenzie? He thought about Irene and her prayers. He could use them now. Why couldn't he catch one break? He was nearly broke—he had no idea how he would pay for a hospital bill. And he'd handed over his ID to the clerk, who was probably putting it in some kind of computer system hooked up to emergency services. Eventually he'd be found by police. He knew it deep in his gut. The end of the line was here.

Lacy's eyes opened. They looked glassy and vulnerable. His heart swelled with love for his little girl. But what kind of life was he giving her? She had her first real illness and she was in the hospital, dangerously sick. He'd always be looking over his shoulder, thinking the police would pick him up any minute. He was failing her as a father.

He pulled over a chair and sat down, leaning his head against the carrier, where she was still safely tucked in. His eyes flooded with tears. "I'm so sorry, sweetheart," he whispered. "All I wanted was for you to have a better life than your mother and I did." He closed his eyes, tears dripping down his cheeks. "Hey, uh, God." He cleared his throat. He had no idea how to pray or what to say. "You know I don't do this," he said quietly. "I don't pray or ask for favors or whatever this is." He opened his eyes and looked at his baby girl again. "Lacy's all I have. I can't lose her. And I can't give her the life she deserves. If she survives this, for her sake I'll do the right thing. I promise. I don't care what happens to me. I just want her to live."

CHAPTER 16

A few minutes after Andrew had fallen asleep covered in a lovely pink-and-white quilt, Joanna heard someone stirring in the Beilers' kitchen. She gave Andrew one last look, then left the addition and opened the door to the main house. Irene stood in the kitchen, her body shivering the same way Andrew's had. An empty mug was on the table. She coughed, her eyebrows raising as she glanced at Joanna. Then she gave her an apologetic look and left the kitchen.

"We were at Rhoda's," Naomi explained as Irene went upstairs to her room. "Irene had a headache and said she wanted to lie down. She fell asleep on the couch and didn't wake up for a few hours. That's why we were late coming home. Although it was a *gut* thing because we were able to wait out the rain."

Joanna nodded. The rain had stopped almost as quickly as started.

Naomi glanced at the staircase. "I should have brought her home earlier, but I didn't want to disturb her. I thought she'd sleep off the headache. Besides, Rhoda seemed happy for the company."

Joanna wasn't surprised to hear that. She remembered Aden's birthday supper and how eager Rhoda had been to help Joanna in the kitchen. Now that she wasn't so self-involved with her own problems, Joanna could see that Rhoda's melancholy was due to loneliness. Rhoda and Naomi had a lot in common—including absent husbands.

"Andrew's ill too," Joanna said. "He's asleep right now."

"In his room?"

"*Nee*, in the new part of the *haus*. He's feverish. I hope you don't mind, but I found some feverfew tea in the kitchen and gave it to him."

"Irene just finished hers." Naomi tilted her head. "Andrew didn't mention you were coming over."

"He didn't know." She threaded her fingers together. "I brought him a picnic for supper. I was hoping he and I could talk."

"Did you?"

She shook her head. "He was too sick. He still feels hot. I think a cold washcloth will help cool him off."

Naomi opened a drawer and pulled out a white cloth. She handed it to Joanna.

Joanna turned on the tap and soaked the cloth with cold water, then wrung it out until it stopped dripping. She turned off the tap. "I better get this to him."

"Are you sure?"

Joanna frowned. "What do you mean?"

Naomi leaned against the counter. "Joanna, are you here for the right reasons?"

Joanna thought about Naomi's question. Now that his mother was here, Andrew didn't need Joanna to take care of him. But she wanted to be here. Not out of guilt or trying to make amends. She loved him, and she wanted to comfort him, whether or not he was still angry with her. "*Ya.* I believe I am."

"Rhoda said there was a nasty flu bug going around. You could get sick."

Joanna didn't falter under Naomi's scrutinizing. "I don't care. I'm not leaving his side until he's better. If that means I get sick, then so be it."

After a pause Naomi nodded, smiling a little. "I'll *geh* check on Irene."

Joanna went back to the addition. Andrew was still asleep. Gently she laid the cloth on his hot forehead, and he didn't move. His skin had a rosy glow from the fever.

She turned and looked at the food she'd laid out earlier. She'd take it to the main house in a little while. The potato salad and the tuna macaroni would have to be chilled, but the rest could go in the pantry. Her hips ached a little as she sat down in a rocking chair near the couch. The rain had stopped and the room was quiet, with the exception of the hissing from the gas lamp and an occasional coughing spell from Andrew.

A short time later she went to Andrew again. She took the washcloth off his forehead and flipped it over to the cooler side. He was still warm, but not as hot as he'd been before he had the feverfew. He shifted on the couch but didn't open his eyes. She looked at him for a few moments, wishing she could take his hand. But she didn't dare. As far as she knew he was still furious with her, and he needed to rest. If she held his hand he might get stirred up, and she didn't want that. Not for her own sake, but for his.

She rose and went to the window in the living room. It was dark outside, and she wondered what time it was. Not that it mattered. She would stay here until he felt better or told her to leave. She put her hand on the brand-new glass. The windows didn't have curtains on them . . . yet. Maybe one day.

Joanna turned from the window and settled back into the rocking chair. She glanced around the room. She hadn't appreciated the work Andrew had done when he'd showed it to her the first time. She'd been too steeped in her own self-pity and fear to pay attention to the details, like the gleaming wood floor, the brand-new woodstove, and a magazine rack near the couch. It would be a good place to keep her cooking magazines. Somehow she knew that's why Andrew had purchased the rack. Again, she thought about how warped her idea of love had been. Being in this small, cozy house Andrew had built with his own hands brought that point home. This was the perfect place to begin a new life. She'd been too blind to see it.

A sense of belonging washed over her in a warm wave. Naomi and Abigail both had faith that she and Andrew would be together again. Now she had that faith too. She glanced at Andrew. Somehow she had to convince him they still belonged together. She closed her eyes. *Lord, help me figure out how . . .*

She opened her eyes to the sound of Andrew mumbling. At some point during her prayer, she had fallen asleep. She went to him and perched on the edge of the sofa. His eyes were closed, and he wasn't saying anything now. She touched his forehead. The feverfew had helped for a little while, but now his temperature was back up. She went to the Beilers' kitchen and made him some more tea, then went back and coaxed him into drinking some, helping him sit up first.

protected

"So hot," he said, throwing off the quilt. His eyes were open now, his face flushed.

"*Yer* fever's higher again. Here." She held the tea mug to his lips, and he sipped. Then he leaned his head back, only to start coughing again.

"I'll be right back," she said. She went to the little kitchen in the addition and turned on the tap. The water sputtered, then flowed freely. She took the washcloth she had used before to cool his forehead, rinsed it under cold water, and went back to Andrew. His eyes were closed again.

"Lean forward a bit."

He mumbled something and didn't move. She put her arm around his shoulders and tried to ease him up. He was too heavy for her. "Andrew . . . you have to help me."

With a groan he sat up a little. She put the washcloth on the back of his neck, and he sank back down against the pillow she'd brought from the bedroom.

"How is he doing?"

Joanna looked up. She hadn't heard Naomi come in. "Still feverish. I gave him some more tea. He might need a different fever reducer, though. We have some at the grocery store. It's Sunday, but Sadie will open it for us."

"It's dawn. I can drive over to the store and get what he needs. Irene too."

"Can you let Sadie and Abigail know where I am?" She was sure they were worried.

"They know. I told them when they called last night. I'll go a little later. I don't want to disturb them too early."

She nodded, then Naomi left. Joanna continued to look at Andrew, who had fallen back asleep. Unable to resist, she brushed her hand against his cheek, which was bristly with a full day's growth of dark blond beard covering his flushed skin. *I love you, Andrew Beiler. I hope someday you can trust me again.*

⁓

Andrew opened his eyes and peered into the darkness. He wasn't sure what time it was, or even where he was for a moment. His shirt was damp, and he removed the cloth from his neck. As he became more aware, he realized he was still on the couch in the addition. He also realized he felt better. He glanced around the room and saw Joanna. So he hadn't dreamed that she was here. She was sitting in the rocking chair, asleep, her body in an uncomfortable position. He was about to wake her, then thought better of it.

He sat up, swinging his legs over the edge of the sofa. The room spun slightly, but he needed to go to the bathroom. He stood, waiting for the light-headedness to settle down, then made his way to the bathroom and took care of business. But on the way back to the couch, he started to sway a little bit. Joanna appeared right by his side.

"You should have woken me up," she chastised. She put her arm around his waist and drew him close to her.

If he'd been of a normal mind, he would have realized she was so thin she shouldn't be able to hold him up, but somehow she was managing. She was stronger than she looked. He leaned against her as she led him back to the couch. He plopped down, then slumped.

"How are you feeling?" she asked.

He looked up at her. "I'm still alive."

She chuckled a little bit.

When was the last time he'd heard her laugh?

"Think you can manage to eat some soup?" she asked.

"Maybe."

"All right. *Yer mamm* made some chicken noodle soup last night. I'll bring you a bowl."

He nodded weakly as she turned to leave. Then he noticed again. "Where are *yer* crutches?"

She gave him the biggest smile he'd ever seen. "I don't need them anymore." Then she walked away. Her gait was a little wobbly, but if someone didn't know what had happened to her, they wouldn't have noticed.

What was going on? His mind was hazy, but he remembered when she'd shown up yesterday. He glanced at the empty coffee table. She must have done something with the food she brought. Why had she done brought it? His head started to throb, and he closed his eyes. Why was she still here?

He wanted to lie back down. His body felt like a team of horses had trampled it. His eyes closed, and he'd drifted off until he heard her come back into the room. When he looked up he saw her carrying a tray with a bowl, a spoon sticking out of it, and a glass of water.

She set the tray on the coffee table and then sat down next to him on the edge of the couch. When he leaned forward to reach for the bowl, she put her hand on his forearm. "Let me."

The idea of her feeding him made him balk. "I can do it myself. I don't need you to feed me." He took the bowl, and his hands immediately started shaking. Fortunately she hadn't filled it too full or he would have spilled soup everywhere.

Without a word she took the bowl from him, then scooped

up some of the soup. Thin egg noodles hung over the edge of the spoon, surrounded by a pale yellow broth. The scent of the soup made his stomach growl, even though he didn't have much of an appetite. When was the last time he'd eaten? He couldn't remember. She held out the spoon. He sipped at the soup, the warm broth soothing his sore throat. But after a few spoonfuls he held up his hand. "I'm done," he said, barely able to sit up anymore.

She set the bowl back on the tray. "Do you want some water?"

He shook his head and stretched out on the couch. She covered him with the quilt, and he started to drift off again. But when she moved away he instinctively reached for her hand. He probably shouldn't have, but for some reason he needed to touch her. *"Danki,"* he said softly.

"You don't have to thank me." To his surprise she sat back down next to him and continued to hold his hand. As he caught her gaze, he saw the love in her eyes that had been missing since she came back from Middlefield. His Joanna was back.

Joanna continued to take care of Andrew the rest of the day. He slept most of the time, but he was able to take some more soup in the afternoon, plus some of the orange juice Naomi had brought. It turned out he didn't need the fever medication, but Irene did. She hadn't come downstairs since she'd been home. Whatever flu bug the Beiler siblings had, Irene had gotten the worst of it.

After Andrew had had some soup, Joanna went into the main kitchen where Naomi was washing a few dishes. "Here's another one," Joanna said, putting the bowl next to the sink. "Can I dry them for you?"

Naomi stopped washing the dishes and looked at her. "*Nee,* it's only a few." She paused. "You look tired."

Joanna nodded. She was exhausted, and in more pain than she'd been in for a while. "I am. I haven't slept well in that chair."

"Then you should *geh* home."

"I will when Andrew is better. His fever is gone, so I think he's on the mend."

"You can at least take a nap in the bed."

"But I want to be by his side when he wakes up."

Naomi rinsed her hands, then dried them on a towel. "Let me fix you something to eat, at least."

"That would be nice." Joanna nodded, went to the table, and sat down.

A few moments later Naomi put a plate of food in front of Joanna, then joined her at the table. After she said grace she picked up her fork to dig into the meal. She felt Naomi's gaze on her. "Is something wrong?"

"*Nee.*" Naomi smiled. "I see Andrew's not the only one feeling better. You don't have *yer* crutches."

Joanna scooped up a forkful of apple salad. "I am feeling better. Not just physically." She took a bite of the salad. It was delicious. "Does Andrew like this?"

Naomi nodded. "We have it every fall, when the apples are plentiful."

"Can I get the recipe? I'd like to make it for him sometime."

"Sure." She paused. "Are you thinking about getting back into *mei sohn*'s *gut* graces through his stomach?"

"It's a start, right?" She smiled and ate another bite of the salad. She swallowed, then spoke. "I'm not sure what I'm supposed to do. I just want him to know how much I care about him. After what I did to him at the wedding, it's going to be a long time before he forgives me."

"I think he might surprise you." Naomi rose from the table. "I need to finish those dishes and check on Irene again. Poor thing, she's really feeling awful."

Joanna finished the salad. She felt bad for Irene, but hopefully she would be feeling better soon. Naomi's words about Andrew gave her hope, though. The picnic was a failure, and she was sorry Andrew was sick. But she was grateful she could be there for him for once. She felt so much love for him, and also a sense of peace. Sure, he only had the flu, but he had needed her. And it felt so good to be needed. When he felt better he might not want her around, but she wasn't going to give up. She hoped Naomi was right.

A short while later she went back to the addition. Andrew was still asleep. She sat down in the rocking chair, trying to be as quiet as possible. But the sound of the chair rockers hitting the wood floor must have awakened him.

"Sorry," she said, looking at him.

"It's all right. I wasn't really sleeping anyway."

She leaned forward. "How are you feeling?"

"Better." His blue eyes widened. "Much better, actually." He sat up a bit and looked down at the quilt covering the lower half of his body.

"That's a beautiful quilt," she said.

He looked at her for a moment, then drew the quilt back. "How long have you been here?"

"Since yesterday."

He frowned. "Where are *Mamm* and Irene?"

Joanna filled him in on Irene's illness. "So *yer mamm*'s been taking care of her while I've been taking care of you." She smiled. "I'm glad you're feeling better. Do you need anything?"

"A shower and *mei* own bed."

"Oh." Her smile dimmed a bit. She stood. "I should be getting back home, then." She waited to see if he would ask her to stay. He didn't. "I'll see you later." She started to leave.

"Joanna."

She turned and faced him, feeling hopeful. *"Ya?"*

"You forgot *yer* basket."

She stiffened a bit, then went to get the picnic basket on the floor next to the coffee table. *"Danki* for reminding me." She met his gaze, gave him one last longing look, and left.

As she went home, she tried to remain upbeat. At least he didn't seem to be angry with her anymore. That, in her mind, was progress.

⁓

After he took a quick shower, Andrew was exhausted again. He was also hungry. He went downstairs to the kitchen and was surprised to see both his mother and Irene there. His sister looked tired, and she was sipping on the same chicken noodle soup Andrew had eaten before. But his *mamm* was munching on red-skinned potato salad. Andrew vaguely remembered that it had been in Joanna's picnic basket.

He sat down and ran his hand through his still damp hair. He felt his mother's gaze on him.

"Do you want something to eat?" she asked.

He nodded. "Did she leave the pepperoni roll?"

He detected a small smile on his mother's face. "*Ya.* She left everything."

A few minutes later he was chowing down on the most delicious pepperoni roll he'd ever tasted. Joanna was a great cook. And a good nurse. He couldn't believe she'd stayed the whole night and day to take care of him. He also couldn't believe how much that meant to him. The anger and resentment he felt for her had cooled, and not because he was recovering from a short but intense illness. But he still didn't trust her. One day of caretaking didn't erase what she had done to him. How much she'd hurt him.

"Joanna's not using her crutches anymore," Naomi said, pulling him out of his thoughts.

"I noticed."

"She seems to be stronger." Naomi took a sip of her iced tea. "In more ways than one."

Andrew looked at his mother. Her hints couldn't have been any more obvious. But he didn't respond. He didn't want to talk about the state of his and Joanna's relationship, even if those brief moments when she'd held his hand, despite his illness, had felt right. What he wanted to do was ask about his father and his cryptic letter.

He also wanted to know why she was still keeping in touch with him. Why they were hiding the truth about what happened in Florida from him and Irene.

Irene pulled the wool shawl hanging on her shoulders tighter around her body. Then she pushed her bowl away. "I'm going back upstairs." Her voice sounded scratchy. She started to get up just as they heard a knock on the front door.

Andrew pushed away from the table. "I'll get it." He was still a little weak-legged, but he felt well enough to answer the door. "Are you expecting anyone?"

Both Naomi and Irene shook their heads.

Andrew went to the living room just as another knock sounded. "Just a minute!" He hurried to the door and opened it. An officer wearing a brown uniform stood in the doorway.

"Hello," he said. Then he glanced at a pad he held in his hand. "Is this the Beiler residence?"

Andrew nodded but didn't say anything. What were the police doing at his home? A thread of panic wound through him. Joanna had left a short time ago. What if she was in another accident? "Did something happen?" he asked, gripping the side of the door.

The man shook his head. "I'm Deputy Riley. I'm investigating the Schrocks' hit-and-run case."

The man was harshly direct, and there was no warmth behind his silver-gray eyes. Andrew's guard went up, although he was relieved to learn nothing had happened to Joanna. But why would he be here asking questions about the accident? "I'm not sure what we can do to help. I don't know anything about the accident. Neither do my mother and sister."

"We've come upon some new information that might lead us to catch the person who did this."

"What does that have to do with us?"

The officer leveled his gaze. "May I come in? I can fill you in on the details."

Andrew hesitated. He'd never dealt with the law before. But if there was something he could do to help the Schrocks, he would do it. "All right," he said, opening the door.

"Andrew, who is—"

Andrew turned around to see his mother turn stark white. She put her hand to her chest. "Bartholomew? Is he . . . ?"

The officer frowned a bit. "Ma'am, I'm here about the Schrock case. I don't know anyone named Bartholomew."

Andrew stared at his mother. She seemed to almost pass out with relief at the officer's news. She quickly regained her composure. "Oh. Sorry, my mistake. Please, sit down." She gestured to a chair near the door. "Would you like anything to drink?"

"Not necessary, ma'am. I'm hoping not to take up too much of your time."

The officer was talking as Irene came into the room. "What's going on?"

"Please," the officer said, sounding impatient. "If you will all sit down, I'll explain."

Irene and *Mamm* sat on the couch opposite the officer, and Andrew took a seat next to them. After seeing his mother's reaction to the police officer, he didn't know how long he'd be able to keep the letter a secret. He was sick and tired of secrets anyway. The truth needed to come out, regardless of what his father had written.

Riley's brow furrowed, and he glanced at his notes again. "Do you know the Schrocks?"

"We all know each other around here." Andrew's tone was noncommittal. He didn't trust this guy, and he wanted him to finish his business as soon as possible. He glanced at Irene, who looked paler than she had before.

"So you're aware of the accident that killed Mr. and Mrs. Schrock?"

"Very aware." Andrew fisted his hands. "I'd appreciate it if you'd get to the point."

"We have a new lead in the case."

"What lead?"

"You'll need to answer my questions first."

Andrew paused, giving the guy another wary look before turning to his mother. "Are you all right?" he whispered to her and his sister in *Dietsch*.

"*Ya,*" Irene said. But her mother only nodded, bunching her skirt in her hands.

"Are any of you familiar with a man named Cameron Crawford?" the officer asked.

What did Cameron have to do with any of this? "He was here a few days ago," Andrew said. "He had a flat tire on his truck and he was waiting for a tow."

"Was anyone with him?"

"His daughter."

"A baby daughter," Irene said, emphasizing *baby*.

The deputy looked at his pad again, made a mark with his pencil, then looked up. "Did he mention anything about an accident?"

"You mean his wife's?" Irene interjected.

"No, although we're aware she died in childbirth."

Andrew frowned. He'd known Crawford's wife had died, but during his daughter's birth?

"How awful," Irene whispered.

Riley's expression was emotionless. "Did you get a look at his truck, by any chance?"

Andrew shook his head, his patience paper thin. "What does this have to do with what happened to Joanna and her parents?"

"You know the Schrocks well, then?"

"Joanna is . . . was my fiancée." Andrew's jaw jerked. "And I'm not answering anything else until you tell me what's going on."

"Fair enough. We got a tip from the auto shop that replaced Crawford's tire. Apparently there was damage to the truck consistent with a recent accident. When the mechanic asked if they could fix it, Crawford refused. We've been asking for information about this case since the accident. Newspaper articles, even a few TV stations picked it up. Fortunately this guy is a news junkie, and he went with his gut and called us. That's what led me here. Other than the motel where Crawford stayed and waited for his truck to be ready, this was the last place he was seen. Do you have any idea where he was going?"

"No." Andrew tapped the toe of his boot against the wood floor.

"He said something about going south," Irene said. "He was ready for a new life for him and his daughter. He had bad memories of Langdon." Her eyes widened. "You think he had something to do with the Schrock accident?"

"Yes," Riley said. "We do."

"That can't be true," Irene said. "I don't think you have the right person."

"Irene," Andrew said, his voice holding warning.

She ignored him. "Cameron is a kind man. He's suffered a horrendous tragedy, and he's trying to take care of his baby. I'm sure the damage to his truck could have been caused by anything."

The deputy looked at her for a long moment, his expression as hard as stone. Irene shrank back, looking more weary and ill than before. Andrew turned to Riley. "That's all we know." He rose from the couch. "I hope you find the person who caused the Schrock accident. I really do. But you won't get any more answers from us, because we don't know anything else."

Again, the deputy didn't move, his gaze focused on Andrew as if he were trying to determine if Andrew was telling the truth. Finally he rose. "If you do hear from Crawford, please let me know." His hardened facade softened a little. "I'm from Holmes County. I know a lot of Amish, and I know you people, as a rule, do not like to deal with law enforcement. But since you have a personal tie to this case, I hope you'll reconsider if you learn anything. I'm sure your fiancée wants closure."

Andrew stepped forward, ignoring the stab of pain he felt at the deputy mentioning Joanna was his fiancée. "Have you talked to her?"

He shook his head. "Not recently. We tried to question her about the accident after it happened, when she was well enough to talk. She doesn't remember much of it, and not enough to help with the case. I don't want to put her through any more stress unless it's necessary." He pulled out a card from his shirt pocket. "I'll leave this with you. If you hear anything or see Crawford again, let us know. You may not know this, but if you decide to help him, you can be charged with obstructing justice."

He heard his mother suck in a breath. Andrew went to her side. "We understand."

The deputy nodded. "Maybe we'll have some good news soon about the case. Our office will keep you posted."

Andrew went to the door and opened it. The deputy nodded and left. When Andrew closed the door, he turned around. Both his mother and sister were upset. "Is there anything about Crawford that you're not telling me?" he asked, looking pointedly at Irene.

Wide-eyed, she shook her head. "*Nee.* And I can't believe he's the one who caused the accident. He wouldn't do that."

"Irene, we don't know anything about him." Andrew rubbed the back of his neck. Crawford's eagerness to leave, his unease around all of them, now started to make sense. He was guilty. Andrew knew it in his gut. *And the man was in* mei haus.

"We should tell the Schrocks," Andrew said. "They would want to know about this."

"But Cameron didn't do it," Irene insisted. She shrank back. "I'm sorry. I shouldn't have said so much to the deputy."

Andrew looked at her. At the time he'd been shocked at her vehement defense of Cameron. But then he started to feel the same way. The man who had been in his house, who had partaken of their hospitality and allowed his sister to care for his daughter . . . He had a hard time reconciling that he was same man who had taken *Herr* and *Frau* Schrock's lives and injured Joanna.

"Will you two tell me what's going on?" Naomi asked.

Andrew filled her in.

"I refuse to believe he's the one," Irene added. "He was too kind and loved his daughter very much—"

"And that's what worries me."

Both Andrew and Irene looked at their mother. She still looked slightly pale, and Andrew wanted to know why she had assumed the deputy was here because of his father. There were too many unanswered questions concerning his parents, and he would get to the bottom of that later. Right now he wanted to know what his mother meant.

"I don't understand," Irene said.

Naomi looked at her, then at Andrew. "You'll understand when you have *kinner* of *yer* own. You'd do anything to keep them safe. To protect them." She licked her lips. "The love Cameron has for his daughter could have driven him not only out of Langdon, but also away from the police."

Andrew sat back, confusion warring within him. His mother's words made sense. He couldn't imagine being a single father, especially at Cameron's age. When Cameron was talking about losing his wife, Andrew had thought about how afraid he'd been when Joanna was in the hospital. He'd been so afraid he'd lose her. *I lost her anyway.*

But not the way Cameron had lost his wife. Or Asa his fiancée. Or even how his mother and father had lost each other. They were still married, at least according to his father.

"What would happen to Lacy if Cameron went to jail?" Irene asked quietly.

"I imagine the *Englisch* legal system would put her into foster care."

"We don't have any proof of that." Naomi put her hand on Andrew's arm. "If we hear anything, we'll report it. It's our duty to do so. But I don't think we'll ever see Cameron or Lacy again."

"What do I tell Joanna?"

"*Nix.* Don't tell her about this." Naomi looked at Irene. "You don't say anything, either."

"How can I keep a secret like that from her?" Andrew ran his hand through his hair. Although they weren't together anymore, he didn't want to keep anything from her. He was tired of lies and deception.

His mother looked at him, pleading in her eyes. "Andrew, I know you want to be honest with her. I understand that. But bringing this up—especially when we don't know the whole story—could really hurt her and her sisters. And what if nothing comes of it? If the deputy is wrong, then you've upset them for nothing. Sometimes we have to do things we don't want to do to protect those we love."

He looked at *Mamm*, and he knew she wasn't just talking about Joanna. And as much as he didn't want to accept it, he also knew she was right about Joanna. Somehow he had to reconcile keeping this from Joanna until the authorities apprehended the perpetrator—whether it was Cameron or someone else.

Andrew looked at his mother again. As their gazes met, they both knew the truth—Cameron had caused the accident. The knowledge was churning in his gut. But there was nothing he could do about it. He could only pray the police would find him. Justice had to be served. Joanna and her family deserved that. And in serving that justice, Cameron would lose his daughter. Despite everything, Andrew felt sympathy for the man.

"I'm going upstairs," Irene said.

After his sister left, his mother started toward the kitchen. Andrew stopped her. "*Mamm*. I need to know what happened to *Daed*."

His mother froze. "You read his letter?"

Andrew nodded. "I guess you were the one who put it on the coffee table."

She nodded.

He took a step toward her. "He said he didn't leave us for someone else, that you are still married. And why did you think the police were here for him?"

She went to sit down on the couch. Andrew joined her. He'd never seen his mother look so sad, even in the days after his father left. "I'd hoped *yer daed* wouldn't have said anything to you. I didn't want you to know about this."

"Know about what?"

"The truth." She looked at him, tears brimming in her eyes. "What we've been lying to you and Irene about all these years."

Andrew clenched his teeth together. "He didn't run off with an *Englisch* woman, then? He wasn't lying about that in his letter?"

"*Nee. Yer vatter* is in witness protection."

His eyes grew round. He wasn't even sure what that was. "Witness protection?"

"To keep him safe. To keep us safe." She sighed. "I met *yer vatter* when I was fourteen. He was fun. Adventurous. *Mei* parents had me when they were in their forties, and *mei vatter* had died when we moved to Florida from Pennsylvania. I was eighteen when *mei mamm* passed away."

He nodded. He'd known his maternal grandparents had died before he was born, but his mother never talked about them.

"I grew up in a very strict household, and as an only child I was sheltered. When we moved to Florida, I met *yer vatter*. He was like a breath of fresh air to me. I fell in love right away. He loved me too. But I didn't know everything about him. I didn't realize that while we were dating, he was selling drugs."

Andrew's jaw dropped. His father was a drug dealer? "Why did you marry him, then?"

"Because he had stopped. He really had. He had renewed his faith and commitment to the Lord. It wasn't until you and Irene were born that the past caught up with him." She looked away. "It always does. The police tracked him down and brought him in for questioning. They arrested him, then offered him a deal—he could avoid jail if he helped them break up the drug gang he'd been a part of. He agreed, and I paid the bail money to get him out of jail. While he was out on bail, someone tried to kill him. We found out the drug dealer he worked for wanted him dead."

"Because he was giving them up."

"*Ya*. And because they were—are—dangerous people. We're sheltered here in Birch Creek. That's how *yer vatter* wanted it. He wanted to make sure his family was far away from the drug gang. We had made plans to move together as a family, but the police had other ideas." Tears flowed down her cheeks. "He had to go into witness protection."

Andrew fell back against the couch. "Why didn't you tell us? Why lie?"

"To protect you and *yer* sister."

"We wouldn't need protecting if he hadn't committed crimes in the first place," Andrew muttered.

"You're right." *Mamm* took off her glasses and rubbed her red-rimmed eyes. "He made some horrible mistakes. He's also paid for them."

"So have you. We all have." He shook his head. "Why didn't he come back?"

"The FBI arrested most of the drug gang. But not all. They couldn't find two of them. To save *yer vatter*'s life, he had to change his identity. He's also being watched by US Marshals. They keep him safe."

"And what about us?"

Her shoulders slumped. "I didn't want to lie to you. He didn't either. But we had to." She looked at him. "You were both young when we left Florida. If you knew anything about what happened to *yer vatter* or what he was involved in, you might have said something. Even now, we can't reveal the real reason he's not with us."

"But doesn't witness protection protect all of us?"

"Only if he follows the rules."

"Is letter writing part of the rules?"

She shook her head. "*Nee.* We take a risk every time we write to each other. But it's the only contact we have. We needed that over the years."

"The return address says he's in California."

"The address isn't real. I don't know where he is. He could be in California, or he could be in Ohio. I have *nee* idea, and that's the point."

"Why aren't we being protected?" Andrew clenched his fists.

"We were under surveillance for a while. That was another thing we didn't tell you. But after a few years they stopped it. We're safe here, especially in the Amish community. That was another thing *yer vatter* made sure of—that I didn't have to leave *mei* faith."

"And he had to leave his."

"*Ya.*" *Mamm* wiped her eyes. "Someday he may be able to come back and reconcile with the church. He'll have to confess, and all this will be public knowledge in our community. I'm not sure if he's willing to do that."

"Because he'll be embarrassed?" Andrew ground out, still hanging on to his resentment.

"*Nee.* Because you'll be."

Andrew shook his head. "Too late for that."

Mamm put her hand on Andrew's. "You need to forgive Joanna, Andrew."

"Because I'm Amish."

"Because when you love someone, you forgive them."

"So you've forgiven *Daed*? Even though he left you alone all these years?"

"I wasn't alone, Andrew." She took his hand. "I have you and Irene. And I have God. He's sustained me through it. And someday *yer vatter* will come back to me—to us."

He pulled his hand out of his mother's. Right now he wasn't in a forgiving mood. She'd had years to come to terms with all of this. He felt like he was on overload. Joanna, his father, Cameron . . . In a matter of days, his life had been hit with an emotional earthquake. "Are you going to tell Irene all of this? Or do you expect me to lie to her like I have to lie to Joanna?"

Mamm shook her head. "I'll tell her when she feels better. Now that you know the truth, she should know too."

Andrew stood. The house felt like it was closing in on him. He had to get out. He started for the front door.

"Where are you going?" *Mamm* asked, rising from the couch.

"Out. Just . . . out."

He went outside, the cold air hitting him. He headed for the barn and to Fred's stall. As he fed his favorite horse, he fought against the softening inside him, not just toward Joanna but also his father. He didn't know what to do with that. He'd resented his father for years. Now everything he'd known about him was a lie. For some bizarre reason he wished he could talk to him. Get his side of the story. It didn't matter, though. Until the FBI or the police or whoever tracked down the other drug dealers, he wouldn't get to see his father.

But now he understood why his mother had been so sympathetic to Cameron. Andrew's father had made mistakes, but he had also suffered for them. He had chosen isolation from his wife and children to keep them safe. And after all these years, he was still faithful to his mother—or so she believed.

After reading his father's letter, Andrew believed it too.

He leaned his head against Fred's side. His mother still loved his father. It's why she forgave him. It's why she defended him to Andrew. When you truly loved someone, you forgave. You didn't turn your back. *You give her the best of yourself . . . even if you don't think it's enough.*

He had to forgive Joanna, and not because he was Amish. Because what his mother said was true—he loved her. After everything, he still loved her.

Somehow he'd have to make sense of the nightmare his life had become. Problem was, he didn't know how.

⁓

"It's been a tough season for the flu," the doctor said to Cameron. "Luckily, Lacy's got only a mild case of it."

Cameron stood next to Lacy's crib, his body shaking with relief. She had been moved to the regular pediatric unit of this small hospital after spending most of the day in the emergency room. She had responded to the fluids well enough that the doctor didn't feel the need to transport her by helicopter to the children's hospital nearly an hour away. Cameron had almost collapsed to his knees when they said they were going to admit her and keep a close eye on her. "So she's going to be okay?"

The doctor nodded. "Her temperature's down to 99, which is good. We'll want to keep her for at least another day to monitor that and get her nutrition back up. She's a little underweight."

Cameron thought about how Lacy hadn't been on a normal

schedule since he'd left Langdon. She hadn't even slept in a regular crib. Their few belongings he hadn't been able to pack into his truck were in storage. Now he wouldn't be able to afford the monthly fee. He was out of money, out of options. But more important, he had made a promise. God had delivered on his end. It was time for Cameron to keep his word.

"We'll have her feeling better soon," the doctor said, extending his hand to Cameron. "Then you can take her home. She'll be a lot more comfortable there."

As the doctor left, Cameron shook his head. He couldn't take Lacy back to that motel. He took one last look at his daughter. *I'd do anything for you, sweetheart.* All this time he thought he was protecting her . . . but he was only protecting himself. He wanted her to have a better life than he had. The only way that would happen was if he let her go and finally did the right thing.

He touched her cheek, careful not to wake her, and left the room. He went down the hall and found a private corner at the end of it, near a window. He pulled his cell from his pocket and stared at it. His chest hurt and his throat squeezed. After this phone call everything would change, for both him and Lacy. Wiping his eye with the heel of his hand, he collected himself and dialed a number.

"Hello?"

Cameron leaned against the wall at the sound of Mrs. Rodriguez's kind, familiar voice. "Hi," he said. "It's Cameron."

"Cameron!"

He startled and pulled the phone away at her loud exclamation. How he managed a half-smile he didn't know. Her excited voice tugged at his heart.

"I'm so happy to hear from you," she said when he put the

receiver back to his ear. "How are you? How is my precious Lacy?"

He filled her in on Lacy's illness but was vague about any other details. She would know the story soon enough. "I know I don't have the right to do this," he said, swallowing. "You don't owe me anything, and I owe you everything."

"Cameron, please." Her voice grew somber, but she still sounded emotional. "Anything you need me to do, I'll be happy to do it. You know you're family to me."

You won't think so after you find out what I've done. "I'm coming back to Langdon. I wondered if you could watch Lacy for me? I have . . ." His chest heaved. "I have something I need to do."

"Of course, of course. And just so you know, I haven't rented your apartment yet. Are you coming back for good?"

He paused. "No. I won't be in Langdon long."

After firming up details, Cameron hung up. He took another deep breath and sighed. He wouldn't call the police until after he dropped off Lacy at Mrs. Rodriguez's. That would be at least two more days. He went back to Lacy's room and stood over her crib. He wanted to touch her again, but she slept so peacefully he didn't want to disturb her. He had forty-eight hours left with her. After that he didn't know if he'd ever see his daughter again.

CHAPTER 17

Two days after his illness, Andrew stopped at the front door of Joanna's house. He paused, afraid to knock. His palms were sweaty, and he felt nervous, much as he had when he first came here after Joanna came home from rehabilitation. So much had changed since then, and not the way he had expected. Or how he had wanted. He knocked on the door. As he'd hoped, Joanna answered it. Her eyes were wide with surprise. He also noticed how different she looked. Relaxed. She'd put on a little weight, so her face wasn't so sunken. She looked, as she always did in his eyes, beautiful. "Hi," he said softly. "I came by to . . . uh . . ." So much for courage.

She smiled. That sweet smile he'd been longing to see. She stepped out on the front porch. She was wearing a light green dress and navy-blue sweater, but she was barefoot. He wondered if her feet were cold, but being without shoes didn't seem to bother her. As she shut the door and moved to stand in front of him, he saw her slight limp. But she seemed strong. Independent.

Dread pooled in his stomach as he thought about the harsh words he'd thrown at her when he was angry. Would she turn him away again? He couldn't predict what she'd do anymore. He forced himself to speak. "I came to thank you for being there for me when I was sick."

Joanna turned to him, her cheeks rosy, her skin back to its usual peachy shade. "You don't have to thank me, Andrew. I wanted to be there. I was glad I could be."

He nodded. Words froze in his mouth again. He looked down at his feet, trying to find the right things to say to her. Sorry didn't seem enough. He had so many things to be sorry for—hurting her, pressuring her, dumping his anger on her, and not being willing to listen to her side. He felt all of it in his heart, but for some reason he couldn't say anything.

"Andrew," she said, facing him. "We can't *geh* on like this. We both know that."

What did she mean? "I don't understand."

She sighed. "Our relationship. It's been wrong from the beginning. Well, not from the very beginning. We got along great when we were only friends." Her smile grew wistful. "But when we started dating, nothing was right after that."

He drew in a sharp breath. So this was how it ended for good—with him messing everything up and her moving on with her life. But he loved her and wouldn't stand in her way. And he couldn't deny that she was right. "I wish things could have been different."

"Me too." She took a step toward him. "I think they can be." She cleared her throat. "Andrew, will you *geh* out with me?"

He frowned. That wasn't what he expected. "Like a date?"

"*Ya.* Tomorrow afternoon, when you're off work."

Joy squeezed in his chest. "I'll take the *daag* off."

"You don't have to."

"I want to." He took one step toward her. There was still plenty of space between them, but for some reason the invisible wall that always went up when they were alone had disappeared. "What time should I pick you up?"

⁓

Joanna pushed the last bobby pin into her *kapp* and looked at herself in the mirror. The butterflies were back. She missed them. While her nerves were ramped up, instead of dread she felt excitement. Anticipation. She also felt confident.

She closed her eyes, remembering Andrew's stunned, then relieved expression when she'd asked him out. She hadn't feared he would say no—well, not too much anyway. She knew they still had love and attraction between them, especially on her part. But they needed to restart their relationship. To do it right this time. To be honest with each other. Today was the first step.

She touched her scar. It didn't bother her anymore. Now she thought of it as a badge, a symbol of what she'd gone through to get to this point in her life. To know that she was strong. Capable. She never would have arrived at this point without going through the tough valley. She wasn't sure she was completely out of it yet, but she was making the climb.

After one last check in the mirror, she left the bathroom and went downstairs. Sadie was visiting Patience today, having revealed that her friend was pregnant. Abigail and Aden were working in the store. And Joanna was ready for her date.

As she sat on the couch, Homer joined her and she petted his head. She glanced at the clock. Five minutes until Andrew was supposed to be here. She got up and straightened the skirt of her dress. Homer barked and she went to the window. She pulled back the curtain as she saw Andrew's buggy pull into her driveway. She smiled. He was early.

Joanna went outside, Homer following her. She met Andrew halfway between the house and his buggy.

"I'm a little early," he said, looking a little sheepish.

"I'm glad you are."

He grinned, his gaze steady with hers. "What do you want to do today?"

"*Geh* fishing."

His eyes widened. "Fishing?"

"*Ya*. At Birch Creek."

"Okay. I didn't know you liked to fish."

"I don't, really." She licked her lips. "But *mei daed* used to take me when I was younger."

He nodded. "*Mei daed* used to take me. In Florida. We fished in the ocean."

Her brow lifted. He never talked about his father. "Uh, well. Since you and I have never fished together, I thought it would be fun."

"You don't think it's too cold?"

It was a little brisk. But the sun was also shining. "I'll wear *mei* coat. You can borrow one of Aden's if you need to."

"Nah, you know I don't get cold easily." He gestured to the buggy. "I didn't bring any fishing poles."

"We can use *mei daed's*."

With a lift of his shoulders, Andrew said, "Show me where they are."

250

An hour later, Joanna and Andrew were sitting on the edge of Birch Creek. The water rushed by, dragging their fishing lines with it. Joanna held on to her father's favorite pole. It was probably older than she was. Andrew was using one of *Daed's* newer ones. Neither of them had caught anything.

"You're kinda bad at this," Joanna said, looking at Andrew with a smile.

"We both are." He peered over the edge of the bank. "I don't think the fish are biting right now."

Just as he spoke the words, something tugged on Joanna's pole. She started to reel it in, but it resisted. When she tried to stand up on the grassy bank, her feet slipped underneath her and she landed on the ground.

"Joanna!" Andrew was right there, his hand at her waist. "Are you okay?"

Joanna laughed. She wasn't hurt, and she didn't care if Andrew saw that she was clumsy. She'd always been a little clumsy anyway, even before the accident. "I'm fine. But you could help me with this fish."

He stuck his pole into a soft spot in the ground and crouched behind her. He wrapped his arms around her shoulders as he took hold of the pole. "You keep reeling. I'll keep the pole steady."

Whatever was on the end of the line was determined to put up a fight. Joanna leaned back against Andrew's chest as she twirled the reel. His forearm tightened as he pulled on the pole, so much that she could see the outline of his muscles. A shiver went through her that had nothing to do with the chill of the day.

The line finally went slack, but Andrew held on to the pole—and to her—as she reeled in her catch. "What kind of fish is this?" she asked as the fish emerged from the water and dangled on her hook.

"Steelhead, I think." He let go of the pole and leaned over her to take the fish. He could have easily stood up and done it, but he kept himself in close proximity to her. The butterflies in her stomach were out of control.

"I'll put it in the creel." He said the words in her ear. Then he stood, put the fish in the creel, picked up his pole, and sat back down, this time much closer to her than before.

They sat in silence, and it wasn't awkward. The rushing water, twittering birds, and rustle of leaves enveloped them. "I can see why *mei daed* liked coming here," she said. "It's lovely."

"Definitely."

She turned to him, expecting him to be staring at the creek in front of him. Instead, his eyes were on her. She glanced away, feeling shy once again. She forced herself to look at him. "Andrew, I'm sorry."

His gaze turned from smoky to concerned. "About what?"

"Asking you to marry me, for one."

"You're sorry about that?"

"I'm sorry about the way I asked you." She angled her body toward him so she faced him more fully. "I put you on the spot and I shouldn't have. We'd been dating only two months."

"I'm the one who handled it badly. I should have told you what I thought." He paused. "How I felt. But I didn't want to mess things up. I wanted to be sure about us."

"And that was the fair thing to do. The mature thing." She sighed. "When the accident happened, I was arguing with *Mamm* and *Daed* about us." She looked away, tears springing to her eyes. "I told *Mamm* if we wanted to get married, they couldn't stop us."

"They wanted to?"

"*Mamm* said we weren't ready. And she was right." Joanna wiped at her eyes, but the tears continued to fall. She held on to the fishing pole. "We weren't. At least, I wasn't."

"I wasn't either." He turned her face toward him. "But I didn't want to lose you. I thought I'd lost you even before the accident, when I hurt you. Then when you were in the hospital . . ." His Adam's apple bobbed in his neck. "I wanted you to know how much I loved you. I thought getting married would make you happy."

"And I kept pushing you away." Her tears were flowing freely now. "I didn't mean to hurt you, Andrew. I was acting stupid and childish."

"I shouldn't have pressured you."

"But I pressured you first."

"Let's agree we both made mistakes."

She nodded. "At least *yers* didn't cause an accident."

His eyes widened. "Is that what you think, Joanna? That accident wasn't *yer* fault."

"*Daed* was distracted. He was telling me not to be disrespectful to *Mamm*." Ugh, why couldn't she stop crying? "He wasn't watching the road."

"Even if he was, he wouldn't have been able to avoid the car that plowed into them. The driver who hit you is the one responsible."

"It doesn't matter. Whoever hit us is long gone by now."

Andrew didn't say anything for a long moment. "You say that as if it's a fact."

She shrugged. "I haven't given it much thought."

"Because you've been busy blaming yourself." He looked at

her for a moment, then ran his thumb over her unscarred cheek. "Why didn't you tell me this before? You shouldn't have had to carry all this pain all alone."

"I didn't want to burden you."

"Joanna, you would never be a burden to me. Ever." He removed his hand and sat cross-legged in front of her. The fishing poles were on the ground, fishing forgotten. "Even if you were, you would be *mei* burden, and I wouldn't have it any other way."

She scrunched her nose. "I'm not sure if that's a compliment."

"It is." His hands were lightly resting on his knees, the breeze ruffling the ends of his hair peeking out from underneath his straw hat. "I need to be completely honest with you, and I haven't been since we started dating." He let out a sigh. "I didn't know what I was doing when I asked you out. I don't know how to be a boyfriend. Or a husband. Even before the wedding I had doubts that I was *gut* enough."

"Really?"

"*Ya. Mei daed* hasn't exactly been a shining example of a family man. At least I didn't think so." He paused. "You can't tell a single soul what I'm about to tell you. Promise me, Joanna."

She steeled herself, wondering what he was so serious about. "I promise."

"I got a letter from *mei* father the other *daag*. Apparently he and *Mamm* have been in touch all these years. He never ran away with another woman. He's been staying away from us to protect us."

"I don't understand."

"I didn't either, at first. And I was so angry with him." His hands balled into fists on his knees. "I didn't want him anywhere near me. But once I heard his side of the story, I realized I was wrong." Andrew's voice grew thick. "He was the perfect example of a husband and father. He made the ultimate sacrifice to keep us safe."

"Safe from what?" She listened as he explained his father's past. Her eyes widened. She didn't know anything about drugs or gangs. But from what Andrew was saying, his father had been in serious trouble.

"Knowing the truth doesn't erase all the hurt, though. At least not now. But I do understand why *mei mamm* stayed with him. Her love for him was deeper than his mistakes and failures." He leaned forward. "I'd like to think our love is like that too."

She closed her eyes, feeling bathed in Andrew's presence. In his love. He hadn't physically touched her as she had craved for so long. That had been another sign of her immaturity—that she needed an outward demonstration of how he felt. His words reached deep inside her soul.

"Joanna?"

She opened her eyes to see him gazing at her. He didn't say anything else. He put his hands on either side of his legs and leaned forward. His lips touched hers, sending the butterflies soaring.

"I hope that was okay," he said as he pulled away.

"Definitely." She smiled.

"*Gut.* I wasn't sure, since this is our first date."

First date? Then she realized it really was. The first time they felt comfortable with each other. That they were truthful with each other. That they could express their love without pressure or guilt.

He reached out and touched her cheek—again, the one without the scar. She took his hand and pushed him away.

He frowned. "I'm sorry. I thought . . . Never mind." His voice sounded slightly exasperated, and he turned away.

"Andrew," she said, straightening. "Look at me."

He did, a mix of confusion and surprise in his eyes when she leaned toward him. "Why won't you touch it?" she asked.

His brow furrowed. "Touch what?"

"This." She ran her fingers over the ridge on her cheek. "Is it that repulsive?"

He shoved himself to a straighter sitting position. "*Nee*, of course not."

Despite herself, she felt the tears sting her eyes.

He lifted his hand, slowly, then cupped her cheek. His thumb hovered over the skin, then skimmed the raised flesh. "There's nothing repulsive about you, Joanna," he whispered. "I never touched *yer* scar because I didn't want to hurt you. I didn't know if you would feel pain from my touch." He released her cheek, then ran his finger gently along the length of the scar. "I also didn't want to bring any more reminders about what happened. You were dealing with enough."

His delicate touch brought a shiver down her spine. He didn't stop at the end of the scar, but kept trailing his finger over her chin to the base of her throat, then pulled away. Then kissed the raised ridge. "I've been wanting to do that since you came home," he said, his voice low. He cupped her face. Then he took her into his arms and thoroughly kissed her, stealing her breath and her heart.

"If this is our first date," she said, breathlessly, "I can't wait for our second."

Andrew laughed. "Me neither."

Andrew held Joanna's hand as they walked toward the barn where her father had kept his fishing poles, tackle, and creel. As far as fishing was concerned, it wasn't a successful trip. Otherwise . . . He smiled. They'd tossed Joanna's fish back into the creek and had spent the rest of the afternoon talking, the way they used to when they were friends. But this time it was different. The conversation was deeper and more connected. The chasm that had separated them for so long had disappeared. Joanna was different. He was different. They'd both been changed by their pain, and somehow God had turned it into something beautiful.

They had also decided to take things slow and to be open in their communication. "You can hold *mei* hand every once in a while," Joanna had said as they headed back to the buggy at the end of the afternoon, putting their decision into practice.

"Don't worry. I plan to." And he took her hand in his as soon as he could. She had such a delicate hand, with long slender fingers, a contrast to his thick, rough hand. Yet they fit together perfectly.

They entered the barn, and Andrew put up the poles and hung the creel on a peg on the wall. He turned to her, not wanting to say good-bye but knowing he needed to go home. "Is it all right if I stop by tomorrow?" he said as they walked out of the barn, slowing his stride to accommodate her limp. "Maybe then we can talk about date number two."

She smiled. "*Ya*. I'd like that." Then she halted in her tracks. A sheriff's vehicle was pulling into her driveway. "Oh *nee*," she said, her voice barely above a whisper.

Andrew put his hand on the back of her waist. She was shaking. "I'm right here," he said as the car came to a stop. "I'm not going anywhere."

The sheriff stepped out of the vehicle and walked toward Andrew and Joanna. "I'm looking for Joanna Schrock."

Andrew was going to respond, thinking Joanna was frozen with fear. But he didn't have to.

"I'm Joanna." She stepped toward the sheriff. "How can I help you?"

"I have some news about the person who hit your buggy. Is there a place we can talk privately?"

"In the kitchen."

Andrew was curious, but the sheriff had said he wanted to talk to Joanna privately. He hung back, trying to decide what to do. Joanna nodded to him, gesturing for him to follow. Relieved, he caught up with her.

Abigail was in the kitchen, and when she saw the sheriff, just like Joanna she froze in place. "What's going on?" She put down the glass of water she was holding.

"They have news about the accident." Joanna limped to Abigail. "I think Sadie and Aden should hear this too."

"I'll *geh* get them." She hurried out the door.

Andrew stood by as Joanna explained to the sheriff that her sister and brother-in-law were working in the store next door. "They'll be here soon. Can I get you anything to drink?" Her voice was calm and steady. Andrew had to hold back a smile. He was impressed with her poise.

The sheriff took off his hat and shook his head. "Thank you for the offer, but I won't take up too much of your time."

Joanna invited him to sit down. As Andrew sat down at the table with him, Abigail, Sadie, and Aden rushed in. "Fortunately we weren't busy," Abigail said. "I turned the sign to 'Closed.'"

Soon they were all seated at the table—Aden and Andrew at opposite ends, the three sisters seated across from the sheriff. The man clasped his hands on the table.

"This case has been open ever since the incident. We've been following whatever leads we could. Initially we didn't have much, but we got a strong lead a few days ago and tracked the suspect from Birch Creek to Chattanooga. We were about to put out a BOLO—"

"Bolo?" Sadie asked.

"That's what we call it when we let other departments know to look out for someone. We ended up not having to send it. The suspect called our office and said he wanted to turn himself in."

Andrew glanced at Joanna. Despite her earlier show of strength, she had turned pale.

"So he was in Birch Creek all along?" Aden asked.

"He's actually from Langdon. His name is Cameron Crawford."

Andrew sucked in a breath. Cameron? He glanced at Joanna. Her eyes were fixed on the sheriff. How was he going to tell her that her parents' murderer had been in his house?

The sheriff scratched his cheek. "He's at the county jail now. We've booked him on both involuntary manslaughter and criminal negligence charges."

Sadie, Abigail, and Joanna exchanged a look. "What is involuntary manslaughter?" Abigail asked.

"It's when a death occurs from recklessness or criminal negligence, ma'am. There are three charges, one for each of your parents. The third charge is for her." He looked at Joanna. "He's also being charged with a hit-and-run. What we need you to do is talk to the prosecutor's office so they can bring charges against him on your behalf. Now, there are two ways you can do this—we can take you in a squad car down to the police station. The prosecutor can interview you there. Or he'll send an attorney from his office here."

Joanna gripped the edge of the table. "To talk to me?"

The sheriff looked impatient. "Yes. We need your statement so we can file formal charges. Right now we can only charge him with the state minimum. If you press charges, he'll get more prison time. You want to see justice done, right?"

Joanna didn't know what to think. She looked around the room, confused and shaken. She had truly believed it didn't matter if they ever caught the person who caused the accident. Now that the man had turned himself in, she didn't know what to think. The sheriff was staring at her, impatience in his eyes. She couldn't think under his scrutiny. She could barely process what he was saying.

"I think *mei* wife and her sisters need time to discuss it." Aden's authoritative voice cut through the tension.

"What's there to discuss?" The sheriff's voice was short. "Crawford confessed. As soon as you're ready, I can take you to meet with a prosecutor."

"What if we don't press charges?" Sadie asked.

The sheriff pushed away from the table. "He'll still serve time. The state will enter their charges. But instead of twenty-five years, he may get only eight." His eyes narrowed. "Eight years for the death of your parents. Do you think that's fair?"

Joanna sensed Andrew tensing beside her. She glanced at him. Something was wrong. He wasn't looking at the sheriff or at her. He was staring at the table, his gaze far away.

"I'll show you out." Aden stood.

The sheriff took a card out of the pocket of his brown jacket. "When you're ready to press charges, call me. I'll come pick you up. Or you can arrange your own transportation. Don't let this man get less time than he deserves."

Aden opened the door for the sheriff and followed him out, Homer at his heels. Joanna looked at her sisters, then back at Andrew. She didn't know what to do. Her sisters seemed confused too. Andrew still stared at the table.

Aden came back inside. "Andrew," he said, motioning for him to join him.

Andrew nodded and stood, gave Joanna a bewildered look, then disappeared outside with Aden.

Joanna looked at her sisters. "What are we going to do?"

Andrew tossed his hat on one of the patio chairs and ran his hand through his hair. He had to tell Joanna that Cameron was at his house. He should have said something to her while they were fishing, but he hadn't wanted anything to intrude on their time together.

"You want to fill me in?" Aden asked, putting his hand on Andrew's shoulder.

"What?"

"You looked like you'd seen a ghost when the sheriff mentioned Crawford's name." Aden's eyes narrowed. "Do you know something?"

"Not really. I did meet him once." He explained how Crawford's tire had blown and Irene had helped him. Then he told Aden about Deputy Riley's visit.

"Why didn't you say something before?"

"Because we didn't know for sure that Cameron was involved in Joanna's accident. We didn't want to worry her and her sisters if the sheriff's department was wrong. I have to tell Joanna now. I don't want her to find out from someone else. I don't want her to be upset with Irene, either."

"She won't be. None of them will. Irene's got a *gut* heart. We all know that." Aden blew out a breath. "So Crawford has a *boppli*?"

"*Ya*, if he was telling the truth that he's the *daed*." But Andrew somehow knew he was. He had seen Crawford with his daughter. Unless he was a brilliant liar, he wouldn't be able to fake that kind of bond with a baby that wasn't his own.

Aden tilted his head toward the house. "They're not going to press charges."

"I know."

"At first a part of me thought they should." Aden's voice was tight. "But knowing he has a *boppli* and is widowed . . ."

"I can understand why he ran."

"You're defending him?"

"Aren't you?" At Aden's nod, Andrew said, "If I had to protect *mei kinn*, I'd do anything I could, and I'd have to figure out a way to live with myself afterward."

"I'm definitely not one to throw stones. I've made more than *mei* fair share of mistakes." Aden paused and looked at the back door. "I wish we could be in there with them."

Andrew nodded. "Me too." But he and Aden both knew only Sadie, Abigail, and Joanna could make this decision. Whatever Joanna decided to do, he would be there to support her.

"What are we going to do?" Abigail asked, her mouth tightening at the corners. She ran her palm across the table. "Should we press charges?"

"He's already going to jail," Sadie said. "I don't think we need to get involved." Then she turned to Joanna. "This affects you directly. What do you want to do?"

Joanna remembered when Abigail had asked her the same question, only it was about her wedding to Andrew. At the time she had agreed to do what everyone else wanted, even though she was full of doubts. She was full of doubts now—and fear, because the niggling in her heart was sending her in a direction she didn't want to go. She had ignored God's prompting, and she and Andrew had been hurt in the process. She wasn't going to ignore him anymore. "I want to find out his side of the story."

"*Nee,*" Sadie said.

"Definitely not," Abigail added. "Let the police handle this, Joanna."

"But—"

Sadie shoved her chair back from the table, the scraping cutting off Joanna's words. "It's finished, Joanna. We forgive him in our heart. That's enough."

"It's not enough." Joanna shot up from her chair, her voice

pinning her sisters in place. "You don't have to *geh* with me. I can do it on *mei* own. But I need to see him."

"Why, Joanna?" Abigail went to her. "What *gut* would it do?"

"He needs to know we forgive him. He needs to hear the words from me."

The door opened a crack, and Aden peeked inside. "Is it all right if we come in?"

Sadie nodded and went to him. "We need to get back to the store. Aden, some boxes in *Daed's* office need to be broken down. Could you help me with that?"

"I'll reopen the store," Abigail said. Then she looked at Joanna. "Unless you need me here."

Joanna straightened. "I'm fine." And she was. The more she committed to her decision, the more confident she became.

Her sisters and Aden left. Andrew stood in the doorway. She went to him and frowned. He looked pale. Wary. And unlike Andrew. "What's wrong?"

"I'm sorry, Joanna. If I'd known I would have said something."

"What are you talking about?"

He went to the table and pulled out a chair for her. She shook her head. "I don't want to sit down. You're scaring me, Andrew."

"I need you to know I'm not keeping secrets from you." He went to her. "I don't want there to be anything between us but the truth. Crawford was at our house last week."

"What?" She couldn't believe what she was hearing. Then she listened as he explained what had happened. How Cameron had a baby daughter. How he was possibly skipping town to protect her.

"He probably didn't want the child to go into foster care," Andrew said. "Maybe that has something to do with it."

"What about the *boppli's mudder*?"

"She died in childbirth."

Joanna's heart pinched. Now she was surer than ever about her decision. "I need to see Cameron."

She saw his jaw jerk. "I don't think that's a *gut* idea—"

She put her finger on his lips. "And I want you to *geh* with me."

He paused, then removed her finger from his lips. "Are you sure?"

"Absolutely."

He tilted his head and gave her a half-smile. "I can tell. I don't think I could change *yer* mind if I wanted to."

"Then you'll come with me?"

"*Ya*. I will."

Joanna blew out a breath. Seeing Cameron would be hard, but it was the right thing to do—not just for him, but for her too.

CHAPTER 18

Cameron sat on the edge of his hard bed in the tiny jail cell. He'd been barely able to sleep since he'd turned himself in the day before. How could he sleep when he had no idea how Lacy was doing? Mrs. Rodriguez still had her, as far as he knew. Every time he asked someone about his daughter, no one would give him any information. More than once he'd doubted his decision to turn himself in. Then he thought about Lacy being in the hospital, about his promise to God, and how relieved his conscience had been when he'd finally made the phone call.

He stood and went to the front of the cell, leaning his forehead against the bars. They had shaved his hair shorter than it had been in years, and it resembled a military cut. This was on the recommendation of his court-appointed attorney, who had talked to him for no more than five minutes after he'd been arraigned. Not that there was much to talk about. He was guilty, he was going to plead guilty, and he would serve his time. Those were the only things he was sure about right now.

He closed his eyes, and although he didn't intend to, he started to pray. *God, I don't deserve to ask this, and I'm not asking for myself. I'm asking for Lacy. She deserves more than foster care. She deserves someone who will take good care of her. Please, take care of my baby girl . . .*

The prayer turned rambling and nonsensical, and he eventually gave up, figuring God wasn't listening anyway. He went back to his cot and lay down. Somehow he managed to fall asleep, because the next thing he knew he heard the jangle of keys.

"You have a visitor," the deputy said.

Cameron got up, let the deputy put handcuffs on his wrists, and allowed himself to be led to what he assumed was an interrogation room, where he would probably meet with his lawyer. Who else would be visiting him? He was determined not to cause any trouble, to be on his best behavior. He didn't want to give the judge a reason to extend his sentence.

When he walked into the room, he saw Mrs. Rodriguez and nearly collapsed from relief, only to have that change to panic when he didn't see Lacy with her. "What's wrong?" he asked, trying to get closer to the older woman.

The deputy pulled him back. "Sit down at the table," he said, taking him to the chair.

Cameron complied, his gaze not leaving Mrs. Rodriguez. Dread churned within him. Something was wrong. He couldn't catch a break. Then again, he didn't deserve one.

"I'll be right outside," the deputy said to Mrs. Rodriguez. "I'm keeping the door open."

She nodded, then looked back at Cameron. Tears welled in her eyes.

"Elaine," he said, using her first name for the first time. The muscles in his jaw jerked in rapid succession. "What happened to Lacy?" He steeled himself for the worst possible answer.

She finally relaxed. "Nothing." Then she smiled. "Your daughter is fine. She's at day care right now." She looked around the room, wrinkling her nose. "I've never been to see someone in jail."

Guilt churned within him. "You shouldn't have come."

"I wanted to. I needed to see how you are doing. I left Lacy at day care because I didn't think this would be a good place for a baby."

"It isn't." He leaned back in his chair, relieved that Lacy was okay but his heart aching from missing her. *This isn't a good place for anyone.*

"The officer told me I didn't have a lot of time to talk to you, so I'll make this quick." She cleared her throat.

Cameron steeled himself for her disappointment, for her anger that he had left Lacy with her, for him being dishonest with her. Any anger she had toward him was well placed, and he would take what he deserved.

"I understand why you left," she said. "I understand why you ran." She leaned forward. "Why didn't you tell me what happened? I thought you knew you could tell me anything. That you trusted me."

"I do trust you. But I didn't want you involved."

"I'm involved now."

The guilt churning within him was excruciating. "I know. And I'm sorry. For everything."

She sighed. "When you and Mackenzie came to my door and asked to see the apartment, I knew there was a reason you were there. There was something special about the both of you.

And the way you cared for Lacy after Mackenzie's death . . ." She drew in a breath. "Remember when I told you you're like a son to me?"

He fought the lump in his throat and nodded.

"That hasn't changed. It won't, no matter what you've done."

"How can you say that?" He ran his hand over his shorn hair, then stopped, unused to the short length. *Mackenzie would hate to see it like this. She'd hate to see what I've become.*

"Cameron, I believe you're a good man at heart. I know you haven't shared parts of your past with me, and I respect your right to your privacy. But I also suspect that what you keep bottled inside is torturing you. I hope one day you can let it go." She smiled, tears brimming in her eyes. "You're so young . . . The burden you've had to bear." She held a tissue up to her nose and blew loudly. "I love Lacy like she was my own granddaughter. I want to take care of her, and you."

Cameron blinked. "What do you mean?"

"My cousin is a social worker, and I've already been in contact with her. There would be paperwork to fill out, and I'll need a background check and a home visit, but if you name me Lacy's guardian while you're . . . gone, she could live with me."

He couldn't breathe. A shiver ran through him as he remembered his prayer earlier that day. He'd never thought God was listening, much less answering. But he had to be sure he was hearing her correctly. "I could be put away for a long time. My lawyer says it could be ten years or more." His voice shook.

"I know. And I would take care of her like she was my flesh and blood. I'll bring her to visit you. She'll write you letters when she's able." Elaine smiled. "I'll even teach her a little Spanish."

Cameron had to keep himself from collapsing with relief, yet he was still troubled. "I don't deserve this."

"It doesn't matter what you think you deserve. This is what I want to do." She reached for his hands, which were resting, still cuffed, on the table. "You're a good man, Cameron."

"Was," he said, clinging to her hand.

"You still are. I want your daughter to grow up knowing that."

"And because of you," he said thickly, this time unable to stem the flow of tears, "she will."

⁓

The next morning Joanna looked at Cameron sitting at the table across from her. He wouldn't meet her gaze. Maybe she shouldn't have come. This was painful for both of them. When she left that morning in a taxi with Andrew, her sisters had begged her not to go. She had ignored them, as well as the doubts she saw in Andrew's eyes on the way to the jail. Now that she was here in this small room, facing the man who had changed her life forever, she wondered if they had all been right. Yet something greater than doubt flickered within her. She believed Cameron needed to hear that he was forgiven as much as she needed to say the words to him.

He was thin. His black hair was buzzed short and he was clean-shaven. The orange jail clothes he wore made his pale skin look sallow. She saw a small scar bisect his left eyebrow and wondered if he'd gotten it in the accident. It was a fraction of the size of her own scar, but it could still be a permanent reminder of what happened. When he finally looked at her, his gaze went to her scar, making her flush.

Thinking about Cameron as a protector of his child was quite different from knowing he was the one who killed her parents. He had taken so much from her family. Yet hadn't he lost just as much?

Andrew sat next to her, his body rigid, like a marble statue. Despite his tension, she drew comfort from his presence beside her, glad he was with her.

"I'm surprised you wanted to meet with me," Cameron said, again averting his eyes. His shoulders and back were slumped, and he was practically hunching over the table. He looked at her, then at Andrew. "I don't know what to say. 'I'm sorry' isn't enough."

Joanna felt Andrew's strong, rough hand clasp hers underneath the table. She held on tight.

"Your family helped me and Lacy," Cameron said to Andrew. He leaned forward with his elbows on the table, running his hand over his shorn head. "And I lied to you. I owe it to you to tell you why."

"Because of your daughter," Joanna said.

Cameron lifted his head. "I spent most of my life in foster care. My parents were losers. I didn't know my dad, and my mom was high on drugs half the time. I spent time with people I didn't know and never really felt like part of a family. I ended up living in a group home the last few years before I turned eighteen. Then I was out of the system. I didn't have much to my name, and I was basically alone.

"I spent the first night in a church shelter." He swallowed, lifting his head a little more. "That's where I met Mackenzie. She was a runaway. Her home life had been even worse than mine."

Joanna didn't move. It would have been easier if the hit-and-run driver had been a cruel person. Not someone with a painful past.

"Mackenzie was seventeen, but she acted older than her age. She never knew her father, and she'd had to take care of her alcoholic mother half the time. Then when her mother remarried, her stepfather . . ." Cameron looked away. "I'm sorry. I didn't mean to give you the whole sob story."

"It's all right," Joanna said softly. "Say whatever it is you need to say."

He looked at her, amazement in his eyes. "How can you be so kind to me after what I've done?"

"Because we've all made mistakes." She released Andrew's hand and leaned forward. "Tell me about your wife, Cameron."

Tears filled his eyes. "Mackenzie and I both started working at the shelter in exchange for a place to stay. We became best friends. Eventually I got a job, she got her GED, and I asked her to marry me." This time his smile was genuine, despite tears falling down his face. "It was the best day of my life when she said yes. We were young, probably too young. But no one understood me better than she did. And I understood her."

She glanced at Andrew and saw the knowing look in his eyes. Now his posture relaxed, and she realized he was thinking the same things she was—Cameron wasn't lying to them. Every word he said rang with truth, and with love for his late wife.

"When she told me she was pregnant, it threw me for a loop," Cameron continued. "Although we were surprised, we were happy. Despite our messed-up childhoods, we both wanted children. We also vowed that we wouldn't raise our child the way we were raised." He lifted his chin. "We would love our baby. Make sure she was safe. She would never know hunger or neglect or have parents who were drug addicts and stepparents who crossed the worst line imaginable." His eyes grew glassy. "Our baby would have everything we didn't."

A lump formed in Joanna's throat. Her parents had loved her, and she had never doubted that love. Never felt any insecurity when it came to her family. She couldn't imagine not feeling loved or experiencing cruelty at the hand of either her mother or father. Yet Andrew had been deeply hurt by his father's abandonment. And although Sadie and Aden never talked about it, she suspected there was something going on with his parents, something that had caused deep wounds in both Aden and his brother.

All this time that she had felt sorry for herself, she hadn't realized how truly blessed she was.

"The pregnancy was normal." Cameron placed his hands on the table and clasped them loosely. "I took a second job and Mackenzie kept hers, and we saved every penny we could. We didn't see each other much, but we knew the sacrifice was worth it. Once the baby was born, Mackenzie would stay home and take care of her. We had it all planned out." His hands tightened together. "That changed after Lacy was born and Mackenzie died right after. She had a blood clotting disease the doctors didn't know about."

Joanna wanted to reach out to him, but she couldn't. "I'm so sorry," she whispered as Andrew nodded his condolences.

"That's when everything fell apart. How was I supposed to do this without her?" Cameron's voice thickened. "That wasn't in the plan. But I had Lacy, and I wasn't going to let her down." He shook his head. "I ended up doing that anyway. When I hit your buggy . . ." He paused, looking at her, tears falling down his face. "I was on my way to work that morning, and I had to turn around and go back to my apartment. I wasn't paying attention to the road. I was thinking about Mackenzie, missing her, angry that she'd left me. I should have pulled over and collected myself, but I didn't. I wasn't keeping track of my speed or anyone else on the road. I hit the buggy—" He put his head in his hands. "God . . . I shouldn't have left the scene." He looked at her, his expression raw. "I was a coward and took off."

She felt Andrew tense, saw him lean forward. When she looked at him, his face seemed to be etched in stone, his brow furrowed in anger over his blue eyes. "It's okay," she whispered, talking to both men. "It's okay."

Cameron shook his head, his eyes snapping with anger. "Don't let me off the hook that easily. I should have stayed. I should have helped you. Maybe your parents would still be alive if I had. But all I could think about was Lacy. If I went to jail, who would take care of her? She'd end up in the system." His jaw clenched. "I know all about that system. I wasn't going to let that happen to my daughter."

The door to the room opened, and the deputy poked his head inside. "Everything all right here?"

Joanna nodded. "Yes. We're fine."

"Five more minutes," he said, then stepped out again.

Cameron looked at Joanna. "Like I said, you don't need to know my whole story. Just know that I realized I couldn't run from what I did, not even for Lacy's sake. What kind of example would that set?" He leaned forward. "I'm sorry I was a coward. I'm sorry I ran. I'm sorry I hurt you and that I took your parents away from you and your sisters."

Tears streamed down Joanna's face. His apology was so sincere her chest squeezed.

"I know words aren't worth anything. Actions are. It was my actions that did this, and I can't fix it. But I can promise you I'll face the consequences. I'm pleading guilty to all the charges. I don't know how much time that will get me, but my lawyer says possibly eight to ten years. It depends on the judge and whether you press charges too. If you want to, I will understand."

Ten years in jail. Ten years away from his daughter. "What about Lacy?" she asked.

His lips lifted in a rueful smile. "My former landlady, Mrs. Rodriguez, says she will take care of her." He shook his head as if he were trying to digest what he'd just said. "It's a miracle. Lacy will have a good home while I'm gone." He paused. "I hope one day you can forgive me."

"That's why I'm here," Joanna said. "I do forgive you."

"I know you have to say that. The Amish always forgive. It's part of your religion."

She shook her head. "It's part of our faith, yes. But that doesn't mean the words aren't true." She leaned forward, connecting her gaze to his, willing him to understand what she was about to say. "God forgives you too. There's nothing you can do that he won't forgive if you ask him."

Cameron shifted in his chair. "If you had said this to me a few days ago, I wouldn't have believed you. God took my wife. How am I supposed to accept that? But . . ." His nervousness returned. "I prayed," he said quietly. "Lacy was sick, and I prayed that God would save her. I promised him that if he did, I'd turn myself in." He looked back at Joanna. "And I did. Then I prayed that God would keep Lacy out of the system. I didn't really believe that would happen. Then Mrs. Rodriguez said she would take care of her. That was a miracle." His eyes pooled with tears. "But if God can do miracles, then why didn't he save Mackenzie? Why did she have to die?"

Joanna felt her own tears slip down her cheeks. "I don't know."

Cameron wiped his nose with the back of his hand as the deputy came back into the room.

"Time's up," he said in a brusque tone.

Cameron nodded and stood, and the man came over to him. He clasped Cameron's wrists in handcuffs and started leading him away.

"I'll be praying for you," Joanna said, moving to stand.

"Thank you." Cameron turned away and left.

Joanna stared at the empty doorway, unable to move. She felt Andrew's hand take hers.

"Are you okay?" he asked.

She started to nod, to say she was fine, but she couldn't. She couldn't erase Cameron's forlorn expression from her mind. He'd lost so much, and now he would be losing precious years from his daughter's life. All because he'd made a mistake, one born out of grief.

So much loss. Her parents, his wife, now his being separated from his daughter. She couldn't hold back the tears anymore.

Andrew rose and shut the door. Then he went back to Joanna and held her. She buried her head in his chest, trying to stem her sobs, knowing this wasn't the place for her to break down. But she couldn't help herself. She let her emotions release as Andrew rubbed her back. When she was finally done, he took out his handkerchief and handed it to her. She wiped her damp face with it. "I'm sorry," she said, her voice thick.

"Don't." He ran his thumb over her cheek. "Don't be sorry."

"I can't help it. I want to be strong—"

"You are. You're stronger than anyone I know. Joanna, I don't think I could have done what you did today." His mouth flattened. "You showed him compassion and forgiveness. You were right. He needed to hear those words. Don't ever think you're weak, not after what you did today."

"I couldn't have done it alone." She took both of his hands in hers, not caring that anyone could walk in on them. "I'm glad you were here with me."

"I'll always be here for you, Joanna. I'm not going anywhere." He peered at her. "Are you ready to *geh* back home?"

She finally knew she would be okay. Forgiving Cameron had set her free. And the weight of self-doubt she'd been carrying most of her life had been lifted. It was hard to let the hurt go. But she'd done it. She wasn't perfect, and she never would be. She would still have healing to do, and she and Andrew still had more to rebuild between them. The grief and pain of the last months were still there, but not as acute. "*Ya.* I'm ready."

<hr />

When Andrew returned home after accompanying Joanna to see Cameron, his thoughts and feelings were whirling. The parallels between Cameron and Andrew's father had stunned him when he heard Cameron's story. Their backgrounds were different, but they had both made mistakes that cost them dearly. They had also done everything they could to protect their family.

He sat down in the kitchen, his head falling into his hands. He didn't know where Irene and his mother were, and he was glad to be alone. The pieces of his life were falling into place, but one part of his heart wasn't healed. It wouldn't be until he could find a way to forgive his father.

Andrew popped up from the chair and searched the drawers in the kitchen. There had to be a paper and pencil somewhere in here. He finally found a large notepad and a stub of a pencil. He sat back down at the table and stared at the blank page. What should he say? *Lord, give me the words.*

Finally he started writing.

Dear Daed,

　　When you're free, come find me.

　　　　　Andrew

He folded the paper into thirds. Later he would give it to his mother. He wouldn't ask for his father's address. His mother had protected it all this time. He would let her mail it for him.

Andrew touched his chin to his chest. He had no idea if his father would respond or if he would ever see his *daed* again. But he knew if he did, he would be able to tell him he forgave him. Until then he would let go of the anger in his heart. Finally, after all these years, he was free.

CHAPTER 19

Joanna looked out the window at the fresh snowfall blanketing the ground. She pulled her sweater closer around her body and let the curtain fall, her heart filled with anticipation. She was alone and waiting for Andrew. He said he would come by, but she had expected him earlier. She wasn't upset at his tardiness, knowing he would want to spend time with his sister and mother on Christmas Eve. His devotion and loyalty to his family were two of the many things she loved about him. He would be here soon enough, and they would spend the rest of the evening together.

Aden and Sadie were at Rhoda's house, and Abigail had decided to go with them when she found out Andrew was coming over. Over the past couple of months, her sister had made strides to get over her hurt from Joel, but Joanna could tell she still struggled. Abigail had been deeply in love with Joel. That was more obvious now than when they had been together. Joanna wanted her sister to know the happiness she had with Andrew and that Sadie had with Aden. She knew Abigail was lonely, and she prayed her sister would have her well-deserved happy ending with a man who would treasure her. In the meantime, Abigail had at least accepted Sadie's invitation to go to the Troyers' for Christmas Eve. She wouldn't be alone on this first Christmas Eve without their parents.

Joanna tried to fight the grief that was never too far from her heart. Although her relationship with Andrew was stronger than ever, that didn't keep her from missing her parents or wishing they were here. Sometimes the grief hit her at odd times, even when she was with Andrew. He never tried to cheer her up with useless words or platitudes. He comforted her with his strong silence, holding her and letting her grieve until the moment passed. She closed her eyes. *Merry Christmas,* Mamm *and* Daed.

Wiping away the few tears that escaped, she opened her eyes and moved away from the window. She glanced at Homer, who was asleep in front of the woodstove. Aden had loaded the firebox before he left, and the room was filled with cozy heat. She walked over to the couch. Her hips no longer hurt, and now the only trace she had of the accident was the scar on her cheek, which had faded a bit over the past weeks. It would never go away completely, and she was at peace with that. She had survived, and now instead of feeling guilty she felt free. She was determined to live her life without fear or regrets.

A knock on the door made her heart leap. *He's here.* She opened it and smiled at Andrew, who met her grin with a cute one of his own. He stood under the porch awning, snowflakes covering his dark coat. "You're late," she said good-naturedly.

He stepped inside and removed his hat. "The snow slowed me down or I would have been here sooner." He kissed her cheek, then whispered, his voice deep and soft in her ear, "I couldn't wait to see you tonight."

She blushed. *Oh my.* Not only was he more demonstrative now, he was also very comfortable showing his affection. Such a difference from a few months ago, when their relationship seemed impossible. Her smile widened as she shut the door and took his coat from him.

He stepped farther into the living room, then let out a low whistle as he looked at the coffee table. "Impressive."

His reaction to the array of food pleased her. She had made three dozen of his favorite cookies—peanut butter, chocolate chip, and snickerdoodle. She had warmed a pitcher of apple cider and placed two mugs, each holding a cinnamon stick, next to it. A fragrant candle was lit in the center of the table near his Christmas gift, a square box wrapped in brown paper and tied with plain string. "I couldn't decide what type of cookie you might want, so I made a few of *yer* favorites."

"I'm eager to try them all."

"You better hurry. I had to keep Homer from stealing them. He can be a greedy thing."

Andrew glanced at the dog, who had barely lifted his head before lying back down again. Andrew had become a familiar presence to him. "He doesn't seem too interested in them any-more. Now, if there had been a ham hock on the table—"

"Then he would have been locked up in my room." She smirked. "After I gave him a little piece, of course."

They smiled at each other for a moment, and Joanna basked in the ease she felt around him. In the past she'd always wor-ried that she wouldn't measure up, that she would do something to disappoint him. Now she knew their love would withstand anything. She wouldn't be perfect. She *would* disappoint him, just as he would disappoint her. It was how they handled the disappointment—and how they forgave each other—that mattered. A hard lesson to learn, but they were both better for learning it.

Before they sat down Andrew pulled a folded envelope out of the pocket of his pants. "Here's the latest letter from Cameron."

Joanna smiled as she sat down. Shortly after Cameron was sentenced to eight years at the prison in Mansfield, Andrew had written him a letter. The two had been corresponding ever since. Andrew shared all the letters, with Cameron's permission. He always asked about her and about their families. This would be his first Christmas alone without his wife and daughter. Another pang twisted inside. "How is he?" she asked.

"Doing okay. He saw Lacy last week. Said she's sitting up, which was hard for him to believe." Andrew shrugged as he unfolded the letter. "I don't know anything about babies, but he seemed happy about it." He handed Joanna the letter.

Dear Andrew,

As always, it's good to hear from you. I hope Naomi and Irene are doing well. Please tell Joanna and her sisters that I send my best. I pray for them every day, and I thank them—and you—for praying for me.

Lacy is growing so fast. Elaine makes sure to send me pictures every week, and she visits every other week. I'm still attending the men's Bible study and have started doing some extra studying on my own with one of my fellow inmates. This might sound nuts, but when I get out, I'm thinking about becoming a pastor. I don't know what church would hire an ex-felon, but if God wants that to happen, it will happen.

Cameron had written a few more things, nothing major, and nothing like the announcement that he might be a pastor. "Do you think he will?" Joanna said, folding the letter and handing it back to Andrew.

"I have no idea. But he's right—if God wants it to happen, it will happen." He put the letter back in his pocket and moved closer to her. "But I don't want to talk about Cameron anymore." He reached for a cookie and took a bite. He closed his eyes as he chewed.

"*Gut?*" Joanna asked, watching his reaction.

"*Ya.*" When he opened his eyes, he met her gaze with a smoky-blue one. "Very *gut.*"

She let out a contented sigh and sat closer to him. There was more than one way to Andrew's heart, but she would always be eager to cook for him, especially if it brought out a bone-melting look like that one. Andrew finished the cookie and put his arm around her shoulders. She leaned her head against his chest.

"Are you happy, Joanna?"

Feeling the warmth of his strong arm around her, hearing the thump of his heart beneath her cheek . . . There was nowhere else she wanted to be. "*Ya.* Very much so."

"Then hopefully this will make you even happier." He removed his arm from her shoulders. When she sat up he angled his body toward her on the sofa, then reached behind her ear. She flinched. He hadn't done this trick in a while, so she wasn't expecting it. When he pulled back his hand, he unfurled his fingers.

"A key?" she asked, looking at the small object in his work-roughened palm.

"*Yer* key." He took her hand and put the key in it.

She continued to study the petite piece of metal. It was too small to be a door key. "What's it for?"

"This." He pulled out a package from behind his back. How did he hide that from her? She had a feeling that in the future she would discover Andrew Beiler had plenty more tricks up his sleeve. He handed the gift to her.

Carefully she unwrapped the plain brown paper, similar to the paper she used to wrap his present. "It's beautiful," she said, looking at a rectangular wooden box about a foot in length and made from sweet-smelling cedar. She looked up at him, a bit puzzled.

"For *yer* treasures."

She was surprised that he'd paid attention to the fact that she saved things. Like the acorn he'd given her in sixth grade, and the flower he'd given her the day she asked him to marry her. She also kept other keepsakes from their dates and had placed everything she saved in an old shoe box in her hope chest. It was nowhere near as fancy—and flawless—as this box, with its smooth surface and perfect small keyhole.

"I had Sol make it. I knew he was a *gut* carpenter, but I didn't realize how *gut* until he finished this. He's very talented with fine woodworking."

"*Ya*, he is." Sol had started making birdhouses in November, and Sadie had decided to sell them in the store. They were popular among the *Englisch* people who visited the grocery. But she had no idea he could make something as fine and detailed as this.

"Open it," Andrew urged, sounding eager.

Joanna inserted the key into the lock and turned it. Inside was a set of round evergreen tea candles. They mingled with the pleasant scent of cedar. Perfect for Christmas. "This is lovely, Andrew. *Danki.*" She kissed him lightly on the lips, which earned her a smile. She set the keepsake box on the table, then reached for his gift and handed it to him. "Merry Christmas."

His grin made him look like a young schoolboy as he pulled on the string, opened the box . . . and pulled out a horseshoe. His eyebrow lifted. "Okay. This is, uh, nice. You know, Joanna. I actually have a lot of these at home. They're kinda important for *mei* job."

"But you don't have one from me. And not one like this." She bit the inside of her bottom lip before saying, "Turn it over."

Holding her breath as he did what she asked, he read the inscription on the other side out loud. "Joanna and Andrew Beiler . . . always and forever." His gaze lifted, his eyebrows arching in surprise above his gorgeous blue eyes. "Are you sure?" he whispered.

"*Ya.*" This hadn't been part of the plan, but she surprised herself and moved from the couch and knelt in front of him, taking both of his rugged hands in hers. "I want to marry you, Andrew." Her mouth grew dry and she tried to swallow. The last time she'd proposed to him had been out of immaturity and impatience. He'd refused her, and rightly so. They hadn't been ready to marry back then. But now the words felt right. Still, her heart hammered in her chest almost as much as it had that day behind the Troyers' barn. "If you'll have me," she said, only able to speak in a nervous whisper.

"If I'll have you?" He laughed and put the horseshoe down.

Then he drew her onto his lap, held her face in his hands, and kissed her until she couldn't breathe. *Ya . . .* He was *very* demonstrative. "Of course I will," he said after he finally pulled away. "Do you have a date in mind?"

"I thought we'd have a January wedding. Or is that too soon?"

He kissed her nose. "January is fine with me."

She nestled against him, and they were quiet for a few moments, listening to the crackling fire in the stove. "Thank you for waiting for me," she said, lifting her head to look at him.

He ran his thumb over the scar on her cheek. "I'd wait forever for you, Joanna."

The words warmed her heart . . . because she knew they were true.

ACKNOWLEDGMENTS

As always, bringing a story to fruition is never a solitary endeavor. A big thank-you to my editors Becky Monds and Jean Bloom for your wonderful suggestions and support. To my agent, Sue Brower, who is always in my corner. To Kelly Long for her friendship and brainstorming/critiquing help. To Tera Moore, for always being there when I need her, despite the miles that separate us. And a special thank-you to you, dear reader, for going on another written journey with me.

DISCUSSION QUESTIONS

1. All her life Joanna has never felt good enough, even though no one else saw her that way. Why do you think she was plagued with self-doubt?

2. Do you think Andrew's proposal to Joanna while she was in the rehabilitation center was genuine? Or do you agree with Joanna that he proposed more out of guilt than love?

3. Can you sympathize with Cameron for leaving the scene after the buggy accident? What would you have done?

4. Do you think Cameron's consequences are fair? If not, what do you think should have happened?

5. Sometimes we don't know the value of something until we don't have it anymore. How did Andrew and Joanna take each other for granted? Have you ever taken someone or something for granted, and how did you stop?

6. Naomi continues to love Bartholomew despite the pain he caused her and his family. How is their relationship comparable to God's relationship with us?

The final story in the Amish of Birch Creek series!

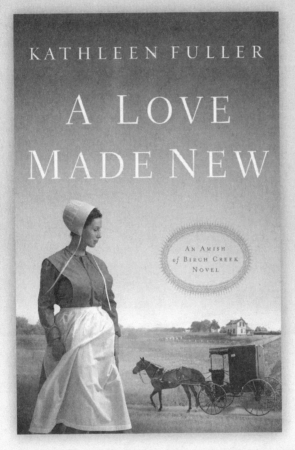

Abigail thinks she's lost her chance at love, but with God all things—even love—can be made new.

AVAILABLE IN PRINT AND E-BOOK FALL 2016!

THOMAS NELSON
Since 1798

ABOUT THE AUTHOR

 Kathleen Fuller is the author of several best-selling novels, including *A Man of His Word* and *Treasuring Emma*, as well as a middle-grade Amish series, the Mysteries of Middlefield.

Visit her online at www.kathleenfuller.com
Twitter: @TheKatJam
Facebook: Kathleen Fuller